SHADOW'S DARKNESS

SHADOW ISLAND SERIES: BOOK TEN

MARY STONE

LORI RHODES

MARY
STONE
PUBLISHING

This book is dedicated to all who've found light, or are still struggling to find it, even in the heart of darkness.

DESCRIPTION

When the dead can't speak, the shadows whisper their secrets.

There's never a dull moment on Shadow Island, especially for its small but growing sheriff's department. This time, Sheriff Rebecca West, along with new deputy Viviane Darby, discover a man hanging from the rafters of the caretaker's shed at Oceanview Cemetery.

Does death follow Rebecca? Or does she attract it?

The scene suggests suicide—an unlocked padlock, a rope, a toppled bench, and the lifeless body. The plot thickens when they unearth the fact that the man's high school love and former wife, claimed by cancer, lies buried close by. Surely, the man took his own life.

Rebecca's gut says otherwise.

When she investigates the dead cybersecurity expert's office the next day and interrupts a burglary in progress, things are suddenly not so cut and dried. Now they're looking for a murderer—one who's gone to a lot of trouble to cover their tracks and make the victim's death look like a suicide.

And he isn't finished.

A cybersecurity expert could make a lot of enemies. The next "suicide" victim had only one. And Rebecca must find and stop him before he strikes again.

From the staggering beginning to the unpredictable conclusion, Shadow's Darkness—the tenth book in the Shadow Island Series by Mary Stone and Lori Rhodes—is a reminder that sometimes, the answers lie in embracing the shadows, because everyone has a hidden side.

1

"What's the point of owning your own company if you can't even pay the mortgage?"

Roger Biggio flinched at the reminder of his failure. His wife was so adamant in making her point that her bottle-blond hair flipped into her face, so that she had to bat it away. His heart sank a bit.

Looking at Patsy's hair, with the gray streaks and dark roots showing, Roger felt another wave of guilt. His loving wife had sacrificed her salon visits when money got tight. Which had only happened because he'd decided to give up his job and start his own company.

Cybersecurity and investigation was a lucrative job in a growing field. Diving into cases of cyberbullying, wire fraud, and computer hacking had satisfied both his technical side and his love of crime stories. His work made him feel like a modern-day Sherlock Holmes. It was thrilling, and he had a knack for it.

For most of his life, he'd made good money with steady raises thanks to dedicated training leading to years of experience. Starting his own company, where he was the boss and made all the decisions, seemed like the next obvious step in his professional growth.

The problem was inflow. He rarely got paid. Leaving his corporate job to branch out on his own meant all the work was on his shoulders, not just the parts he was good at.

Roger had to advertise, schmooze within his network, handle all the bookkeeping, and keep his certifications up to date since there was no one to remind him. He didn't have a human resources department...or any other employees, for that matter.

While he didn't have the client list or the recurring contracts that his old employer had, he'd made a name for himself in the field and was certain his reputation would be enough to sustain him once word got out.

When he first struck out on his own, picking up individual clients hadn't been too difficult. But those jobs were smaller and didn't pay as much.

The tide turned when he recently landed a big contract from the local hospital. They'd noticed inventory discrepancies in their in-house pharmacy and wanted Roger to go through the system and find the problem. It meant long hours, but the job paid well. Of course, he wouldn't get the balance due on the contract until he'd filed his report. And he wasn't quite ready to do that.

"Just because I can't pay it now doesn't mean I can't pay it in the future. Every business runs at a loss for the first couple of years. We just have to get through this, and then we'll be fine."

He knew he sounded like a broken record, repeating the same thing over the last year and a half. Why wasn't she getting it? The business was still pretty new, so of course things were slow now. But every day was an opportunity to generate interest. Roger was certain the day was just around the corner when he'd have the steady list of clients he needed to maintain a healthy income.

"What future?" Patsy threw her hands out, not listening to him once again. "How are you going to have a future after we get kicked out of our house when the bank forecloses on it?"

"I can always sleep at my office." The response was thoughtless and idiotic. He knew it as soon as the words left his mouth and his wife's face crumpled. This was going to get ugly.

"*You. You* can sleep at your office. The office you pay for even when you can't pay the mortgage here. For our home. Where we're *both* supposed to live." She crossed her arms, her hands gripping her elbows.

"That's not what I meant, babe." He sighed and scrubbed his hands over his face. "I just meant that, as long as I have my business to fall back on, things will get better. And I'm willing to work day and night to prove to you how serious I am. We just have to tighten our belts a little bit for now."

"How about instead of sacrificing our home for your business, you give up your office in town and just work from home? That rental is where you spend most of our money, and it's an unnecessary expense. You have everything you need here." Patsy sounded patient, rational, and nothing like her normal self.

"I can't. I need that office space. Besides, I want to keep a solid work-home divide. Otherwise, I'd always feel the need to work, never relax. I've heard that from others."

"Divide."

Roger recoiled. He'd pushed her too far. He knew it. But he had to make her understand how much potential he had with this career path. And the office was an added layer of security, keeping their home separate and private. While his clients were always happy with his work, the targets of his investigations were less than thrilled to have a light shined on their activities.

Patsy ran her fingers through her hair, combing it back from her face. She looked gentle and serene. But then the sparks in her beautiful hazel eyes died as she went completely still.

Hell was waiting in that silence. He mentally prepared for her to lash out at him. Animated Patsy was a joy to behold. Quiet Patsy was a Bouncing Betty ready to detonate.

"You have your damn *divide* firmly in place already." She turned and walked to the foyer.

He rushed to follow her. This was not a good sign. Not good at all. She should be yelling, maybe even throwing stuff.

"Hon—"

"I've made countless sacrifices to help your business succeed. I want you to succeed. But every decision you make, you make on your own. Every time something must give, I'm the one to give it. Well, I'm done giving."

She laughed, but her hands trembled as she picked up her purse and slipped on her shoes. He stood watching her, unsure what to say or do. Thoughts raced through his mind, but none were up to the task of appeasing Patsy.

"I have nothing left to give. Not a care. Not a damn. Not a single fuck left. Go live in your office. That's clearly where you want to be and where you're happiest. Go play big shot businessman for your clients with all your expensive trappings. I'm tired of playing a game I can't win."

She straightened, and he prepared to dodge whatever she hurled at him. But she never even looked back before walking out the door, closing it softly behind her.

The quiet click of the latch sliding into place sent a chill down Roger's spine.

Last month, they'd had a big fight. A real doozy. She'd later labeled the argument his "trifecta of insensitivity."

Roger had been working long hours and treated himself to an afternoon off, playing a round of golf on the mainland. When Patsy found out, she lost it. She screamed about how she was working long hours and scrimping to help their budget and he decided to blow a chunk of change on eighteen holes.

Then, in typical fashion, she layered on all her other concerns. He was reminded how he hadn't taken out the garbage for the last three weeks. How he couldn't be bothered to put his dirty clothes in the hamper she'd moved for his convenience. How he hadn't put a dirty dish in the dishwasher for as long as she could remember. All of it had bubbled over and spilled out in a rush of emotions.

But they'd talked after she cooled down, and Roger was working every day to be a better husband and partner. He was devoted to Patsy, and his stress about work wasn't an excuse to neglect his responsibilities...or her.

She always hollered at him when he screwed up. That was how he knew this time was serious. This gentle, collected approach was new and terrifying. Roger stood there for several more minutes, shifting his weight from foot to foot and watching the door, waiting for his wife to return.

Since she hadn't yelled, it meant she'd come back. Right? Of course she would. He took a deep breath and turned away from the entrance.

Patsy loved him and always came back after a fight. She was off collecting herself.

He couldn't let her see him standing in the foyer waiting for her like a sad puppy. He had to play this cool. Maybe if she saw how unfazed he was, she would finally have some faith too.

It was late. By this time of night, he and Patsy were usually in bed. The fight probably got out of hand because they were overtired—that, and he'd chosen his words poorly. Like always. But he knew how to fix that.

Grabbing a snifter of whiskey, he beat a hasty retreat to his office. His tongue always betrayed him because he was terrible at spur-of-the-moment reasoning. He needed time to find the right words to convey his deepest thoughts and feelings. Pulling out his chair, he dropped down at his work desk, prepared to write a sincere apology and explanation to his one true love.

His home office setup was basic—high-tech on the inside, worn and dirty on the outside. He had a more expensive, showier desk in the office his clients visited in town, and he'd gotten a particleboard substitute for home. It was a bit crowded with three monitors, two horizontal and one vertical, but it had everything he needed to get the job done.

But his home retreat with all the gadgets and tech was somehow different tonight. Roger felt as worn and dirty as his equipment looked. Perhaps he was the human equivalent of a cheap desk, a particleboard husband. Patsy was his everything, and her unsettling calm had turned his world upside down.

Roger's favorite part of his private setup was the multi-colored keyboard. It was too flashy for his public-facing persona, but it made the time he spent working at home more enjoyable. At least it had, until tonight.

When pressed, the keys had a crisp snap that echoed throughout the house, informing his wife when he was busy without him needing to say a word. But tonight, there was no one to hear them. And the glowing keyboard felt more like warning lights than high-tech gadgetry.

Opening a word processing document, he started pouring his heart out to his wife. He wasn't sure how long he'd been typing, minutes or hours, before he heard a sound somewhere in the house. He paused for a moment and listened. Footsteps in the living room.

His fingers moved faster. He'd already written his apology, but now he was compiling all the proof he needed to demonstrate to Patsy that his business was lucrative. He needed to do it in such a way that it still protected his clients' anonymity.

One thing Patsy had never understood—because he'd shielded her from it—was how dangerous his job could be. When millions of dollars and professional reputations were on the line, his targets could go to extreme measures to bury the truth.

He copied over his invoices, showing how much he expected to make in the next few months. It was more than enough to cover all their bills. In fact, it was more than he'd been making at his last job. Once the hospital contract was finished, he'd have enough to not only repay Patsy for everything she'd given up, but to treat her to professional hair coloring for the nice cruise he was going to take her on.

Roger reflected for a moment before deleting that part. He couldn't give away his surprise Christmas present so early.

He kept one ear tuned into her whereabouts. She was wandering around the house a bit. He fought against himself, trying to stay focused on what he was doing and not worry about his wife.

From the doorway, he sensed her presence, though the expected yelling hadn't started yet. Guilt twisted Roger's stomach. Could he have pushed things too far? Made her feel like he didn't actually care? That wasn't what he wanted. He loved Patsy with all his heart. Once she read the love letter and saw how bright their future was, she'd understand.

"One more minute, baby, please. I promise I'm not ignoring you. When you see this, what I've just written, I think you'll understand and hopefully even forgive me. We won't lose this house. I can prove it." He hit the print button before glancing over without fully turning his head.

Her petite shape was a shadow in the doorway. He'd forgotten to turn on the light when he'd come into the office, so she was backlit from the hallway lights. She moved closer, likely to read what he'd sent to the printer. A sharp pinch in his arm made him jump.

Stunned, he rolled his chair to the side, swiveling to face her. The movement must've been too abrupt. Or he'd drunk that whiskey too fast. The world wobbled around him.

"What the hell, babe? That hurt."

He had to struggle to lift his eyes to stare at Patsy. For some reason, his lids were so heavy. He craned his neck up instead, his head falling back on his leather headrest.

She was still...so quiet.

Her shape seemed wrong, somehow. Her shoulders were too wide. She was opening my desk drawers and looking under my keyboard. What was she searching for?

After a few clicks on my keyboard, she glared at me with eyes I didn't recognize. She reached behind her and pulled out something that looked like...a thick, metal pole or...something.

"What's going on? Babe?" Roger's legs and arms tingled. A chill spread from his limbs to his chest. His wife stood there, looming. No. That wasn't right. His wife was a tiny woman, thin. Not broad and...

"Oh, we're not close enough for you to call me *babe*, Mr. Biggio. And since you're expecting your wife, I need to move quickly. How do I access your cloud server?" The voice came to him, warbled and distorted. It reminded him of the tin can telephones he'd made as a child. His mind wandered back to calmer times, playing with his childhood friends.

"Wha...I don't...why?"

"Give me the access codes to your server where you store all your work."

Wait. That's not Patsy's voice. Why couldn't he think? The pinch! His adrenaline started pumping as he realized the stranger had drugged him in his own house. "Who are...I don't..."

"Damnit. The drugs are kicking in too fast." The object in their hand was silver, shiny, cylindrical.

The stranger leaned over the desk, moving the gadget over the monitors. Even through his fog, Roger recognized it. A large magnet. As it was placed on his PC tower, his letter to his wife rippled as the hard drive struggled against the electromagnetic interference. Briefly he wondered why his printer hadn't spit out the letter yet.

Like a human wave at a sports stadium, each screen turned black, one after another, as the operating system was wiped clean. But the stranger hadn't gained access to Roger's encrypted cloud backup system. His PC might be toast, but Roger prayed this person wouldn't get their hands on his client files.

His half-numb legs kicked reflexively, lifting him out of his chair. His balance wasn't there, though, and he fell back. The chair spun under his weight, rotating him back toward his desk. A photo of his wife from their last vacation together rested next to his blue computer screen.

Patsy. He had to get away, get to Patsy. Make everything right.

"Whose why?" Roger's brain was foggy, his tongue thick. He struggled to use the right words. "The ow my arm."

Using all his concentration, he managed to get upright. The man—he thought it was a man with short hair—stepped back, laughing at him.

Roger tried to take a swing at him but missed and stumbled. His shin smashed into his desk. The glow from the monitors, the only source of light in the room, wobbled. The world danced once again, and Roger didn't know how to make it stop.

He couldn't feel anything. No dizziness. No panic. No pain. Even the adrenaline was fading as the beat of his heart slowed. Whatever had been in that syringe made his brain and body start to disconnect.

The strange human shape reached for him again as Roger pitched forward. A terrifying, tingling darkness clouded his vision, but he spied Patsy's beaming smile beside his monitor. As a lone tear trickled down his cheek, he prayed Patsy would forgive him.

2

S eriously?

Seriously?

Sheriff Rebecca West simply couldn't believe what was happening on her island. Was it truly cursed, like so many of the town folk seemed to believe? Or was it just her? Was she the curse that brought death to this tourist town?

Does death and destruction follow me everywhere I go? Am I the cause of all the bad things that have happened on this otherwise peaceful island?

All she and her newest deputy had wanted to do was visit the grave of the former sheriff, Alden Wallace. After that, they'd simply sought out the caretaker to discuss the unkempt condition of the cemetery.

Instead, they'd found…this.

"Never a dull moment on this side of the desk."

Deputy Viviane Darby had a way of succinctly characterizing the horrors of her new role. Her troubled brown eyes were locked onto the bloated, blotchy face of a man hanging from the rafters inside the caretaker's shed at Oceanview Cemetery.

Rebecca worried this could be yet another victim Viviane knew. In some ironic twist, the man had taken his final breath at a graveyard, where Rebecca and Viviane had been the ones to find him.

Better us than some innocent who'd be scarred for life.

There was something peculiarly gruesome about any strangulation death exaggerated by hanging.

Any body part that was tightly bound swelled, deformed, and changed colors as the trapped blood died and pressure built within the veins. The skin of the face warped out of shape, and parts not normally seen became exposed. Delicate membranes swelled, expanded, or even popped while the outer layer of intact skin folded as it stretched.

Especially in the August heat.

For many people, seeing a face so badly disfigured would trigger an instinctual fear response. Rebecca's deputy was holding up well so far.

Rebecca was also proud that Viviane wasn't automatically considering this a suicide, even though initial impressions leaned in that direction.

A professional law enforcement officer didn't have the luxury of assuming anything, and each death had to be approached with an open mind and a meticulous eye for detail, regardless of how obvious the circumstances might appear on the surface.

Inside the work shed, concrete scraped beneath Rebecca's shoes as she shifted to take pictures of the rest of the scene. With an unusually high ceiling but a small footprint, the wooden building seemed impractical. So much so that locals mocked the shape, joking that the roof was extra high to allow ample meeting space for all the spirits of the departed.

Rebecca shook her head at the thought, goose bumps rising on her arms.

In the hour since she and Viviane had discovered the

body, Rebecca had called in the crime scene techs and the M.E. before cataloging the evidence.

A body, a rope, and a knocked-over bench. The bench matched the shed's worktable, in age and wear, and had been moved out of the way until it could be carted off to the forensics van. Viviane had found the padlock for the double doors on the ground a few feet away. It was unlatched but didn't appear damaged when she bagged it.

Questions rapidly formed in Rebecca's mind. Who was the dead man? The lock could've been picked, or perhaps someone had a key. Did the cemetery simply symbolize death, or was there a deeper connection?

The decedent's identity would have to wait until Dr. Bailey Flynn and her assistants were ready. Currently, Bailey was having a debate with the crime scene techs about the best way to get the body down without destroying any potential evidence.

The techs had already collected samples of the bodily fluids evacuated at the time of death, most of which had pooled on the concrete below the corpse. That elimination was the only mark on the ground to indicate that a death had happened here. There were no footprints, drag marks, or anything else.

Despite the tidiness of the scene, Rebecca had insisted on pictures being taken from every angle, and she had made sure to get her own. Not because she doubted the techs' abilities, but because she felt better having her own copies to review while the case was still fresh and raw.

"We're done with everything below the body." Justin Drake, the unofficial spokesperson for his group of techs, pointed to the wooden rafter where the rope was stretched tight. He was the only chatty one on his crew. Rebecca liked him.

"Then can I get the gurney in here and position it under

the body?" Bailey walked in, pulling the strap of an N95 face mask over her tightly braided black hair.

When Justin turned to Rebecca, she took one final look around. "I don't see any issue with that."

"Let's lay down plastic first." The tech waved his hands, outlining the area he wanted covered.

Bailey's gloved hands thumped as she clapped her palms together. "Good plan. You never know how squishy or squirty these bodies will be until you get them horizontal."

"Squirty!" Viviane squeaked, then cleared her throat, looking around desperately for an excuse to leave.

"Deputy Darby."

Like the female lead in a slasher flick, Viviane slowly turned her head to face Rebecca.

"Why don't you clear out, so they have room to work? You still need to fingerprint the lock and draw a rendering of the scene to scale."

"Yes, ma'am." Needing no further prompting, Viviane fled the building.

Bailey, with the help of Justin, laid out the plastic sheeting they would lower the body onto. "Breaking in the rookies is always so much fun. Remind her that the sooner she learns to laugh in the face of death, the easier it'll be for her to deal with the nightmares our jobs bring. Vi's a soft one. She's going to struggle with that."

Rebecca stepped out of the way, closer to the door. "Yeah, but if I break them too hard right out of the gate, I'll be the one getting my hands dirty and dealing with the smelly stuff while they huddle around the cruisers trying to look busy." She pointed over her shoulder where Viviane had been joined by Senior Deputy Hoyt Frost, Vi's training officer. His long, lanky frame made him easy to find in any crowd.

"Oh, don't blame Frost on me." Bailey struggled to get the gurney in and properly aligned without disturbing the plastic ground covering. "His infamous weak stomach was well established before I worked with him."

A snicker escaped her assistant, Margo Witt, a thirtysomething, physically fit woman with a freckled face. Bailey deliberately ignored her.

"So! About that rope!" Bailey finished smoothing out the plastic tarp. "Justin, are you willing to get him down while we catch?"

After another round of debates that Rebecca stayed out of, the beam was removed and lowered with the body onto the gurney. They'd determined that the beam wasn't structural to the shed, so removing the entire thing prevented spraying sawdust around the potential crime scene.

Once Bailey was back in her lab, she could carefully remove the rope from the victim's neck and give it to the techs for testing. Just from looking at it, Rebecca guessed the material was natural fiber, probably hemp.

With the rope preserved so it could be examined by the forensic techs, Justin mouthed, *Timber*, and the corpse and wood beam were lowered.

The stiff corpse had to be shifted and carefully adjusted as it came to rest. The beam complicated matters, since there was little room for both the body and the long piece of wood on Bailey's cart. With the time already two hours past noon, the day was plenty warm, plumping the body slightly with decomposition.

But at least they'd found it before the bugs did. It could have been so much worse.

"I'm guessing time of death was about twelve hours ago. He's in full rigor." Bailey grunted as she maneuvered the body.

Even freed from hanging, the man's chin remained tucked against his chest, obscuring his face and trapping the rope. Still, Rebecca continued to take pictures.

Bailey pulled her hand from the man's back pocket and held up a wallet. "This might be helpful."

Already gloved up, Rebecca reached for the evidence.

"Finally got him down?" Frost asked, joining them.

If Hoyt had been standing straight, he would have needed to duck through the door. But he almost always walked in a slouch. He was a good man to have at her back, except when the sight or smell of dead bodies had him gagging.

His weak stomach was one of the many reasons he'd refused the office of sheriff, despite serving as a deputy longer than anyone else on the team. He hadn't changed his mind when Rebecca had pointed out that sheriffs did less of the *squirty work* than their deputies. In reality, the man simply didn't want the job.

"Boss, thought you'd want to know the new guy's here." Hoyt pointed over his shoulder, turning his body with the movement to give Rebecca a better view.

After years of the sheriff's office running with a thin crew, she was finally hiring some trusted officers. Finding someone she could ensure was not corrupt had been the hard part. Worries over hiring compromised employees had led her predecessor to institute a hiring freeze long before she'd joined them.

Rebecca was pulled from her thoughts about staffing when Hoyt pivoted to talking about the identity of their victim. "Even without seeing his face, I can tell you that's not the caretaker, Abe Barclay. Abe's a big guy, as in heavy." Hoyt rubbed the back of his neck while still keeping his distance from the body on the gurney.

With so many unconnected threads being tossed her way at once, Rebecca chose to focus on the one Bailey had handed her first. She flipped open the wallet and pulled out the driver's license, crouching to examine the dead man's face. Now that he was on his back and gravity no longer tightened the noose, he was starting to look human again.

Rebecca glanced up at Bailey. "Didn't happen to find a suicide note in his pocket by chance?"

The M.E. shook her head. "Just the wallet."

Though Rebecca took another few moments to check all the compartments inside the wallet for a note, aside from the driver's license, twenty bucks, and a few credit cards, she came up empty.

"Our victim's name is Roger Biggio." She held the license closer to the man's face. "The face is a bit twisted, but he still matches his picture."

Hoyt gazed up at the high ceiling as if deep in thought. He knew just about everyone on the island. "Doesn't ring a bell."

"Then run that name for me. And send Jake over. It's his first day…maybe we'll see how he handles the mess. Since it's our shift overlap, have Viviane track down Abe the caretaker. And make sure she asks when he was last in this work shed. Also find out who else might have a key to it."

Hoyt stayed still, his eyes twitching as Rebecca lobbed tasks at him. She raised an eyebrow, waiting to see if he was going to ask her to repeat any of it.

"On it, Boss." He took a step toward the tree where Viviane stood sketching the scene, then he paused and turned to where a tall man in a crisp, new deputy uniform was watching them with the piercing, pale blue eyes of a husky.

It looked like Hoyt would choose heading to his cruiser until he pivoted and marched toward the new deputy instead.

Bailey had a twisted smile when she looked up at the sheriff. "Is it pick on Frost day? 'Cause I have to admit, that's my favorite day of the week."

"Just giving him some payback." Rebecca took the

evidence bag that Justin Drake held out, giving him a nod of thanks before filling out the label. "He's been having entirely too much fun hazing Darby. Nothing she can't take, but I like to remind him not to turn it my way. Besides, he needs to get better at delegating tasks instead of doing the lion's share of the work himself."

Bailey shook her head without disturbing her intricate French braid. "Frost really should know better than to pick on the person whose job it is to delegate the work."

Rebecca grinned, showing her teeth. "He's been in a bit of a mood since I came back."

"Yeah, he wasn't in a great mood when we hauled your broken and bleeding body off that island in a medevac either. Or when I talked to him still covered in your blood." Bailey subtly looked around, seeing how many people were within hearing distance.

It was just them, her assistant Margo, and Justin, who was working in a corner. Bailey's other assistants were waiting just outside the door to allow her space to work.

"Have you talked about it yet? You and Hoyt?"

Rebecca didn't want to recount how scared and pissed he'd been at her sending him and everyone else away on the boat while she stayed and watched their backs. At the time, she'd made a joke about playing Gandalf, making sure no one else could pass, while Hoyt piloted the boat to safety.

But like the wizard in the books and movies, she'd fallen as well. If Bailey hadn't been on scene when they found her, she would have bled out on that tiny spit of land surrounded by dead cartel drug runners. Even now, almost a month later, she still didn't like looking in the direction of Little Quell Island.

Fragments of images flickered in her mind. A shot ringing out. Ryker dropping lifeless. Darian's jokes, even as blood poured from a wound somewhere she couldn't see.

Hoyt's angry face. Locke's look of fear and determination. Guilt was a bitch, and it weighed heavily on her each time she closed her eyes.

"We hashed it out, the two of us. But that's not the only thing bothering him. We've had a lot of changes in just a few days, and of course, we had to hire some new faces. Something Wallace had refused to do because of political pressure," Rebecca again took note of who might be listening, "and *unreliable* deputies."

She pointed at the man striding toward them now, the one Hoyt had told her was here.

Bailey watched the new deputy approach. "This one's good?"

God, I hope so.

"He's a highly regarded deputy, brought to us by a glowing recommendation from Agent Rhonda Lettinger of the Virginia State Police."

The early afternoon sun made Jake Coffey's light-brown hair appear almost blond. He bobbed his head hello to everyone as his frame filled the doorway to the small shed. Having worked for the state police for the last five years, including a few scenes on Shadow Island, he likely knew everyone already. As he moved, his pale eyes shifted constantly, taking in his surroundings without pause.

That was one of the things Rebecca had noticed about him the few times they'd interacted. Not his hair, eyes, or even his impressive height and build. It was the way his gaze was always moving, always assessing. That was why she'd approved his request to transfer into the department from the state police. Having Rhonda's recommendation clinched the deal.

Once she read his résumé, his habit made sense. Jake Coffey was ex-Army, like Darian had been. The major difference was Jake had been military police and never deployed to a combat zone. Instead, he'd spent most of his service in Germany, working crime scenes and, as he put it, "hauling asses out of places they had no place being."

"Sheriff." Jake greeted her, then gave a friendly nod to Bailey. If the condition of the body bothered him, Rebecca couldn't tell. "Dr. Flynn, always good to work with you. I hear the sheriff found us a hanging vic." His voice was so even and calm, they could've been chatting about the weather.

"He's not hanging anymore, Deputy Coffey. It's good seeing you again, though. Watch out for this one. She's a real taskmaster. I'm going to have to take Biggio and his beam back to the lab before I can get this rope off, though." Bailey glanced around. "And it looks like everyone could benefit from me getting all this out of the way. It's crowded in here with all these rookies."

Jake grinned at the jibe but turned to Rebecca. "Deputy Frost mentioned that the victim's name is Roger Biggio."

Rebecca watched his eyes slide to the side, and she followed his line of sight toward the rows of headstones outside the shed. "That's right."

"There's a Lauren Biggio buried right over there. They might've been related or even married." Jake then pointed out the gold band on Biggio's left hand. "And I noticed a car parked near the gate. I ran the plates while I was waiting for you, and it's registered to Roger Biggio."

Bailey grunted. "Okay, maybe *rookie* is the wrong term. You're just the new guy."

Jake gave her another nod, the all-purpose gesture of soldiers that could mean nearly anything.

Rebecca cocked an eyebrow at her new hire. She was impressed by his level of perception. "Very observant. I'll have Frost check into Lauren. I'm having a little fun busting his balls today. You can dig through the car and see if you find anything that gives us a clue about what happened here."

"That what he used to climb up there?" Jake pointed at the heavy wooden bench that was near the body before they moved it. Based on current evidence, Biggio had stood on it, secured the rope, and kicked away the bench to hang himself.

"Could be." Rebecca passed her camera to him. "I know your uniform is brand-new and spiffy, but this isn't a messy scene. Once Bailey clears out of here, how about you go ahead and get pictures of the bench he used? We may as well take advantage of your height and get some pictures from higher up. Perhaps there's something we're missing at these lower angles. And there's a ladder if you need it."

Jake accepted the camera with a smile and shifted his focus toward the rafters twelve feet up. "Always glad to be someone's eye in the sky." He looked where the one beam had been removed.

"Good to see you're finally growing your department." Bailey projected her voice over the crinkling plastic of the body bag on the gurney as she started tucking Biggio away for transport. The lengthy beam cozied up next to him made adjusting the body bag a bit tricky. Closing the zipper was out of the question.

Rebecca glanced around at the crew she'd assembled. "Hopefully, if we get enough trained deputies running patrols, you'll only have to come out here to hang out, instead of working all the time. We'll have enough of a police presence that the criminals will go somewhere else."

"Now that's what I'm talking about! Islands are supposed to be for fun in the sun and drinking with friends." Bailey zipped the bag as far as she could, leaving the rope to extend out and over to the beam by Biggio's side. She leaned forward, dropping her voice conspiratorially. "But it's okay to admit the real reason you decided to hire him."

Rebecca raised her eyebrows in question.

Bailey glanced over at the deputy who was climbing the ladder with the camera. The new uniform pants clung like a second skin to the muscles in his legs and everything else as he leaned to get several angles of the other beams and some aerial photos. Rebecca saw where the other woman's gaze was traveling before she turned back. There was a wicked gleam in her brown eyes.

"You only hired him because his name is Coffey."

Rebecca laughed and shook her head. "No comment."

3

Rebecca handed Hoyt the responsibility of watching the techs as they scoured the area. They'd done a grid search of the cemetery and a thorough review of the shed and Biggio's car. Even though this was an apparent suicide, Rebecca wasn't taking any chances that foul play wasn't involved.

This was Shadow Island, after all.

Every footprint, piece of landscaping equipment, scrap of garbage, and loose item was photographed, logged, and bagged for processing.

Leaving the scene in Hoyt's capable hands allowed Rebecca to visit Biggio's next of kin to give them the news of his suicide. That person was his very much alive wife, Patsy. They had a home address in Coastal Ridge just across the bridge to the mainland.

Viviane and Hoyt remained on the island looking for any connection between Roger and Lauren Biggio. If she got an opportunity, Rebecca could ask the widow about the grave marker. She hoped they could also find some reason Biggio would drive out to their cemetery to take his own life.

As she made the drive across the bridge, Rebecca couldn't shake the feeling that something was off about Biggio's death. Why would he drive out to Shadow Island to kill himself? Had he even killed himself? If he didn't, then someone was either Herculean strong or wickedly clever. There were too many questions and hardly any answers.

Since she was out of her jurisdiction, she'd called the Coastal Ridge Police Department and asked to be met by an officer trained in death notifications. She spotted the cruiser waiting a few houses up as she pulled onto Biggio's street. It started rolling forward, meeting her as she parked at the address that appeared on both Patsy's and Roger's drivers' licenses.

Two uniformed officers stepped out of the vehicle, one giving her a nod as the other casually swept the area. "Sheriff West? I'm Officer Hooper." The shorter, dark-haired one introduced himself as she walked up, stopping at the bottom of the driveway and out of sight of the large bay windows that faced the street.

The neighborhood was a nice one. Not gated, but those weren't typical in this area. The houses were unique and custom-built, standing at least two stories tall, with wide, paved driveways and connected garages. Though none appeared to be older than a hundred years, some still sported the tall white columns and sprawling porches the area was known for.

There were no kids' toys in the front yards, and most of the backyards were fenced in or ringed by hedges. It was the type of place that spoke of money and maturity, not family barbecues with the kids running through sprinklers. This was the neighborhood parents hoped to be able to afford after their kids went off to college.

"Officer Hooper, good to have you with me. You up to speed on what we're about to do?" Rebecca glanced up at the house. She didn't want the woman to be scared by police converging in front of her residence, so she waved for him to start walking with her.

"Yes, ma'am. We're here to notify Patricia Biggio, aged forty-four, of her husband's death. Do you know if she has any medical issues?"

Hearing him ask that relieved some of the tension Rebecca had been holding in her shoulders. They were going in blind on this, but at least he was trained in compassionate communication. There was never any telling how the family would take the news when they got the notification. Some refused to believe it, some got violent, and some fainted or had heart attacks.

Rebecca shook her head. "None known. We also didn't find anything indicating they have children living with them. This is a normal notification, but be ready for anything."

"That's why my partner's going to wait at the car. In case we need extra help. Otherwise we won't crowd her."

It was a good strategy, and one she preferred to use when possible. Until now, she hadn't had the labor force to do such things. That was finally changing, though. With Greg Abner officially returning to work part-time, they had overlapping schedules with at least two people on shift and a third on call when needed.

Luckily, the crime scene had been discovered during a shift overlap, so she hadn't needed to wrangle any off-duty deputies. Most of Shadow's cases happened during the daylight hours. After dark, there wasn't much for people to do on the island.

With Hooper at her back, Rebecca stepped onto the porch and rang the doorbell. She heard heels on wood floors before the door swung open and a petite woman stared at them with confused eyes.

"Officers, is there a problem?" She stepped forward, waiting for an answer and peering up and down the street.

"Are you Patricia Biggio?" Rebecca asked, even though the woman matched the license photo except for the dye job that had grown out.

"I am. Is there something wrong?" She shifted back. "I've just gotten home. Please, come in."

Patsy stepped out of the heels that didn't match her business suit, and Rebecca noticed the suit didn't really match her either. It was a bit too tight in the shoulders and a little too long in the legs. It also looked like the hem had been done with safety pins.

"We're here to deliver some news." Rebecca stepped just inside the door and shifted to the left to allow Hooper in while still giving the woman space.

"News? Do I have an outstanding ticket or something? I'm sorry, I've just come home, like I said, and it's been a rough day."

"Would you care to sit down while we talk?"

Patsy glanced from Rebecca to the uniformed officer. The muscles in her throat tensed as she braced herself. "No. I think I prefer to stand right now."

Just rip off the Band-Aid.

"Ma'am, we regret to inform you that your husband Roger has died. We're in the process of investigating his death."

The woman's eyes narrowed slightly. "Is this some kind of joke? Are you friends of his?" She peered at Rebecca's sheriff uniform and then Hooper's. "Is that why you're not wearing matching uniforms? He's trying to get back at me for our fight yesterday?" Patsy spun on her heel and stormed off into the house. "Roger, this isn't funny! Get out here and explain yourself!"

Rebecca followed her, keeping a few paces behind. "Ma'am, this isn't a joke. Your husband isn't here."

"Roger!" A higher pitch crept into Patsy's voice as she ran through the house, calling for her husband.

Hooper stepped up to Rebecca and tapped her back. Side by side, they walked through the foyer and into the den.

Patsy's voice was coming out of a short hallway to their right. She spun out of a doorway, flinching when she saw them, before running frantically from one room to the next, shrieking for a husband who would never answer.

Rebecca's heart went out to her. As a team, she and the officer stepped closer once the woman finished her circuit of the house.

"I don't understand. Roger's not here, and his computer is off. But he never turns his computer off. That's where he leaves me notes. He must still be at work." Her hand trembled against her forehead as the color drained from her face, and she kept looking around. As if she were waiting for her husband to pop out and yell, "Surprise!"

But that was never going to happen.

"No, Mrs. Biggio, he's not. He's dead." Hooper moved to assist the woman to the den behind them. "Why don't—"

Patsy collapsed and slid down the wall.

Rebecca managed to catch one arm, Hooper the other. Together, they kept her from banging her head and managed to pull her back up to her feet as she regained strength in her legs. Despite the strain that catching the woman put on Rebecca's healing ribs, she was grateful that the moments when she experienced pain were few and far between now.

"The couch." Hooper pointed with his chin and called his partner to get an ambulance sent over.

Thankfully, the woman weighed almost nothing, and they easily got her situated. Rebecca sat beside her while Hooper got her a glass of water.

She was mumbling incoherently while tears streaked down her cheeks.

"Is there someone we can call? Family or a friend?"

"Sister." Larger tears welled up in Patsy's eyes as she lifted her face to Rebecca. "My sister. She's in my contacts on my phone as Delly." She pointed to the little table by the door. Patsy tried to rise, but Rebecca placed a firm hand on her arm, preventing her from standing.

Hooper set the glass of water in front of her and walked over to make the call before returning. "Ma'am, do you have any objection to me walking through your home? I'd like to look for anything that seems out of place. Would you be okay with that?"

"Wha…? Um, sure. I have nothing to hide. Go ahead and look wherever you want." Meeting Rebecca's gaze, Patsy searched her eyes for answers. "How can he be dead? Are you sure you have the right person? How did he die?"

Rebecca handed the woman a tissue. "We don't have a lot of details yet. His death appears to be a suicide, but we won't rule it as such until we conclude our investigation and get the medical examiner's full report."

"Suicide? Roger? No. He'd never."

"Mrs. Biggio, can you tell me where you were last night?"

"My sister's house. Roger and I had a huge fight. The biggest. I left to get some space and clear my head. I…I told Roger I was done with him. He was being so selfish and pigheaded." The tears flowed down in a rush, bouncing off Patsy's lips as she poured her heart out.

"What was the fight about?" Rebecca asked softly. Even though Roger's death appeared to be a suicide, she had to remember that many homicides were committed by a victim's loved one.

"I wanted him to be more conservative with our finances. To be home more often. We couldn't keep up with his spending. I didn't want to ruin his dream, I wanted to make things sustainable. His image was so important to him, though. He had to be seen as this...success. I don't know why, when so many people are already working from home. There's nothing wrong with working from your home office. Is there?"

"I'm sure there isn't."

Hooper came out of the hallway, his face stony. Rebecca guessed he hadn't seen anything that would prove helpful.

But now that Patsy was talking, there was no getting her to stop.

"I mean, look at me." She pointed to herself and gave a pained chuckle. "I had to borrow my sister's clothes to go to work today. But not her shoes. They don't fit. So I wore mine. Do you know who noticed? No one. No one cares. I was still dressed and did my job well. Why...why couldn't he do that? Then he'd be here with me."

"How long were you and Roger having troubles?" Rebecca had to lean over to hear Patsy's reply as the bereaved woman shook her head against her knees.

"Not often. It was just money arguments once in a while. Sometimes I'd get so mad about that, I'd yell at him for silly stuff, like not taking the garbage out. But I love my husband. He loves me. He would never leave me." She started rocking slightly. "Money's tight. We're behind on our mortgage. But if he'd give up that damn office in town, we'd be fine. I make enough to support us, but not his flashy downtown office and all the business accessories he insists on."

"Where is his office loc—"

Patsy suddenly jerked upright. "His office. If anything could have driven him to suicide, it would be in his office. He always kept me out of his work stuff. Said it was for client confidentiality. I think it was so I wouldn't know how poorly he was doing after he struck out on his own, starting his own business."

"What kind of work did he do?"

"He was a cybersecurity and forensics expert. He started a business called CyberGuard Forensics. When he worked, it was good money. But he was still building his client list." Pushing her hands against her knees to stand, Patsy swayed a moment, and Rebecca reached out to catch her in case she fell again.

But the woman had gotten her second wind and walked purposefully to her purse. She dug through the bag and called back over her shoulder to where Rebecca waited. "I left in such a huff last night, I didn't realize I'd grabbed Roger's key ring and not my own. They're basically the same, except his has his office keys."

She drew a shaky breath and walked back to hand the set of keys to Rebecca. "Anything you need from his office, take it. His computer here at home is linked to his work computer at his office in town, but otherwise, his business stuff is kept there, all his paper files and everything else."

"If he owned his own business, would he have a life insurance policy as well?" Rebecca glanced at Hooper. He'd finished his walk through and shook his head. He hadn't found any signs of foul play in the house. If she couldn't convince herself this death was a suicide, she'd need evidence to get a warrant so the house could be searched more thoroughly by the forensic techs.

Patsy's face crumpled. "Yes. He does. Before you ask, I was his sole beneficiary. But I'm pretty sure there's a suicide clause in it for the first five years. It hasn't even been two years yet."

"I can call your insurance company and find out, if you'd like."

Again, the grieving widow rallied, showing how strong-willed she was. "I'll call them and let them know. You can have full access to the policy. And CyberGuard. I'll talk with the rental agent over there as well."

"Thank you." Rebecca offered a genuine smile. "That's very helpful."

"He used to say he didn't want to discuss his cases with me. I knew in part it was to protect me. In his business, he made a lot of enemies. People lost their jobs because of what he would find out about them. People were arrested too. And there were threats. I don't know if that will change your mind or not, but I can't believe, I won't believe, that my husband chose to end his life."

"Can you think of any reason he would be at the Ocean-view Cemetery?"

"I don't know why he'd go to any cemetery. Is that…is that where you found him? Did he leave a note?"

"That's where we found him, but there was no note. Did you happen to find one here?"

"I don't…I got home right before you knocked. I didn't… didn't see anything." Patsy's unfocused eyes trailed around the room. "If he left any kind of message, it would be on or near his computer."

Before Rebecca or Hooper knew what she was doing, Patsy had left the room. Rebecca followed her into a home office.

Patsy went to hit the power button on the PC tower, but Rebecca stopped her. "Wait. We may need to fingerprint these items."

"But I need to see if he…if he…" The sentence trailed off, and Rebecca felt the woman's pain. Patsy was barely holding it together.

"Okay, but I'll boot it." Rebecca pulled a pen from her pocket and used just the tip of it to depress the thin, shiny power button.

The monitor woke up but remained black. Rebecca, Hooper, and Patsy all stood for a long moment...waiting.

"That's strange." Patsy's voice cracked.

"That's all right, Mrs. Biggio. I can take this, and we'll do some diagnostics, if you'd like."

Patsy's face was pale. "Yes, please. I don't think I can. I just...I just don't know." She wrapped her arms around herself, suddenly looking lost as she stared around the room.

The walls were decorated with images of tropical scenery and dozens of pictures of her and Roger smiling as they posed together, as a couple or with friends. A home filled with a husband who had vanished without explanation.

"I don't know anything anymore."

4

Hoyt Frost watched as Viviane squared her shoulders and stretched her spine to stand as tall as possible while peppering the cemetery groundskeeper with questions.

Abe Barclay had pulled up almost fifteen minutes ago and had been a pain in the ass ever since. And even though each one of his responses had been disrespectful and somewhat hostile, Viviane hadn't let it get to her. Instead, she'd followed Hoyt's directive to "keep it fast and keep him on his toes" to the letter.

Hoyt was proud of her. And as he watched, Abe's behavior made him consider whether the man was somehow involved in the victim's death.

"Where were you from eight p.m. yesterday until now?" Vi held a pen over her notepad, eager to write down any information the caretaker shared. It wasn't the first time she'd asked the question, and Hoyt wondered if Abe would be more straightforward this time.

Nope.

Abe's eyes barely flickered at Viviane before settling on Hoyt. "I've been working my ass off since that damn hurricane blew through here. I've got trees down, debris every-where, and the storm surge flooded a few of the mausoleums and washed all the mulch away. It's been nonstop since then."

Viviane lifted the pen. "Mr. Bar—"

"Not to mention the prep work I have to do with fall coming." Even though Viviane was asking the questions, Abe kept his focus on Hoyt. "Chainsaw needed sharpening. Skid steer needed gas. You know I'm just a department of one."

Hoyt wanted to smack the sexism right out of the guy. He was supposed to be looking up Lauren Biggio on the ceme-tery website but had been stuck here and had to pass that task on to the new hire. Abe couldn't tell them anything about the deceased woman because, in his words, he was "just a glorified lawn guy."

"I'm sure filling a machine with gasoline is very taxing, Mr. Barclay, but I need you to answer my question." Though Viviane's brown eyes glowed with irritation, her voice remained firm and strong. "What time did you leave the cemetery last night? You say you've been very busy, but I'm not seeing evidence you've done any of the things you claim."

Abe turned his back to Viviane, addressing only Hoyt. "I worked 'til six. There's no time clock or nothing, so I don't know how you expect me to prove that. I did stop at Seabreeze for dinner. I was too hungry and didn't want to fuss making something when I got home."

"Did anyone see you there? Do you have a receipt?"

"Betty saw me. She was miffed that I was so dirty from work and said I stunk. Broad needs to learn how to talk to a man. I don't know how she came to run that place, but she's rude. Maybe she needs a man in her life."

Hoyt knew talking trash about Betty's diner was a sure-fire trigger for Vi, and he had to work to hide his smirk, wondering if she'd cuff Abe right then and there.

Viviane stepped between him and Barclay, demonstrating

more composure than Hoyt felt. She might actually be better at this crap. "Betty *owns* Seabreeze."

Abe finally glanced down at Viviane. "Huh?"

"She's the owner, not the manager. What time did you leave there?"

"It was around seven thirty, I s'pose. Service was slow, as always, or I'da been home sooner."

"Where did you go when you left the diner?" Despite Abe's efforts to ignore her, Viviane stayed on task.

"Home. Like I said, I've been busting my balls around here, and I was tired. Went home and cleaned up. Watched some TV and went to bed."

"I'm assuming you were alone in bed and have no one to verify that."

Hoyt had to turn his head away and fake a cough to cover the laugh he could no longer stifle.

Abe finally met Viviane's intent stare. The veins in his temples were pulsating, and Hoyt briefly worried the man might go into cardiac arrest. He hoped the caretaker wouldn't need mouth-to-mouth, because he and Vi would have to rock-paper-scissors for that task.

"No, no one can prove I was home. But that don't make me guilty of nothin'."

Just as Hoyt had trained her, Viviane pressed him further, keeping him answering so he didn't have time to come up with a lie. "Have you ever seen this man before? He ever come to the cemetery?"

Barclay wiped sweat off his forehead with a bandanna, tucked it back into his pocket, and leaned over to look at the tablet with Roger Biggio's license photo on it. "Sorry, Deputy Frost. I don't recognize the guy at all."

"Her name's Deputy Darby. She's the one asking you questions." Hoyt pointed at Viviane.

Abe was acting like the misogynist he was. His refusal to

address Vi in any capacity, to not even make eye contact with her, spoke volumes about the man. It was bullshit, and Hoyt didn't know how women put up with it.

As her training officer, Hoyt could've stepped in, taken over, and sent her off to work on something else. But he refused to make things easier for Abe, and Viviane did need to learn how to deal with this disrespect while in uniform. Besides, Rebecca had told him to listen in when Viviane interviewed the guy. He wasn't looking for another fight with his boss.

All the while, Viviane was standing calm and cool in the ninety-degree heat, and Abe was sweating like a whore in church. "Do you keep any rope in your shed?"

Barclay didn't answer immediately, and Viviane patiently waited.

"Rope? Nah, can't say that I do. Have no call for it. It's mostly shovels, rakes, and stuff to keep the plants from encroaching on the markers."

"Then what's the skid steer for?"

"I'm not getting any younger. That thing saves my back. The backhoe attachment makes it easy to haul mulch around, move all the debris away, and lift heavy stuff. In the winter, I use it for the heavy wet snow. It's got a nice, tight turning radius that lets me navigate around all the markers." Abe absently gestured over his shoulder to the rows of headstones.

Viviane gestured toward the backhoe attachment sitting next to the shed. "And that's to dig the graves."

Barclay nodded. "Yeah. My shovel days have been over for a long time. I use the bucket more often, though."

"And you're sure you've never seen the decedent before? Visiting a grave or attending a funeral?" Viviane continued to press for answers about Roger Biggio. Her usually cheery expression had hardened into a steely mask of focus and competence.

"Oh, I don't hang around for the funerals. Stay clear of those as best I can. Too many crying women." He chuckled and eyed Hoyt. "You know what I mean."

"People are supposed to cry at funerals, Abe. It's called mourning and shows respect and love for the deceased." Hoyt's voice was flat, even though his internal struggle to not punch the man was firing at all cylinders.

Had this small-minded man been standing there watching as he and Angie cried together over Alden Wallace's grave? Abe had worked here long enough he might've even seen Wallace crying over Rita's grave when he'd buried his wife. And the jerk thought it was funny to see people in pain like that?

Who the hell hired this ghoul?

Viviane glanced at Hoyt and casually shifted so she was standing in his eyeline. It calmed him down and made him smile.

"Can you explain why your work shed was left unlocked?"

"I didn't leave it unlocked. Never do. When I left yesterday at six, I double-checked it was nice and secure. That's part of my rounds." He dug around in his pockets. "Got the key right here." He pulled out a simple key ring with different-sized and shaped keys on it, and a diner receipt fell out as well. Abe didn't bother to pick it up. He waved a hand at it. "There's proof about my dinner last night."

Change pants much?

Although Viviane's wrinkled nose led Hoyt to believe she was having the same thought, she kept it professional. "Why is there only one padlock key?" Viviane stepped forward and pointed at the round-headed key.

Abe flipped the ring around and snorted. "Because the

jerks I work for think I can't keep different keys straight, so all the padlocks have the same key. The others here are for the mower, toolbox, and of course the truck." He jiggled the keys as he pointed at the beat-up white Ford parked near the entrance. "'Course, if ya'll did your jobs and kept those dang kids from breaking in and—"

"You're referring to the vandalism from four years ago with those kids trying to summon the Witch of Shadow."

"That's right. Surprised you remembered that." Right away, though, the amazement left Abe's face, replaced by a knowing smirk. "Then again, you are a woman. Y'all always remember every little thing from the past."

Before Viviane could respond, Hoyt stepped around her and snatched the receipt from the ground. "We'll reach out if we need anything else from you. You can go now, but you'll need to come to the station to give us your fingerprints for exclusionary purposes."

The threat didn't seem to bother Abe as he walked off, still smirking.

"I can stand up for myself, you know." Viviane's nostrils flared, though she kept her voice under control. "You didn't have to protect me from him. Or any other misogynists. And just so we're clear, I wasn't crying earlier."

Hoyt frowned. "I know you can stand up for yourself, and I wasn't protecting you. I wouldn't expect any less from the kid who grew up at the station. Cry if you need to. No one with a brain would think ill of it. God knows we've all shed plenty of tears over the last few weeks. Months."

Viviane's lips lost their hard line. She cocked her head, and he was reminded, once again, of the kid she used to be when she hung out with her mother at the station, playing detective. "Then why were you so cold with him?"

He clenched his jaw a few more times, trying to calm down. "Because my wife and all the other 'crying women' who've come here for funerals, memorials, or to have a chat with lost ones aren't here to stand up for themselves. We are, though, and he needed to be put in his place."

The thought of that smug bastard watching his wife grieve fueled his anger like a prickling heat. Hoyt yanked off his hat and turned to point. "My father-in-law is buried right over there. Angie comes out for his birthday and wedding anniversary. She's not afraid to cry in public, and I won't have someone mocking her for it. If I ever catch him saying anything about how my wife grieves, I'm going to knock his head back on straight."

Hoyt's gaze followed Abe as he took his time going back to work. "I might have to start driving a patrol through the area next time she does. Just to make sure he's not watching."

Viviane nudged his ribs with her elbow. "Or I could. Just until you calm down." She smiled. It wasn't her million-watt smile, but the one she reserved just for friends.

"Yeah, that's probably a better idea. Wouldn't want him to accidentally trip over a headstone a few times and bruise that soft face of his." Hoyt grumbled and turned away from the object of his ire. "I'll remind you in September. Her dad's birthday."

"Anything for Angie." She bumped him again and started walking toward Jake, who was sitting in Viviane's cruiser, doing research. "And to keep me from having to be the one to arrest you for assault."

"Sometimes I miss the days you could get away with smacking someone in the teeth for insulting your spouse." The corner of Hoyt's mouth lifted. It was no match for her smile, but then, he could never be as cheery as Viviane. "But don't worry. I know better than to do it in front of witnesses."

"That's what Mama always taught me too." Viviane's smile

widened, showing all her teeth in a way that made him think of Rebecca.

The two women looked nothing alike. The only thing they had in common was their height, slightly taller than average, and their tendency to wear their hair pulled back.

However, Viviane had been learning a lot from the new sheriff, and Hoyt was grateful for it. She was a rookie now, but he knew when it came time to pass the reins over in the future, their little island would be in good hands.

"Yeah, you remember that. 'Cause Angie knows the same thing." He snorted with laughter as he realized he suddenly felt a little sorry for Abe Barclay. The man's own bigotry kept him from seeing the many amazing, strong, talented, intelligent women who lived on the island.

"That's 'cause she was raised right."

Hoyt slapped his hand down on the cruiser, jamming his hat back onto his head. "Okay, Coffey, tell me you have something for me so I can get out of here."

"There was nothing in the car. No rope, no knife, no suicide note. The door was left unlocked, and the keys were on the seat. Which isn't unusual for a suicide, but it's also common for a carjacking gone wrong. Techs are trying to get prints now, since I had to come and research the other lead I found."

Jake looked up from where he was slouched in the passenger seat, his knee resting on the open door. The car laptop was twisted around so Hoyt could see it.

Hoyt did his best to look unimpressed and motioned for the man to continue. "What lead?"

"Lauren Biggio, born Lauren Kline, married her high school boyfriend Roger Biggio. After battling ovarian cancer for three years, she succumbed to it ten years ago. Per her wishes, she was buried here. Shadow Island was one of her favorite vacation spots. The couple had no children. She does have an older sister who lives in Norway now."

Hoyt leaned against the SUV, arms crossed. Staring at the uneven rows of grave markers, some ancient, some entirely too new, he understood why Biggio might've chosen to come out here if he planned to end it all.

Survivor's guilt was a hell of a thing. Something Hoyt himself was still struggling with. After his recent talk with Rebecca about it, he knew she was haunted too.

"He must've brought the rope with him. Barclay said he doesn't keep any rope in his shed. This might've been what he planned to do all along."

"But he's got a wife." Viviane shook her head. She'd braided her hair and wrapped it tight to fit under the uniform hat, but loops were starting to frizz out from the heat and humidity.

Hoyt stared at the stone monuments. The sun had baked them all day, and now waves of heat were radiating off them, like ghosts preparing to rise for the night. "Boss is notifying the wife now. I'm sure she'll try to determine if she could be a suspect."

"A suspect?" Vi's chin came up. "But it looks like he really did die by suicide."

"It's not suicide until it's been proven. And Bailey hasn't called it one way or the other. We don't make a determination until all the facts are in. Even when it appears obvious at first glance." Hoyt noted Jake's subtle nod of agreement with his summation. "Until then, we treat it as a homicide investigation."

He was glad they had enough deputies to cover all the shifts now. Even better that they all seemed to know how to do their jobs well, even if the newbies needed a little seasoning. With the never-ending lineup of cases, though, Hoyt was certain they'd get plenty of that soon enough.

5

R ebecca sat in her cruiser and inspected the sprawling business park where Roger Biggio had rented office space. Once Patsy had given her the keys to CyberGuard Forensics, she didn't see any reason not to check it out immediately. Since Roger's office wasn't far from his home, stopping by would save her a return trip.

As she scanned the nearly vacant parking lot, the details they'd accumulated so far ran through her head. Often the pieces of a case didn't seem to fit together. With this case, they seemed to fit together too well. Maybe she was becoming a cynic, but then, the job could do that to a person.

She'd just concluded a call to the Biggios' insurance agent and verified all the information Patsy had provided. Patsy didn't make sense as a suspect. She knew the policy had a suicide clause. There would be no point in staging Roger's death when she'd never collect. If the woman had wanted to cash in on the insurance, she'd have been better off making her husband's death look like an accident.

But Rebecca was going to check every box during the investigation.

It wasn't like she had anything to go home to. A reheated meal and another round of physical therapy exercises while sitting on her couch was her recent routine.

She missed Ryker desperately and couldn't shake her guilt over what happened to him. He never should've been out at Little Quell Island. But if he hadn't shown up in his new boat when he did, the cartel would have slaughtered all of them. Ryker had been hospitalized and Darian Hudson had paid the ultimate price. And while Rebecca was finally healed from the many injuries she'd received, the emotional wounds would be with her much longer.

Ryker and Rebecca had only recently shared their feelings with each other, but his parents had received her coldly, not saying a single word. The pain of their silence had stung more than all her injuries combined.

Rebecca looked at the cup of frozen coffee she'd grabbed on the way to the office park, took a sip, and decided to make another phone call.

"Senior Deputy Frost speaking. How may I help you?"

"Frost, it's West."

"Hey, Boss. Let me put you on speakerphone. We've got some news." There was a click, and she heard chairs moving in the background. Probably Jake and Viviane shifting closer so they could have a conference. "We're all here. Even this new guy who thinks he's doing a real bang-up job on his first day."

Clearly, the hazing was in full swing.

"If you don't want the newbie to quit on the first day, keep it up, Frost. If I read between the lines, I'd say Jake is doing a good job."

"Well, he hasn't shot himself in the ass yet. Or anyone else," Viviane chimed in. "That's really all you can expect from those state guys."

Rebecca noted Jake's silence as they took turns ribbing

him, which said a lot for his character and more for his professionalism. This type of banter was common in their line of work. Rebecca hadn't seen a single sign of it turning toxic with her crew, so she chose not to put a stop to it.

"And I hate to admit it," Hoyt's voice was less cheerful this time, "but Jake also found useful information on Lauren Biggio, whose grave we saw at the cemetery. Go ahead, tell her what you found."

Jake gave her the rundown of Lauren Biggio, her life before Roger, how she'd vacationed on the island as a child, her marriage to Roger, and the yearslong battle against the cancer that finally claimed her. He also explained how he'd only found keys in Roger's car before it was hauled off to the evidence garage.

"Good job, Jake. Did the rest of you manage to learn anything, or is Jake the only one who knows how to work?"

"I know how to work." Hoyt was quick to defend his dedication, but she still heard the distinctive sound of him leaning back in his chair. "I didn't see any reason to stress over it when we've got these two young 'uns who still need to prove themselves. I spent all day scrolling through Facebook."

Rebecca laughed at that, knowing he was most likely telling the truth. "And what did you find on Facebook?"

"That Level 372 of Candy Crush is really hard."

She shook her head, mostly at the idea of Hoyt even enjoying a game about matching colored candy. The man considered his phone a tool. Not a source of entertainment but a link to work that had to be tolerated. It was the same way he felt about all forms of social media.

"And what else?"

"That Biggio fell in love with Lauren at the tender age of fifteen but didn't ask her out until junior prom. From that day on, they were inseparable. After getting married, they moved to Suffolk, where they tried to start a family. Being unable to conceive naturally, they went to the doctors to find out why. At the age of thirty, they figured it out. Lauren had stage three ovarian cancer. Surgery and chemo couldn't save her, but it did give her a few more years to be with the love of her life and devoted husband."

Rebecca made an educated guess. "Did you find her memorial page?"

"I did." Hoyt's voice got louder, his chair squeaking as he leaned forward. "And his personal page as well. He's not much of a poster or a sharer, but there were some pictures of him and Lauren. She's tagged in every post. Pretty lady with dark hair, near as tall as him, and they were always smiling at each other. Nothing like his new wife. She's on here, too, but always posed pictures, and not a lot of them. Very, very few in fact. There might be a bit of favoritism going on."

"Well, Biggio was a cybersecurity expert. He might not have felt safe about sharing much any longer. Or he wasn't as in love with Patsy as he was with Lauren." Rebecca took a sip of her frozen coffee treat. "When I talked to her, she mentioned they'd gotten into a huge fight last night about finances."

"Do you consider her a suspect?" Viviane's voice was loud. She was probably leaning right over the phone.

Rebecca thought that through. "I doubt it, but we must follow every lead. She seemed genuinely shaken up by the news. She was also very cooperative, if a bit frantic. We had to call the paramedics and her sister to get her to finally calm down after we started looking for a suicide note."

"Could've been trying to get away with a lie and wanted it to look like she was about to pass out." Jake had been quiet so long, she'd almost forgotten he was still there.

"I wondered about that. But if she was faking it, she was good enough to convince the EMTs too. Her blood pressure was high enough that they were trying to persuade her to be admitted. That's when I left. And she gave me the key to her husband's business and access to their life insurance policy as well."

"Not something most guilty people would be willing to do. This is starting to look like a straightforward suicide after all, Boss."

"On the surface, it seems that way. But something doesn't feel right about any of this." Rebecca glanced at the time, realizing she needed to assign responsibilities. Locke was on vacation visiting friends, so she was down a set of hands. "Frost, you go on and head home. It's been a long enough day for you. Viviane, you know how to sort the pictures, so you can take care of that. And show Jake how we do it as well. Abner will be there in a couple of hours. You guys can always call me if you need anything."

"On it, Boss!" Viviane's footsteps cut off abruptly as Hoyt switched the call back to the receiver.

"You coming back anytime soon? You've been on the clock as long as I have."

Rebecca shrugged. "I'm going to check out CyberGuard Forensics, Biggio's office. I'll probably bring his computer and some files in as evidence. After that, I'll schedule the techs to come out tomorrow to do a sweep, depending on how Bailey classifies the death."

"All right. Holler if you need anything."

"You, too, Frost."

After Rebecca let the line go dead, the weight of the silence pressed against her. With a deep sigh, she dropped her face into her palms. For the first time in her life, she found herself praying for a suicide, not out of callousness, but from a fragile heart uncertain if it could bear the burden of chasing another shadow in the dark. Or another loss.

6

Now, if I were a nosy, uppity, holier-than-thou dickhead who got his rocks off by destroying other people's lives, where would I hide my important paperwork? I stared down at the desk in his private office. The asshat had a waiting room, as if people were lining up for his services. But I'd heard business wasn't that great. As I scanned the room, I marveled at the wastefulness.

I laughed and dropped into Biggio's chair. This one was even more pretentious than the chair in his home office. The back of it stretched way up above my head. There was a short footstool under the desk, too, but it was out of reach.

Disposing of Biggio had been exhausting, even for someone as physically fit as myself. After hauling him to the cemetery and staging his suicide, I'd had to hoof it back to the mainland to retrieve my own car. It was late by then and I was spent. But I knew the cops would be investigating the despondent man's suicide, so now I was in his office tying up loose ends.

Before I dealt with the paper files in his locked cabinets, I searched for his access codes to a cloud server. Someone in his line of work must have backed up his important information somewhere. But ole Roger had succumbed to the drugs too quickly to provide any answers. And so far, my search of his home and office had been fruitless.

Hoping the cops wouldn't be able to access his backup system, I used my magnet to wipe the office computer clean like I'd done at his house. I wasn't here to retrieve files. I was here to remove any incriminating details they contained.

While the magnet interfered with the hard drive, I took in the rest of the space. His desk was elevated like a throne. Sitting here, I had to lower my head to look at the shorter chairs across from me. A king looking down on those he found unworthy.

For my part, I used the same tactics, making my inferiors crane their necks up to look me in the eye, to beg me not to do it. Maybe Roger and I weren't so very different after all. In that case...

I spun and looked behind the desk. The late sunset of summer created more daylight than I wanted. But I'd made sure my presence wouldn't be detected here. Biggio's financial troubles were hardly a secret, and my intuition had been right that he'd been unable to pay his bills for his security system.

To avoid detection by any security cameras in the office park, I'd come in through the window. Same as I'd done at his home. All the blinds in the office were closed, and I pulled out my tiny flashlight and crouched down before turning it on.

The lock on his filing cabinet was laughably simple. Mostly there to deter people from trying and not really enough to stop a person who actually wanted access. And I definitely wanted to get inside this cabinet.

Inside it, I was certain I'd find the report Biggio was compiling on my accomplice, who'd been siphoning drugs from the pharmacy where she worked. Some of those drugs were making my job easier while others were for her own recreational use, but I feared she might become a liability.

She wasn't a pro like me and might crack under questioning. Although she appeared cool on the outside, I suspected she would throw me to the wolves if it meant saving her own ass. Yeah, I'd need to keep a close eye on her in the coming days.

For now, I needed to see if Biggio had made the connection between my supplier and me. Though it was the least of my concerns, information like that would create problems with law enforcement. The Yacht Club's vengeance was worse than time in prison.

Powerful forces of Shadow Island kept plenty of guys like me on call, men whose jobs were to sever loose ends. Those assassins were only an encrypted message away from being summoned to make an example of me. I knew they'd wipe me off the face of the Earth just as I'd wiped so many others in service to the Yacht Club.

Each time I'd eliminated a threat, I'd been meticulous. Hell, my method of hiding bodies was pure genius. But literally being in bed with my accomplice had complicated matters, and that was why I was standing in Biggio's office, searching for any incriminating evidence against either one of us. There could be no loose ends, and I needed to know if this prick had connected the dots between me and my partner.

I reached into my tool bag and pulled out the mini-pry bar. All it took was a slow push and a wiggle before the cabinet door popped open. *Voilà!* Biggio's super-secret stash of papers. I pulled them out and laid them on the floor to read by flashlight. None of them contained what I was looking for. And I hadn't found anything in his house either.

Had my supplier overreacted to the threat Biggio posed?

I'd offed the man based on her fears. Maybe she was just a paranoid slut, because there was nothing incriminating here. Maybe he had other files elsewhere.

Footsteps sounded in the outer hallway. Most of the other businesses in the park closed more than two hours ago. Holding my hand over the switch to muffle the sound, I clicked my flashlight off and kept my eyes focused on the waiting room, which was between this room and the hallway entrance.

That outer office door was solid wood, so no light streamed in from the hallway. But under the doorway to Biggio's private office, a shadow moved in the waiting room. As quietly as I could, I rose to standing, leaving the loose papers on the floor. The scratch of a key in the lock came next.

Shit.

I wasn't done in here. I'd have to make this quick and quiet. *Not my preferred method.* I pulled my favorite knife from my tool bag. Stepping out from behind the desk, I pressed my back against the wall next to the door.

7

As the door to CyberGuard Forensics swung open, the hairs on the back of Rebecca's neck stood on end. Tiny wisps that had slipped free of her ponytail waved in warning as well.

Something was wrong, but her eyes found nothing to focus on. Unease trickled through her nerves, sending adrenaline coursing. Her right hand dropped to her holster as her left hand went for her radio.

She searched the room, unlit except for the dim light of the outside world. It was dusk out there now, the purple reds of the sunset and the amber of the parking lot lights hidden behind heavy blinds on every window. Using her right foot, she kept the door open.

The air-conditioning pumped cool air into the room. Under that rhythmic noise, she was certain she perceived another sound. One she could not place.

It was an office with a welcoming waiting room consisting of two leather couches and a short coffee table, a tall wingback chair with brass studs, and a tall side table tucked next to it. Basic office prints by classic artists graced the walls. The whole vibe gave off old-fashioned study, down to the crystal barware in a tall antique buffet in the corner.

To her left, past the makeshift bar, was another room. Seeing no other doors, Rebecca surmised it was Biggio's private office.

Using her left hand, she snapped on the overhead lights, flooding the waiting room with crisp, cool-white light.

Once again, her focus moved over every piece of furniture. Except for the wingback chair, everything was set firmly against a wall, giving no place for anyone to hide. Stepping smoothly, she slid past the couch until she could see behind the single chair and verify there was nothing behind it.

As she maneuvered around the furniture, she saw behind one of the blinds. There was no glass in the window frame.

Feeling a little foolish, she stuck her head out of the missing window. Taking in the face of the building, she noticed other windows, a somewhat boring facade, but nothing to indicate why the window would be the best entry point.

Then she realized there was *nothing* on this side of the building, and that was exactly the appeal. No cameras. No people. No witnesses.

This guy was fast and efficient.

THAT WAS where the real breeze was coming from, not the artificial air. That was what she'd felt when she opened the door. The barest hint of fresh, warm air that had no place in this building so far from the exterior doors.

Someone had cut the pane out in order to gain access to CyberGuard Forensics. Perhaps the intruder had been at Biggio's home. They might even have killed him. Since Patsy had taken Roger's office key, she wondered if the intruder had used the window because they hadn't obtained the dead man's keys.

But why doesn't a cybersecurity guy have an alarm system?

She filed the thought away as a question to pose to Roger's widow.

Pulling her head back inside, Rebecca slid her gun out of the holster and double-checked that her radio was dialed to the Coastal Ridge PD as she turned the volume all the way down.

When she raised her gun to eye level, the 1911 felt strangely heavy despite the comforting, familiar grip. There was nothing wrong with her sidearm. She knew it. Still, holding it steady so she could look down the sights, waiting for a target to come into view, was a struggle.

Her gaze shifted from what was in front of her to her right. She was gripping too tightly. Her shoulders were too tense.

Calm down. Don't clench, don't pull.

Her training had prepared her for what she was about to do.

Water lapping at her back.

Wesley Garrett. The first bullet took him down. The next four shots hit him in the chest, stomach, legs, and throat. So much blood.

The thought was so random but so fierce that Rebecca paused outside the door. Her breath came faster and faster. There was no pain from her ribs to snap her out of it this time. No pain?

Wait. If my ribs don't hurt, then that's not my *breathing I'm hearing.*

Rebecca jerked back, twisting left at the waist. She was barely out of the doorway when a gleaming blade sliced the air near her face. As she tried to bring her gun around, the dark silhouette of her ambusher loomed in her peripheral vision.

Clenching the radio tighter, Rebecca's instincts turned it into a makeshift weapon. Without fully aiming, she swung, surprised when her knuckles crashed against the hard bone of a man's fabric-covered jaw instead of his torso. It wasn't a solid hit...more a desperate reflex. But she felt the slight shift in his stance, a hint that she might've thrown him off.

The sudden movement cost her, though.

When her attacker fell forward, Rebecca stumbled, her right wrist clipping the doorframe. Her gun plummeted to the ground with a damning thud. Her options changed in an instant. Distance would be deadly.

Dropping the radio, she grabbed at him. Her fingers latched onto his black shirt, and she tried to slam him up against the wall, hoping he'd lose his grip on the knife. Her momentum was too much, and it propelled her into the outer room. He jerked back, and she struggled to keep her feet under her and maintain her grip.

His cloying breath filled her nose. His brown eyes were frenzied, riddled with madness and glee. The white flesh around his eyes wrinkled as he tried to shake her off. There was only one thing she could think to do.

Squeezing her eyes tight as her grip slipped, Rebecca brought her head down, slamming her forehead into his nose. The sickening crunch and his muffled yelp of pain gave her the upper hand...for a second.

He recovered swiftly, his palm landing heavily on her shoulder and shoving her back.

Then, as if a switch had been flipped, he abandoned his attack, hurling himself through the window and taking the blinds and curtains in his chaotic exit.

Gasping for air, Rebecca stumbled after him, kicking her radio in the process. The curtains were snagged on the twisted blinds, blocking her from the intruder's escape path. Following him out the window wasn't her best option.

Remembering kicking her radio, Rebecca spotted it next to a side table. Snatching her gun and the radio, she pressed the button and turned to run for the door.

"Officer needs assistance. Suspected burglary in process. Subject has escaped. I repeat, officer needs assistance."

8

_____

"**Y**ou headbutted him?" Viviane chuckled. "Hardcore, Boss."

Rebecca sighed and struggled to keep the phone pressed against her ear as she sat on the bumper of the ambulance. They'd insisted on giving her a cold compress for her wrist. Now she had to sit still and hold it in place.

"It was the only thing I could think of. Not the best idea, since those bones just healed. I struck him pretty hard, but he was wearing a ski mask, so I couldn't gauge the damage. And I never even would've pulled that off if the guy hadn't been shorter than me."

"That's one way to use your head."

She groaned into the phone. "That pun was so bad, it hurts worse than my wrist. You've been hanging out with Frost too much. It's time to switch you to a new training officer."

"Nah, we've always hung out. There're more than twenty years' worth of his terrible puns and jokes stuck in my head."

"Well, at least I'm not to blame for the corruption, then." The Coastal Ridge PD was still walking around the parking lot, checking in with Rebecca before being sent out again. Their response time had been amazing, but even Rebecca, who'd only been a few feet away from him, hadn't caught up with the intruder.

Because of that, she'd been unable to give them an idea of which direction he'd gone. All they could really do was stop any short guy on the street to see if his nose was broken. At least she'd been able to do that much. Since he'd taken the knife with him when he dove through the window, they didn't have it to fingerprint.

"I'm just so annoyed he got away. By the time I made it through all the hallways to get out of the building, he was gone. The security patrol thought I was the intruder, so that wasted time too."

"Letting the men get away. Story of my life, right there. Which, in my case, is a good thing, because when I have my hands on the bad boys, it only gets me in hot water."

"Viviane, please, can we keep this on topic? Although, I'd like to hear more about your sordid dating past later." Rebecca chuckled and dropped her head, noticing the tiniest throb in her forehead for the first time. There wasn't even a noticeable bump. Bone versus cartilage wasn't really a fair fight.

"Sorry, Sheriff. I'm getting a bit loopy here. Being a deputy requires me to be 'on' more than as a dispatcher. Do you think he was Biggio's killer or a burglar with shitty timing?"

"Cause of death hasn't been declared by Bailey yet. But I also don't believe in coincidences this big."

"Did you get enough of a look to create a BOLO?"

"Well, the eyes I saw were a muddy brown. The skin around his eyes was light, so he's probably Caucasian. And he was pretty buff."

"Short, buff white guy with mud-brown eyes and a

recently broken nose. That's at least a memorable description."

"Yeah. Too bad he didn't leave any bodily fluids on the scene. And his mask likely absorbed any of the blood from his nose. Or it didn't bleed. He was dressed head to toe in black, with some kind of pouch around his waist."

"You mean like a fanny pack?"

"No, not a fanny pack. Something bigger." Rebecca thought about it. The entire fight between them had lasted only a minute. Even if she'd seen his face under the ski mask, she might not have been able to give a good description. "Maybe a tool pouch of some kind. He did cut the window out of the sill. You can't do that with your bare hands."

But why had he come through the window instead of the door? She knew Patsy had accidentally taken Roger's keys when she'd left the house. Was that why? Had the intruder also been at the Biggios'? If so, what was he after? And had he found it?

A minute. Two tops. That was all it had taken.

If she hadn't hesitated, would she have been able to shoot him before he tried to slice her open, before the gun had been knocked from her hand? Then again, if she hadn't paused when she had, she might have taken that knife to the chest, since she wouldn't have heard his breathing in time to dodge the attack.

This time, her instincts had worked for her. And she'd gotten lucky last time when Locke tased Rod Hammond. That was twice recently she'd hesitated in a life-or-death situation. She was the sheriff and couldn't afford to flinch. But ever since returning from medical leave, she couldn't seem to help herself.

If she'd caught any of her deputies hesitating the way she had, she would've benched them. It was a good way to get yourself killed in the line of duty. Or worse, someone else.

But she was the sheriff. Could the station handle it if she had to take time off again? She'd already upped her therapy visits to include an extra session over video conferencing every week.

"Boss, can you hear me?"

Rebecca snapped out of her swirling thoughts. "Sorry, I was caught up in trying to recall the whole incident. What did you say?"

"I asked if you've shared all this with the boys in blue over there."

"Yes. I gave my full statement already. Until we know if the cases are related, Chief Morrow of Coastal Ridge is going to investigate this as an armed burglary and assault of an officer. He's got his team going over the scene, and he's going to send Biggio's files and computers to the lab. It's Morrow's case now anyway. He was quite adamant about the fact that I'm a victim here and his personnel will handle it. Which I'm fine with. We have enough work already."

Viviane chuckled again, but the sound hinted at bitterness. "That's true."

Rebecca nearly tossed the cold pack aside, then thought better of it and held it to her forehead instead. The cold would take down the mild swelling and help her focus. "I'm hoping Bailey will be able to get to Biggio's autopsy soon. Then we'll know what we're dealing with. Is Abner in?"

"Sure is. He and Jake are talking like old friends. At least, I think they are. I bet you already knew Jake was an MP, didn't you?"

"Oddly enough, I did know he was military police. It was on his résumé."

Viviane's tone was hushed and conspiratorial. "Did you know he speaks German?"

"That I did not know."

"Well, this might come as another surprise, but Abner

also speaks German. Apparently, he's been learning online for the last few years. I don't know what they're saying, but they're smiling and laughing, so it's either something good or something bad."

"Viviane."

"Yeah, Boss?"

"Go home. You're rambling."

"Yeah, Boss!" Viviane hung up.

Going home sounded like a good plan. Getting to her feet, Rebecca looked around for the EMT so she could tell him she was leaving.

Her phone rang, aggravating the headache that was beginning to bloom. She immediately recognized the number for the Coastal Ridge Hospital switchboard. Had Bailey decided to work late and finish the autopsy? That would help move things along nicely.

"Hello, this is Sheriff West."

"Rebecca? It's me. Ryker." His familiar voice was like a balm to Rebecca's fraught nerves.

It had been so long since she'd heard from him. It felt like ages had passed since trying to find him in the hospital and being greeted by the stone wall of his parents. And although she'd phoned him many times, he'd never answered. Never called her back.

That didn't matter though. All that mattered was that he'd called her.

Hearing his voice sent a thrill through Rebecca. "Ryker, hi. How are you? It's so good to hear from you. Do you need something?"

"Yeah. Can you come to the hospital, please?"

9

In what might've been viewed as an abuse of power, Rebecca ran her lights the entire drive to the hospital and flashed her badge every time she had to ask for directions to Ryker Sawyer's room. But in her defense, Ryker hadn't explained why he needed her, so...

She knew he'd been in one of the long-term rooms upstairs. But she had few details beyond that. The rest could be sorted out later. Right now, she just needed to see him.

As she threw open the door to his room, a man in a long white doctor's coat standing by a whiteboard looked over at her. His eyes crinkled at the corners as he beckoned her in with a smile.

"Ah, you must be the girlfriend. You got here much faster than expected. Not surprising, I suppose, since you're the sheriff. You get to drive as fast as you want. I was going over the in-home care Ryker's going to need once he's released."

"In-home care?" The cloth partition was pulled, blocking Rebecca's view of the bed. She walked in, peeking around the corner of the fabric.

At the sight of Ryker, she nearly gasped in surprise.

Ryker looked…fine. In fact, he looked damn fine. His hair was messy, but he was dressed and sitting in the chair next to the bed instead of stretched out on it like she'd expected. She suddenly had cotton mouth, and he looked like a tall glass of water she couldn't wait to drink.

His suitcase and a small box filled with a stationery set were on the floor next to him.

"Come on in." Ryker waved her to the other chair, grimacing down at the clipboard on his lap. "I'm almost done here. Then we can leave."

What? Leave? She didn't understand.

"Only if she agrees." The doctor cautioned, pointing a heavy finger at Ryker. "I'm Dr. Olsteen, by the way. Ryker's neurosurgeon."

"Agrees to what?" Rebecca stepped around the man, hating herself even more because Ryker's injuries had required a neurosurgeon be involved in his care. He'd been shot in the chest and sustained a hard blow to the head, resulting in a traumatic brain injury.

During his month-long recovery, Rebecca hadn't received a single phone call from him. Early on, he hadn't been in any condition to call anyone. And when she'd visited his bedside, she'd felt the weight of his parents' disapproval. She'd essentially been blocked from visiting after that. HIPAA, the hospital staff had told her, but she knew the truth. Ryker hadn't wanted her around.

But now…?

What's going on?

"I can be released from the hospital, but I can't go to my home because I live alone. I know this is a lot to ask, but do you think you could stay with me? Or I could stay with you? My memory is still spotty sometimes, and I need someone to make sure I'm recovering well."

"For at least the next three weeks." The doctor stressed the last two words.

Confused, Rebecca moved next to Ryker and tried to hide her shock when he took her hand and kissed it.

Where were his parents? Why her?

"I…um…yeah, of course." The complications of the request ran through her mind, aided by the surge of adrenaline she'd been under since getting his call. "You can stay at my place. It would work better there. I've got the two beds, if needed, and the shower right next to the kitchen in case you need help. I don't know what kind of bed you need, or if you…"

She trailed off, not sure if she was explaining things anymore, or just making them more awkward. There was no way she was going to say no to Ryker when he needed her help, despite not knowing where their relationship stood.

"Oh, he shouldn't need help with anything like that. Strength, stamina, dexterity, and coordination are all there. I want him to take it easy, no bending over if it can be helped. He also needs someone to be with him to make sure his memory is working properly. And to verify he takes his meds on time and doesn't get confused." The doctor pointed at the clipboard in Ryker's lap. "It's all written down there. He'll need someone to check in with him every few hours."

Rebecca nodded as if she understood. "Memory?"

"Yes. His short-term memory seems to be working fine now. But it could relapse, and if it does, we'll need to know about it. If he gets confused while having a conversation, loses something he just had his hands on, asks a question he should know the answer to, stuff like that. And of course, let us know if his eyesight becomes blurred or gets worse."

"Gets worse?"

The surgeon skimmed his discharge notes. "That's the problem with this type of trauma. He won't know if he's unwell until he's extremely unwell. Someone needs to be around to notice if he's having visual or cognitive issues."

Rebecca opened her mouth to ask if he needed round-the-clock care. How would she manage that and work? And why only call her now? Minutes before discharge? Where were his parents?

Before she could ask the litany of questions floating through her mind, there was a tap at the door.

"Knock, knock. Ryker, you ready to go?" A nurse walked in, pushing a wheelchair. "I heard your ride was here, and I know you're champing at the bit after being locked up for so long."

Ryker laughed and pushed to his feet, turning around to sit in the wheelchair as he pulled the suitcase into his lap. "It feels like it's flown by, Addison."

"Well, it would for you. You were asleep for most of it. Okay, then, let's get you rolling. You must be the wonderful girlfriend we've heard so much about. I'm glad to see you're up and moving too. Things must've been so busy after getting back to work yourself." Addison lifted a judgmental eyebrow. "That's why you couldn't come and visit?"

What? Did Ryker think she'd been too busy to make time for him? She'd have kept vigil by his bed if she'd been allowed.

But she hadn't been allowed. And each time she called, she'd been told that, since she wasn't a family member, his health information couldn't be released to her. She'd been blocked from his life and thought he hated her.

And now...?

Rebecca pressed her fingertips to her temple as she attempted to process the current events. "I'm still recovering, actually. But I was assigned physical therapy at home, so I wouldn't have to make too many trips to the mainland."

"Oh?" The nurse looked her up and down. Her expert

eyes landed on the slight swelling on her forehead, then latched onto the dark spot on her wrist. "What happened to you?"

Rebecca glanced at Ryker, but the woman stood between them. "Some broken bones mostly. The doctor wouldn't let me drive until those healed enough that I could get off my pain meds. She released me to go back on light duty a few days ago. But it's better than desk duty. The mark on my forehead is from fighting off a burglar a couple hours ago. And the wrist is from hitting it on a door while defending myself. It's nothing."

The nurse's gaze followed Rebecca's hand as she pressed it against her newest bump.

"And you fractured your ankle?" Ryker laughed, trying to lean around the nurse to get a look at her. "How'd you heal up so quick?"

"Quick?" Rebecca forced a chuckle "Ryker, it's been a month since I wheeled myself into your hospital room and found you gone."

Addison finally moved out of the way, and Rebecca could see Ryker was as confused as she'd been when she'd first walked in. The nurse broke the silence. "Ryker, that must have been when you were moved to the other room and out of critical care."

Rebecca hadn't meant to spill it all, but the confusion, Ryker's nonchalance, and Addison's initially snarky attitude had pushed her over the edge. Tears burned in her eyes.

"I thought you blamed me for everything that happened and that you didn't love me. That you hated me. And that was why you never answered when I called you and why you never reached out to me. I thought you'd been released since your room was empty. But then you didn't answer your phone..."

"No!" Ryker pushed out of his wheelchair so hard the

nurse had to catch it. The doctor, looking incredibly uncomfortable now, retreated farther into the room to get out of the way as his patient lunged for Rebecca. "I never thought that. Never felt that. Rebecca, I love you."

She still didn't know what had really happened, or even what was going on right now. It didn't matter. Not in that moment.

Rebecca grabbed Ryker's face, pulled him close, and kissed him. The doctor, the nurse, the suitcase he dropped on her foot, none of that mattered. Ryker said he loved her. He didn't hate her. And he wanted to be with her again.

His arms wrapped around her back, pulling her closer as she reveled in the feeling.

And then an electric pain raced up her chest.

She gasped. "Ribs!"

Ryker instantly released her. "Oh, sorry. Shit. Are you okay?"

He tried to pull back, but Rebecca grabbed his shirt, ducking her head to nuzzle his neck. "Better than I have been all month." His arms came back up, gently holding her around the shoulders. "I missed you."

"I missed too. When I was awake, I no idea you were being not finding out what was going on here. My mom can protect. She told you, right?"

Rebecca pushed away from Ryker and looked at his neurosurgeon. "Um, is he okay? Doctor?"

Ryker glanced between them, unaware.

Dr. Olsteen nodded while scribbling some notes on the chart. "When his blood pressure and stress levels are elevated, his speech may be impacted. He might drop words from sentences or substitute the wrong word or simply speak gibberish. It should go away over the next few weeks, but let us know if it gets worse or if he begins slurring his words. That could indicate a brain bleed."

Panic was like a slap to the face, but Rebecca pushed it away. "Are you sure he's okay to be released?"

"I know it doesn't seem like it, but he really is. Just try not to let him get worked up."

Rebecca rubbed her face against Ryker's neck. Leaning like that was slightly painful, but it felt too good being held.

Ryker's confusion was almost amusing. "What's going on? Are you saying I'm not making sense?"

Dr. Olsteen waved his pen at Ryker. "We talked about this earlier. You won't realize it's happening. That's one reason you need to stay with someone, so they can monitor these kinds of behaviors."

"I feel like everyone is in on a joke except me. But I guess I'm the punchline, huh?" He flashed a smile, and Rebecca's fears from the past month were swept away. "Let me be brief. I will talk to Mom. I'll fix it."

"Ryker, you can stay with me, so don't take this the wrong way. But if your mom is so concerned, why aren't they taking you in while you recover?"

He took a few deep breaths and then answered slowly, pausing to make sure he made sense. "My parents actually had to go out of town on business. They wanted to hire someone to come watch me, but I refused." Glancing at his physician, he shrugged. "Doc, can you tell my girlfriend what happened?"

"Let me start at the beginning, then, to make sure she's completely caught up."

Rebecca released a puff of air that felt like it'd grown stagnant in her lungs. "Good idea."

The neurosurgeon appeared unfazed by their spontaneous declaration of love and Ryker's mixed-up speech patterns. "Ryker arrived here with a gunshot wound to his chest and a depressed skull fracture from a severe blow to the head. The fracture pushed bone fragments against the brain and caused a traumatic brain injury. We had to operate to elevate the skull back into position."

Rebecca ran her hands through Ryker's short hair, feeling the scars beneath her fingertips. "I'm so sorry."

Olsteen glanced at the chart, but Rebecca doubted he needed to check it. "The bullet in his chest was removed. He was very fortunate there, as it didn't hit his lungs or heart. But he was in a coma for a few days following the surgery on his skull. When Ryker awoke, he presented with short-term memory loss. Every two hours, he'd forget what had happened."

A brain reset. She'd heard about that. "I'm so sorry," she said again.

Ryker squeezed her shoulder. "Stop saying that."

The doctor rubbed the back of his neck as he rolled his head to release the kinks. "The MRI showed a traumatic brain injury. With his parents' consent, we put him in a medically induced coma. Sixteen days later, he woke up again. Since then, we've been monitoring his progress. As of today, the swelling has gone down enough that he can be discharged."

Rebecca pulled back as the surgeon continued speaking, staring at Ryker and realizing how close she'd come to losing him. "In a coma...twice. I suppose that's a pretty good reason for not calling me." She grinned up at the man holding her as she got lost in his eyes.

"That, and I lost my phone in the ocean. Or it's in police lockup somewhere. I'm still not sure."

When Ryker smiled again, Rebecca found herself inspecting every movement of his face. Traumatic brain injuries could affect so many different things. "It's a miracle you pulled through as well as you did."

"Well, according to the stories my dad told me, my super-hero girlfriend fought off an entire crew of assassins single-handedly to make sure I got to safety." His hand hovered over her face, nearly touching her. "Did something happen to your eye? It looks odd."

She pinched her lips together. No one else had commented on the slightly different shape of her face that she noticed every time she looked in the mirror. A somewhat more angled slope along the side instead of a smooth curve. It was touching, somehow, that Ryker had perceived it.

"The socket and cheek were broken, but they're mostly healed now. Does the eye look bad?"

"Badass." He kissed her cheek. "How about we go home, and then we can get caught up on everything that's happened?"

Home. That sounded like a damn fine plan to her.

10

"Is there anything better than beer-battered fish at the end of a long night?" Viviane grinned as she popped a hush puppy in her mouth. It was a quiet evening at the Seabreeze Café.

"How about a beer with beer-battered fish in the middle of the day right before you jump in the boat to go fishing? Not a care in the world except if the fish are biting." Hoyt sipped from his glass. "But this is good enough. I've had enough of boats for a while. Shrimping hasn't started yet, anyway, and tuna put up too much of a fight."

"Since when are you not up for a fight to land a big fish?" Viviane added more tartar sauce to her plate.

Hoyt snorted into his beer, frothing it up enough that it hit his nose. He brushed the back of his hand across his upper lip. "Since I started working sheriff hours and haven't had a chance to recover yet."

"Yeah, but Rebecca's back now."

"There was a reason Alden would spend so much time sitting at restaurants, at his desk, and calling things in. Heck, even now we had to take a moment to confirm Abe's alibi with Betty. No rest for the weary. The shifts are at least twelve hours and up to sixteen. Alden was smart to conserve his energy."

Viviane waved a napkin at him. "It's not like you didn't have to cover for Alden when he was out either."

"That's true." Hoyt wiped his face properly. "Those were usually a couple hours here and there, though. He never really got hurt on the job."

"Well," Viviane dropped her voice, "not to speak ill of the dead, but he wasn't as active and involved as Rebecca is either."

The old man had been her hero when she was a child. As an adult, though, she saw him through a different lens. Everything she'd learned about him said he was a man who'd lost his way trying to deal with something bigger than himself.

"Take this from an old man who's only getting older. Just remembering what I could do ten years ago compared to now makes me worried about how I'll feel when I'm the age Alden was."

That didn't sound like the Hoyt she knew. "Oh, you're not *old*. You—"

"Hush up and don't go taking away my favorite excuse. I waited fifty years to be able to use it. I'm going to get good mileage out of it for the rest of my life."

Viviane, eyes sparkling, tipped her milkshake. "Yes, sir. Though we all know you only play the age card so we'll treat you better."

Picking his glass up again, Hoyt tapped it against hers. "That's right. Mind your elders, now. And don't forget, Rebecca is twenty years younger than me and thirty years younger than her predecessor. She's not nearly as worn out as I am. That's one of the reasons why I expect so much from her."

"Yet you're still the one who takes us newbies out for dinner once we've proven ourselves." She grinned at him as she swirled her straw in her cup. Hoyt had been complaining about being an old man for as long as she could remember.

"That's a me thing, not a sheriff thing. It's important to have a bit of bonding with your coworkers. I took Rebecca out for dinner too." He looked lost in thought for a moment, then shook his head. "That was right before the hurricane. Hopefully, this dinner ends better than that one did."

Viviane remembered that vividly. How Rebecca hadn't known what to do and came to them, without shame, to ask for guidance. That was when Viviane knew Rebecca was the perfect person for the job. "Okay, the hurricane part was no good, but I think she really proved herself. Not to us, but to the rest of the town."

"Let's hope so. Election's coming up in November."

"She'll win. Hands down." Viviane wiped her hands on her napkin, not a single doubt in her mind. If there was one thing she excelled at, besides picking up new skills in record time, it was keeping up with the local news. Not rumors, but the actual events, as well as what people were saying about them. Between her and Greg Abner, they knew everything that was happening out in the open on the island, and quite a few things that people might've hoped to keep hidden.

"Things have been crazy since she arrived. But none of that has been because of her. In fact, she's risen to the occasion every time. You know I listen to the gossip. The only thing that has people worried is that she's not a local. What if she decides to leave without finishing her term?" Viviane popped her last hush puppy into her mouth.

Hoyt gazed into the middle distance. "She's got Ryker."

Viviane's lips quirked down as she chewed. "Maybe. Rebecca's been moping around, alone. I haven't seen or heard a word about him. Every time I stopped by or called, his mother sent me away. I think she's been doing the same with Rebecca."

Would Rebecca be willing to stay on the island with such loose ties? Viviane wasn't sure. But she hoped Rebecca would want to make the island her home.

Having polished off her hush puppies, Viviane slowly dragged a few fries through some ketchup, thinking about the sheriff. "She'd stay for us, right? We're her friends."

"You, me, Angie, your mom. That's about all she has right now." Hoyt sipped his beer and eyed her quickly disappearing fries.

Viviane shoved her plate a couple of inches toward him. "Help yourself. But not the crispy ones." She grinned, but it was all teeth and very little humor. "I think she has more friends than we realize. But we need to make her feel appreciated and cared for. Otherwise, you're going to end up being the sheriff. And we all know you don't want that."

"If that happens, I'm going to deputize your mom, then step down so she can take over." He swiped a fry. "I might even ask her to rehire me after that. And thank you kindly."

That admission made Viviane laugh into her napkin. "My mom as sheriff. Oh my god. Could you imagine?" The possibilities for that were endless and amusing.

"She'd have the whole town cleaned up in a month."

"And lawsuits going on for the next twenty years." Viviane shook her head, still laughing. "I love my mama, but she hates red tape and paperwork more than anything. She'd arrest all the bad guys and troublemakers, throw them in jail every time she saw them, and let the courts sort it all out. If they're in jail, they can't break the law or hurt anyone. That's what she would say."

"She might even lose the paperwork that stated they were in jail." Hoyt nodded in agreement.

"Lock the cell and throw away the key." Viviane sighed

and leaned forward to speak quietly. "I've only been on the beat a couple of weeks, and that already sounds good to me. Like this case. If this is a suicide, why are we wasting so much time and resources? Or do you think there's more to it?"

When she'd joined the force, she'd been looking forward to taking down the group that had terrorized her island and her generation so much. The Yacht Club had been the bogeyman of her teen years.

Better not dress too slutty, or the Yacht Club will come for you.

Don't stay out too late, or the Yacht Club will find you.

If you're on the beach at night, the Yacht Club will see you.

She wanted to make sure no one else would endure their formative years always looking over their shoulder the same way she had.

"There could always be more to it. But we need to concentrate on the evidence in front of us, not speculation."

Viviane, still thinking there could be more behind the scenes, shifted her focus back to the case in front of her. Hoyt was right. "You think Rebecca's burglar is really a killer?"

"It makes logical sense." Hoyt shook his head. "It's too big of a coincidence that a man commits suicide and the following evening someone breaks into his office. And the burglar is someone willing to commit assault instead of running away. That points to homicide."

11

I pulled up to the cemetery once again. There were no nearby streetlights. No houses in the vicinity either. My headlights had been turned off earlier so as not to draw attention. But the moon was nearly full and gave me more than enough light as I tailed my quarry.

She shouldn't have any reason to come to this island in the middle of the night, let alone the cemetery. The last few days she'd been acting strangely, and I was glad I'd decided to follow her. This trip proved what I'd already suspected—that my accomplice couldn't be trusted.

She parked next to the only truck in the parking lot. Abe Barclay's. Without bothering to look around, she walked through the gate into the cemetery.

I parked on the side of the road partially hidden by some bushes. Hopping out of my car, I ran to catch up.

Her arrogance was working to my benefit. I didn't even have to slow down as I ran across the moonlit ground to catch up with her. The night sky was filled with thin, wispy clouds that sailed across the sky, blocking out the light in random pockets and causing shadows to waver across the ground. Even the sky was on my side.

What had brought her here tonight? Perhaps she wanted to see where Biggio had taken his last breaths. He'd been a danger to her, one I had eliminated. Upon hearing rumors that someone was looking into discrepancies in the pharmacy's inventory, she'd enlisted me to silence the threat.

Eliminating the cyber snoop did her a favor, but hanging the man in Abe's work shed served me too. I'd chosen the site for Biggio's end with purpose.

After helping me to conceal so many dead bodies—the corpses of men and women who stood in the Yacht Club's way—Abe had suddenly become skittish, which was bad, and then he asked me for more money, which was worse. The man needed a clear message about the consequences of insubordination. Biggio swinging from the rafter in his shed was the blowhorn for that message.

As my accomplice continued her confident stride through the cemetery, I was stumped by the reason for this late-night trek. She couldn't be trusted. I knew that. I'd known that even when I agreed to work with her.

That mistrust went for all people like her. Which was why I was following her now. My pursuit had already proven I was right to be suspicious. She lived and worked on the mainland, so there was no good reason for her to be here.

I followed behind her, one row of gravestones at a time. Darting forward when the moon was behind clouds and waiting behind cover when it glowed brightly.

What the hell is she doing here?

I really thought I knew her. Well, I'd seen her naked, if that counted for anything. Which I guessed it didn't.

Ahead, I could hear her talking with a man. The pair of voices floated back to me, indistinct.

I ran, not wanting to miss any of it. If she was meeting

Abe, I needed to know why. And that had to be him. Who else would she meet here?

"Why did you want to talk about our mutual…friend?" Yep, I recognized Abe's voice.

"Keep your voice down." She hissed at him like a cat.

As I ducked behind a wide, low-growing tree, I saw his face. He looked pissed.

He opened his mouth, probably to rebuke her for speaking to him like that, but she barreled over him. "He doesn't know I'm here, but I had to come and warn you. You know he dumped that body here to send you a message."

That made Barclay smile. "Yeah, I assumed that was his answer to me asking for more money."

"Then you know we need to get rid of him."

"You think so?" He walked away, heading to the other side of the cemetery.

She trailed after him, not done harping. "Yeah. And if you were smart, you'd think so too. He screwed up on this one. Leaving the body where the cops could find it. It's going to end up coming back on me. And if it does, this is my ticket out of jail." She handed him something. "You must have something on him too."

They continued to talk, but I couldn't make out what they were saying. The moon was too bright, and I had to wait for another cloud before I could chase after them again.

By the time I caught up, they were inside a mausoleum. The glow of Abe's flashlight got brighter as they walked out, and he stopped to lock the gate behind them.

I knew that was where Abe hid things he didn't want anyone else to find. It was where I'd stash his payments and he would leave me the burial schedules I needed. Biggio's death was a special case because his body was meant to send a message. Normally, I couldn't leave my kills where the cops might find them. That was why the cemetery was such a useful location.

A used grave was a great place to stash some extra corpses. Abe had proved invaluable at digging up freshly filled graves and adding a victim of mine or two. And if there weren't any fresh graves, very few people paid any mind to the long-dead family plots toward the back. Plus, who'd ever think to search in someone else's grave for one of my victims?

The setup had been perfect…until now.

My two accomplices no longer looked so chummy. She had that furious, familiar expression on her face, like whoever she was talking to was the dumbest, laziest slob on the planet. Abe wasn't the kind of man to take that from a woman. Whatever scheme she was trying to create was bound to fall apart if she kept at him like that.

But the fact that they were meeting at all was cause for concern.

"Don't be stupid! He's going to end up getting caught. And he'll take us down with him if we don't protect ourselves." She slammed her hands on her hips, making her boobs bounce. Suddenly, Abe didn't look quite so angry. "How many cops were here today? Do you want them pounding on your door tomorrow, ready to arrest you for murder? 'Cause I know I don't."

As she started to turn, I dropped down to hide behind a large angel statue. Neither of them made a sound, so I didn't think they'd seen me.

"They think it was a suicide." Abe walked right past me, rubbing his hand over his neck. "You women spend too much time worrying."

They were making their way back to their vehicles. Decision time. I could follow her, follow him, or double back and see what she'd given him that he felt important enough to stash in his hiding spot. The key he'd provided me worked all the padlocks in the cemetery—though I'd only ever used it on the mausoleum before leaving Biggio's body in Abe's locked shed.

But maybe the reason they went into the mausoleum was to retrieve something, and not to stash what she'd offered him for my head. Abe knew where my victims' bodies were hidden.

Could he have given her that damning piece of information in exchange for the object she handed him? I always expected her to backstab me one day, but I'd concealed my business dealings, and I didn't think she had any hard proof against me.

Yet somehow, she'd learned Abe was working with me.

Neither of them appeared to be holding anything, but she carried her purse like she was protecting its contents. It was the huge, bulky brown one she insisted was fabulous because of its ugly orange pattern. That hideous thing could have anything in it. A fucking dead body could practically fit in there.

With these two talking when they shouldn't even know each other, my life was about to get more complicated. They were planning to incriminate me. Thankfully, I knew how to deal with people who tried to take me down.

They were at their vehicles. I'd have to run to catch up to them. Knowing she was the brains here, I decided to follow her. I could always come back later to check the mausoleum and have a chat with Abe. If they were going to try and double-cross me, there was plenty of room left in this cemetery for both of them.

12

"Morning, Sheriff. You're in early." Bailey's hands pulled and twisted as she carefully scooped intestines from a scale so they could be bagged.

"Yeah, well, I wanted to get this done before breakfast so I wouldn't pull a Frost and get your shoes all messy."

Rebecca hid her grin behind a paper surgical mask. Just to be on the safe side, she pulled out a set of gloves from the box on the wall before making her way over to join the M.E. at the table.

Bailey was wearing her standard bunny suit, so Rebecca's threat about ruining her shoes was empty. Disposable booties covered her feet. The M.E. shook the freshly packed viscera at her. "*Mmm*, makes you want to go grab some breakfast sausage links, doesn't it?"

"I was thinking something more European, like bangers. Their skin's got a nice crisp snap to it." Rebecca snapped her gloves in place then paused for a moment. "Those are the English sausages, right? Bangers?"

"I think so." Bailey shrugged and dumped everything she was holding into the abdominal cavity of the corpse on the table. "I'm not much of a foodie. A sausage is a sausage to me. So long as it browns up right and the kids'll eat it, that's good enough."

"Either way, I was lying. I ate before coming in. Ryker made us omelets this morning."

"Oh ho! That explains the spring in your step and smile in your eyes. But doesn't explain why you're already out of bed and over here. If I had a chance to stay snuggled up with my hubby, you wouldn't see me here. *Mmm*, bed." Bailey trailed off, and her eyes got dreamy before they moved back to Rebecca. "Just make sure you don't overdo it. You're still recovering. So don't get too frisky."

Rebecca laughed, hating that her cheeks were heating. That had crossed her mind, but the way Ryker had passed out last night after she'd gotten him back to her house had been all the reminder she needed to take things slow.

"No worries there. Ryker's still recovering too. The doctor said he can't do any strenuous activity, and that includes me ripping off his clothes and throwing him on the bed. Did you know he was still a patient upstairs 'til yesterday?"

Bailey stopped working. "Yes, I was aware." Her concerned eyes shot over to the calendar that hung on her work desk. "You didn't know? It's been three weeks already."

"Closer to four. Yeah. I've been in the dark about his status, then he suddenly called me last night to pick him up. The doctors said he could go home, but only if he had someone to watch over him. So he's staying with me."

"You're watching over him?" Bailey frowned. "No offense, Rebecca, I'd want you at my back for nearly anything else in this world. But how are you supposed to take care of him when you work so many hours? And odd hours at that. I have kids, and I know how hard that can be. Not that I'm saying Ryker is a toddler or anything. You get what I'm saying."

"I get it. Trust me, I do. I don't plan to do this on my own. I'm not stupid." Rebecca snorted, puffing out her mask, then realized that was a bad idea this close to a corpse. She backed away.

The M.E. snickered at Rebecca's move.

Trying to restore a bit of dignity, Rebecca pressed on. "I already made arrangements with some people to swing by the house every few hours. We set up a rotation schedule this morning. Between his friends and mine, there'll be someone there pretty consistently through the days. Heck, he'll probably get sick of having too many folks around."

Bailey looked relieved. "And that's why I'd always want you at my back." She moved her fingers, tucking the bag of already examined internal organs into place. "But you're not here for this guy. Or your love life, which thankfully doesn't need an autopsy or the morgue. Let's get to talking about your case."

Stripping off the outer layer of gloves, the doctor tossed them in the garbage and pointed at the other table.

"Time of death was an hour after midnight on Monday. Give or take fifteen minutes. There were no major weather changes, so that helped me pinpoint the exact time. I'm leaning toward it being a homicide. And not by hanging. The hanging was real enough to kill him, but Biggio didn't do it to himself."

After the run-in with the intruder at CyberGuard Forensics the previous day, Rebecca wasn't shocked. She reached for her notepad and began taking notes. "Are you saying the hanging was staged?"

Gloved up and ready, Bailey pointed at Biggio's neck. "You can see for yourself. There's a single band, in the V-shape we're looking for, which goes up behind his ears. This is a sign of a hanging as opposed to a strangulation, which would be straight back or even down."

She trailed her fingers over the solid purplish-red line. They hadn't been able to see this at the site because the noose had been too deeply embedded in his throat.

Rebecca crouched to inspect the mark. "Then what makes you think it's a homicide instead of suicide?"

"There's only one line. No other marks on his body from rope burn." Bailey looked up at her. "I don't care how determined you are to kill yourself, when the time comes, and you're being strangled by the noose, your body is going to fight to survive. You're going to thrash, kick, and twist your head around. And your hands are going to claw at your neck."

Rebecca moved around, looking for any other marks besides the nearly perfect line.

As she did, Bailey mimed grasping a rope and pulling it away while stretching her chin up high. "Which would leave scratches on the neck and multiple burn rings around it. He had none of those signs."

Bailey was right. There were no scratches, no rope burns, no abrasions even. "But there's no evidence his hands were bound. So why didn't his body react in a normal way?"

"And that's the sixty-four-thousand-dollar question." Bailey waved her hand over the corpse like a game show presenter. Amusement danced in her eyes, and Rebecca realized Bailey was testing her. "There are no blows to the head, so he wasn't knocked unconscious. That wouldn't have stopped him from death throes anyway."

Rebecca couldn't see how he could have hung himself—holding the noose in place, stepping off the bench, and hanging placidly until he died from lack of oxygen.

"There's more. He didn't have rope burns on his fingers or hands." Bailey lifted Biggio's well-kept hands and stretched out their digits. "Can't say for certain these hands never touched that rope, but I can't find any signs that they did. He certainly didn't dig at it. No fibers whatsoever are on the pads of his fingers. Then there's this." Bailey leaned over the body and pointed at the upper arm.

"What's that?" Rebecca moved around to get a closer look at the odd mark. There was faint bruising in a near-perfect circle with a red pinprick at the center.

Bailey brightened and once again waved her hands like a presenter, letting Rebecca know she'd found another clue. "Initially, I thought it was an insect bite. That was how it first presented. But I think it's an injection site. That perfect circle doesn't happen naturally very often, especially with a mark dead center."

Rebecca grunted at that and straightened to see Bailey nodding even as she asked her next question. "He was drugged?"

"Had to be. It's the only thing that makes sense. I've already sent his blood for analysis. We should know more when we get those test results, but I'm betting they'll find something pretty strong if it kept him from moving at all while he hung there, docile, being strangled to death over the course of several minutes. If I see what I'm expecting, then I'll be ruling this a homicide."

Bailey's preliminary findings put a whole new spin on the investigation but also confirmed Rebecca's earlier suspicions. *Score another one for my gut.* If this was murder, Rebecca needed to talk to the forensic techs.

"I'll check with the lab to see if they have anything yet. At the same time, I'll ask if they've found any skin cells in the rope. And if they have, forensics can compare that DNA to Roger Biggio's."

Rebecca had checked the entire work shed herself, and no syringes had been recovered. Running through a mental inventory from the scene, she couldn't think of anything similar that could have been used as a syringe either. The same was true for the cemetery grounds and Biggio's car.

A couple of possibilities ran through her head. Option one, Biggio was drugged elsewhere and brought to the shed. Option two, Biggio was drugged at the shed, and the perpetrator took the syringe with him when he left. But both those possibilities meant someone had gone to a lot of trouble to cover their tracks and make Biggio's death look like a suicide.

The murderer clearly didn't understand Rebecca would find him anyway.

13

The forensic lab wasn't far from the morgue, but once Rebecca got there and started asking around, she found that none of the blood work results were in yet. Tests had their own timeline and didn't care how quickly anyone needed them. Instead of waiting around for those, Rebecca decided to track down Justin Drake, her favorite crime scene technician.

She found him sitting at a desk, his chin buried in his hand while glaring at his screen.

"Hey, Justin." Rebecca stood next to him, tucking her hands into her pockets. "Do you have any results back from either the cemetery or the CyberGuard Forensics burglary?"

"Not a ton, but one thing was interesting, so I did some more digging. After getting all the tools and machinery from the cemetery processed, we found a hair in the skid steer's bucket. The hair belonged to your dead guy, Roger Biggio. I can't imagine he voluntarily stuck his head in the bucket while he was alive."

"Well, I guess that matches what Bailey just told me. She's ruling his death a homicide." Rebecca walked back and forth through Justin's small office, trying to sort through the puzzle pieces.

Justin watched her pace. "You think the killer used the bucket to lift Biggio's body so he could hang him from the rafters?"

"Makes sense, oddly. The shed entrance was plenty wide enough with those double doors. And with the reach of the bucket, he wouldn't even have had to drive the vehicle inside. Were there any prints found on the grab handles or any of the control mechanisms inside the steer?"

"No, we never get that lucky. Let's count our blessings with the lone hair."

Rebecca filed that bit of information away and shifted to the other crime scene. "What can you tell me about CyberGuard?"

"So far, I've learned that Biggio was incredibly proficient at his job and that he took his profession seriously. I've had software running since last night, trying to guess his password, but no hits yet. Until then, I won't be able to track down any backup servers, cloud or otherwise."

"You've got nothing for me?"

Justin looked up at that and frowned. "I thought this was Chief Morrow's case."

"It's mine, too, now that we know Biggio didn't commit suicide. The burglary and homicide are linked." Rebecca bobbed her head at the monitor before him. "Which means whatever's on there could be the reason Biggio was murdered."

"Well, I'm not at a complete loss." He gestured at the computer. "Looks like someone took a powerful magnet to the PC, and it messed up the hard drive. This might end up having to go to the hackers up at the FBI, but we still have all the paper files Biggio kept locked up."

"A cybersecurity guy had paper files?"

"I'm not sure if they're the kind of files you want, but he has his client list on paper."

"Does that seem a bit weird to you?"

Justin shrugged. "Not really. Lots of people like to have a paper backup. With this guy, maybe it was because he knew technology better than most. Also, these papers have been handled more than a few times. Some of the folders are empty while others are jammed full. I could speculate that the empty folders represented clients he was hoping to get or maybe recently secured but hadn't started working on yet. But that's just a guess."

"I suppose that makes sense."

He shook his head. "We won't know about his files until we get through his encryption. Meanwhile, Biggio had flimsy locks on his filing cabinets. Anyone could've picked those or forced them open. That's what we're guessing happened. Your guy, the burglar, used a pry bar on the lock."

"Biggio was so focused on the online threat he didn't bother to secure his files better?" Rebecca read through the printouts. They featured lists of names, both people and companies.

"Some people are laser-minded like that."

Could that have been what happened with Biggio? He was so hyper-focused on his clients and their security that he never thought about his own files or his physical safety? And if that was true, was his home any more secure than his office?

14

Contemplating the realization that Roger Biggio was murdered, Rebecca left Coastal Ridge to return to the station. The normal tension around solving a case was magnified by her personal concern surrounding Ryker and his recovery.

While she was on the mainland, she'd stopped and picked up a few things to make his stay at her house easier and more comfortable. The rental property had been stocked for only one person. That was good enough when it came to cooking and hosting. Unfortunately, there was a lot missing from the bathrooms and bedrooms to accommodate a long-term guest.

She found Turkish cotton towels, sateen sheets, down-filled pillows and comforters, and a top-of-the-line, programmable, two-week medication scheduler with an alarm feature. Even if his brain injury caused him to forget, the machine would remind him to take his pills.

All those things combined might have been going over-board. Rebecca realized that as she was carrying in four huge sacks. And she'd need to load up the washing machine before she could even get back to work.

Ryker'd been sleeping, so she hadn't gotten a chance to show him her purchases. This was possibly a good thing. She didn't want to seem like she was trying to smother him.

Of course, with the number of pillows and blankets I bought, he might think exactly that.

Rebecca swung open the front door of the station. Elliot Ping, Viviane's replacement as dispatcher, perked up and smiled.

"Morning, Sheriff. Ready for the day?" He reached down to buzz her in, but she waved him off.

"As ready as I'll ever be." Swinging her hip, she used the fob on her keychain to unlock the half door and scoot into the bullpen.

Jake Coffey's deadpan expression was one of the best she'd ever seen. "Especially after working late into the night." He dropped down into his desk, the one that used to be the spare beside Locke. "But coffee is here to save the day."

"Are you referring to the life-saving drink or a deputy with the same name?"

"Ha. Both."

Rebecca blinked a couple of times before realizing the seating arrangement in the bullpen had changed. Hoyt's big, heavy, silver thermos sat on Darian's old desktop. And the desk Hoyt had vacated now held a little potted plant marking that spot as Viviane's.

Unbidden, the deputies had rearranged themselves to give Jake Coffey space without asking him to "step into Darian's spot."

If anyone was going to take Darian's seat, Hoyt had more right to it than anyone, and Viviane was Hoyt's trainee, so her seat beside him made sense.

Rebecca couldn't help cracking a smile as she tipped her

travel mug at Jake. "Coffee does make things easier to deal with."

"My dad used to say the same thing." He gestured at the stack of papers in her hands. "Got something new for us?"

"I was going to wait for the morning shift to show up." Rebecca waved at the empty desks behind him.

Jake shrugged. "I've been here about an hour and haven't seen them yet."

"They're out writing up an accident report." Elliot twisted in his chair to join the conversation. "Happened a while ago."

"Good to know it's not always drug gangs and murders down here." Jake shook his mouse to wake up his monitor.

"Yeah, despite the stuff that makes the headlines, we're mostly dealing with the usual. Accidents, lost dogs, noise complaints, drunk tourists—"

The buzzer sounded, interrupting Rebecca's train of thought.

"Mrs. Walsh complaining that her neighbor parked too close to her petunias." Viviane walked around the wall to join them.

Hoyt was right behind her. "*Again.* That's the one you have to remember, Jake. Mrs. Walsh calls in at least once a week. And we have to remind her every week that it's perfectly lawful to park on the shoulder of a two-way street on the right side."

"Good to know." Jake jotted the tip in his notepad. "Mrs. Walsh, petunias. Anything else?"

"Oh, so much else. This is a small town. You'll learn the names of all the moaners soon enough. Also, Labor Day is coming up. The last of the desperate beachgoers with children will be flocking to the shores. But you're probably used to that already."

"Yes, sir."

Hoyt clapped Jake on the back as he passed, then veered

sharply left to sit at his new desk. He looked uncomfortable at first, a sad smile on his face as he leaned back in the chair that used to be Darian's. "But, Sheriff, you'll be happy to know our little Vi got a new merit badge today."

"For traffic citations?" Rebecca made an educated guess.

"Failure to yield." Viviane mimed putting a pin on her uniform blouse.

Rebecca passed over the stack of papers she'd been holding. "Well, this is a badge you've already gotten. But always an important one to practice."

"Combing through lists of names?" Viviane flipped through the pages.

Hoyt relaxed in his chair, sipping from his thermos as if he hadn't a care in the world.

"That's right." Rebecca smiled. "You and Frost get to go through those names. Call them up and see if any of them were working with Roger Biggio's company, CyberGuard Forensics. An update on this case...Bailey has settled on one a.m. Monday morning as the time of death. Also, she does not believe it was a suicide."

"No shit?"

When she turned to look at Jake, he drew a line on his neck. "The V was too straight, wasn't it?"

Only the second day on the job, and he'd once again proven his attention to detail. "That, and there was a tiny mark on his shoulder that could be a drug injection point. Bailey's waiting on toxicology. Forensics is attempting to crack Biggio's work computer too. Turns out he was pretty good at his job, and they're having a tough time gaining access. Looks like someone might've taken a strong magnet to the hard drives."

"Then where did these names come from?" Hoyt waved a lazy hand at the list Viviane was flipping through.

Rebecca rubbed her temple. "His filing cabinet, which was

broken into after his death. We're also not sure if Biggio was drugged on-site, at his home, or somewhere else. So we'll need to get the forensic team out there at some point to take another look around his house."

"Did the burglar get what he was looking for before you stopped him? That's the question." The senior deputy cleared his throat. He waggled his fingers at Viviane, and she handed over half of what she was holding. "I'm guessing you're taking Jake and heading out?"

Hearing his name, Jake stood.

"Yup. It won't be as much fun as going through a long list of names, but I need him to do a deeper search through the Biggio residence. We've got CyberGuard under lock and key while we take everything out of there and process the scene. This guy attacked an officer, so he's not above attacking a grieving widow either."

Viviane nodded. "That's true."

Rebecca turned to her newest deputy. "Bring your personal effects, Jake. You're going to be protecting Patsy Biggio."

15

R ebecca and Jake each took their own cruisers over to Coastal Ridge.

For her part, Rebecca felt like she'd spent the entire week crossing the bridge. Still, it was a nice enough drive that she took the opportunity to roll down the windows and let the briny breeze in. Wispy, stretched-out clouds were scrawled across the sky. Sunlight spiked off the crests of the waves as the ocean churned underneath. For a few miles, she was able to relax as the wind whipped through her hair.

Her tires hummed as they hit the stretch of grooved lines used to channel water off the road. As a kid, that had been the sound that let her know vacation was about to start—or end—as they took the bridge.

One hand on the steering wheel, she propped her elbow up in the open window and took in the sights. Seagulls and pelicans lazily surfed the updrafts, dipping and bobbing as they swayed side to side, looking for a meal. Their excited calls to each other, probably the bird equivalent of "get off my lawn," added to the zen-like quality of the scene.

If Jake hadn't been in his cruiser behind her, Rebecca

totally would've stuck her hand out the window and let the breeze push it up and down the same way she had done as a child. Her tires hummed again as they left the last section of bridge and transitioned back to the boring pavement of town.

Straightening, Rebecca rolled up the windows before the heat of the city could roast her. Still, the smile stayed on her face for the rest of the ride to the Biggio house, where the weight of responsibility settled onto her shoulders again. It was time to get back into work mode. She sighed.

Pulling up to the curb, she took her sunglasses off and tossed them onto the passenger seat. She'd need them again when she drove over the bridge to go back home. Hopping out of the SUV, she paused long enough for Jake to join her. Together they crossed the quiet residential road, Jake falling back a half step to let her take the lead.

On the walk up the drive, the front door swung open to reveal a woman who looked remarkably like Patsy, though quite a bit taller. With arms crossed, she stepped out onto the front porch, shutting the door behind her. Her hair was a lighter shade than Patsy's, especially at the roots, but they had the same nose.

"I'm Delilah, Patsy's younger sister." The woman spoke a little over a whisper. "Patsy's inside. Officer Hooper called to let me know you were on your way over."

"How's she doing?" Rebecca lowered her voice to match the protective woman who was squaring herself up, even if subconsciously, in front of the door.

"She's holding herself together. But if she scrubs the kitchen again, we're going to have to repaint the cupboards. And maybe the walls too."

"Stress cleaning. I totally get that."

It made sense, but if this was a crime scene, Patsy could have destroyed any evidence that had been left.

"Look, I don't mean to be rude, but what are you here for?" Delilah looked over her shoulder. "Do you have more questions or new information?"

"I do have some news. I'm sorry."

The sister flinched. "Come on in." She turned halfway to the door but hesitated. "Don't…please don't judge my sister. She's…been having a rough time."

"Ma'am, I assure you, we won't judge her. Everyone grieves in their own way." Every time the woman opened her mouth, Rebecca became a little more worried. The last time she'd been here, they'd needed to call the ambulance. Could Patsy have gotten worse?

Delilah reached for the door and paused again. Then she sighed and opened it, leading them inside.

Clattering emanated from the kitchen, and Delilah directed them there. "Patsy, some people from the sheriff's are here. Are you up to talking to them?"

"Of course! Send them on in."

The walk inside to the kitchen was a short one, where boxes and wrapping paper piled around Patsy Biggio and her hair—what little that was left of it—quickly came into view.

"I'm not going insane." The woman laughed.

Rebecca realized her eyes were wide and her jaw was hanging open. For someone who had seen so much, she was not prepared for the micro-bob and deep-burgundy dye job—that most certainly came from a box and was applied with a shaky hand—that the widow was now sporting. Hysteria and grief could make even the most balanced people start to lose it.

Jake laughed, and Delilah and Rebecca both spun on him.

He ignored them, beaming with amusement. "A bit of stress cleaning getting done?"

As Patsy nodded happily, he pointed at his light-brown hair. "And a new do? My sister does the same thing when she's stressed. Which is why I always have her over every time something goes wrong. I give her dinner and ice cream, and she makes my whole apartment sparkle."

Patsy laughed and waved a hand at Delilah. "See! That's what a good sister does, Del. You should be happy I'm cleaning."

"Making order out of your chaos. That's how my sister always puts it." He smiled at Delilah and her shoulders relaxed. "Totally normal and healthy way to deal with things. Ordered house, ordered mind."

"Yes! That's it." Patsy's smile grew shaky as she fingered her hair. "I might've gone a little overboard on the hair, though."

Jake waved her off, joining her at the kitchen island. She gestured toward the barstools, and he casually pulled one out to sit on. "Like we don't all do that when we go through a major change. You should see what I did when I got out of the Army. Had a mohawk up to here. And dyed the ends... only the ends, mind you...a bright green."

Laughing, Rebecca pulled out a stool. "I think I can picture that on you. Mine wasn't as extreme because I wanted to get back to what I used to have. I hit the salon as soon as I got out of the hospital last time. If I could've moved my arms, I would've done it myself. Now I'm wondering if I should've gone with something a little bit flashier. Or new."

With every sentence uttered, Patsy was acting slightly less manic.

Jake had picked exactly the right tone. Easy camaraderie and shared pain to help Patsy feel like she wasn't so far outside the norm.

Delilah finally joined them, looking amused. "Oh my god. Patsy, do you remember what I did when I caught Cliff cheating on me?"

Patsy paused to think, then laughed as riotously as her

sister. Rebecca and Jake sat watching, amused, as the sisters laughed together, having to lean on each other to stay upright.

"You rearranged your entire apartment. And got a tattoo on your butt!"

"It wasn't on my butt! It was *above* my butt, thank you." Delilah giggled into her hands, covering her face. "A phoenix bursting out of an egg, of all things."

Picturing the middle-aged woman with a tramp stamp of a mythical creature, Rebecca could see that Patsy came by her coping strategies naturally.

"But you didn't show up at my doorstep to talk about my hair or my sister's butt, Sheriff. What was it you needed?" Patsy was still smiling as she turned her attention to Rebecca.

Not wanting to draw it out, Rebecca laid out the facts as clearly as possible. "Early last night, Roger's office was broken into. I was there at the time and confronted the thief and chased him off. Between that and other evidence, we've ruled your husband's death a homicide."

The amusement fell from the women's faces. Patsy stared at Rebecca while her sister watched her protectively.

"I knew he didn't take his own life. Roger wasn't a quitter. He's already gone through so much. We've gone through so much together. I couldn't picture him throwing in the towel. Between the two of us, I was the one more likely to give up. Not Roger. Never Roger." Her smile was a bit watery, but she still managed.

"Do you happen to know if Roger had a security system at his office?"

Patsy shifted uncomfortably. "He used to. It was one of the things we had to stop paying for with finances so tight."

"Because of the break-in at CyberGuard Forensics, I'd like to station one of my men here. Deputy Coffey doesn't have to stay in your house. He can stay outside, if you prefer. It's up to you. But—"

"She can come stay with me." Delilah took Patsy's hand and smiled at Jake, who beamed right back. "My house could use a good scrubbing anyway. And I have ice cream."

"Who killed my husband, Sheriff West? Do you have any clues?"

Rebecca wasn't going to admit that Patsy might've erased some of the evidence they needed in her cleaning binge. "We do have some clues. So far, we're not sure exactly who they point to. This might be uncomfortable to think about, but we learned that Roger's ex-wife was buried in the cemetery where we found him. Do you know of any reason he might have been there?"

Patsy didn't look disturbed by the question at all. "I have no idea. We used to go to Lauren's grave on her birthday every year. For the last two, Roger didn't go with me. He was busy with work."

"You'd go to your husband's ex-wife's grave alone?" Rebecca found that hard to believe.

"Not ex-wife. First wife. She died while they were married, so she's not an ex. And Lauren was my best friend. That's how Roger and I met. They were high school sweethearts. Lauren and I roomed together in college. She always said I was her platonic soulmate. We stayed close after she and Roger got married. Then Roger and I leaned on each other to get through her loss. One thing led to another, and we fell in love."

Patsy shrugged and pointed at a picture on the wall in the front room.

Rebecca turned. There were Roger and Patsy Biggio with an arm each around a woman standing between them. The trio was posed and smiling at the camera.

"Then why doesn't Roger post as many pictures of you

online as he did with Lauren?" Jake's question was casual and got right to the heart of the matter.

Patsy frowned, lost in memories as she stared at the picture of her dead friend and husband. "Lauren's parents never understood how Roger and I could get together like we did. They were too hurt from losing their daughter. I can't blame them. Their grieving led to their divorce. Our shared grief led to us getting married."

Rebecca thought she understood. "You didn't want to hurt them further?"

Patsy blew out a breath laced with heartbreak. "Roger and I thought it would be cruel to rub their noses in it, us being able to move on when everything fell apart for them. We both stopped posting. And to be honest, we're not kids anymore. Hardly anything we do is worthy of sharing with the world."

That all made a sad kind of sense to Rebecca. Now that she knew what the "first wife" looked like, she saw her face over and over again in the house. Posed with either Roger or Patsy, candid shots of the women as young adults, and just as many with all three of them smiling. It would be easy enough to double-check what she'd said, and Rebecca made a mental note to do that.

"If CyberGuard was broken into, do you think his death is related to his job?" Patsy pushed her bangs back. Not used to the short length, she failed to tuck a strand behind her ear properly and didn't notice it slide forward again. "He was always so dead set," she flinched at the wording, "on keeping his work separate from his homelife. I thought it was an excuse to keep a fancy office and pretend to live beyond his means."

"It could be related. We're not sure yet. Did he ever talk about his work?"

"Rarely. Never before a case was finished. One time,

Roger had to testify in Norfolk about a teen girl being cyber-bullied by a classmate her senior year. He uncovered some social media history and confirmed that the cyberbullying was happening and traced the anonymous posts back to one person. The bully was expelled from her private school and lost a college scholarship after charges were filed against her for stalking, communicating threats, and identity fraud."

Rebecca smiled. "That's important work."

Patsy attempted to brush her hair behind her ear again. "That girl's father punched Roger in the face when he was leaving the courthouse. The police grabbed him, and he was charged with assault. Roger refused to press charges, but it didn't matter. It was witnessed by the cops and in a federal building. The case went forward without Roger doing anything."

"Can you remember his name?"

"Of course. It made the news. It was Brian Dunmore, former football player for Virginia Tech."

Rebecca pulled out her notepad and jotted down the name. "Is there anything else you can remember? Any other clients?"

"*Hmm*, he was recently doing something for Coastal Ridge Hospital." Patsy rubbed her eyes, as if she could call forth scraps of conversations she'd had with her husband.

"Any other clients? Or people he might have mentioned?"

"There was one case he told me about. I remember it because they were local, and Roger was worried about it. That's why he told me. An executive from a Virginia-based investment firm hired him to investigate one of their employees, a day trader named Niro Donato. Roger put together evidence of insider trading and bribery. The guy was fired because of what Roger found."

Rebecca wrote that name down too. "You seem very familiar with the case."

Patsy's eyes narrowed in anger. "It stands out in my memory because he ran into my husband at a restaurant one time. He said Roger ruined his life. He was arrested, and his wife divorced him, took their two children, and moved out of state. Roger didn't feel remorse. I didn't think he should either. All my husband did was find out what was really happening and report it. Donato did all that to himself, but he wanted to blame a good man for his downfall."

"Did Mr. Donato say anything else?" Rebecca's tone was neutral, but Patsy's hands were balled into fists and her knuckles had gone white.

"That bastard told Roger he would get his revenge one day. What if this is what he really meant?"

16

————

Viviane and Hoyt were alone in the bullpen going through the list of names Rebecca had supplied. Locke was still off visiting his friends, and Vi was glad he was taking some personal days. Thankfully, no crises had arisen to leave them shorthanded.

Hopefully, she hadn't just jinxed their current case with that thought.

"Well, that's interesting." Viviane was so used to talking to herself in the empty office that she didn't even notice Frost looking up when she spoke.

"What's so interesting?"

Viviane jerked her head up. Frost was leaning over to see what she was looking at. "Oh, um. One of the names on here is Deborah Niece."

"Deborah? From Shadow Homes Real Estate Agency?"

"That's the one."

"I haven't talked with her since Natalie Lamar's death." Hoyt stood up and took the two steps he needed to read over Viviane's shoulder. "Why's her name in here?"

"I'm not sure. Biggio has information on her, her business, her dad, and her ex."

"Oh, what was that slimy bastard's name?"

Viviane snorted. That was exactly how she would describe the man. He'd been a womanizer as well as a crappy real estate agent, always hitting on his clients. "Melvin Niece. He skipped town before the divorce was even settled."

"You hungry? I'm thinking of going down to the renovated, newly owned, and murder-free Seafood Shack to get some fish tacos."

Thank goodness for new management. Mike Smith, a murderer in hiding, had run the Seafood Shack before and killed one of his employees to escape arrest, which had put most of the department off eating there for a while.

Viviane actually heard Hoyt's stomach growl. "What? I couldn't hear what you said over your stomach making all that noise."

He laughed. "Feed me, Darby."

"We finally get a tiny lead, and you want to go get fish tacos?"

"Look, to be clear, those two things have nothing to do with each other. I wanted to go get lunch way before you interrupted my daydreaming." He glanced at his watch. "It's already one o'clock."

Viviane blew a raspberry and rolled her eyes. "Don't give me that. Daydreaming. You were sitting there going through all the names, same as me. You're merely pretending to be lazy, so I'll feel obligated to pick up any slack. But we both know there isn't any slack because you do your job."

Hoyt pressed a hand to his chest in mock shock. "Again, to be clear, you don't need to *feel obligated* to pick up my slack. You're required to pick up my slack. That's one of the benefits of being a training officer. Having a mewling little rookie to do all the grunt work."

With another roll of her eyes and an exaggerated sigh, Viviane shook her head. "Not fair."

"And if I haven't given you any slack to pick up, I should fix that now. I'm going to run out to get some lunch. You want anything?" Done with his theatrics, Hoyt straightened and went to his desk.

"No. I want to have a talk with Deborah and see what she can tell us about why she's on Roger Biggio's list."

The senior deputy locked his desktop computer, pushed his chair in, and settled his hat on his head. "You can do that too. That'll help us figure out what these lists are about and why he has all these names."

"Wait." Viviane squinted her eyes suspiciously. Only last week, she'd gotten chewed out, twice, for interviewing a witness on her own. Surely this had to be a trick, or another part of Hoyt's half-lame, half-cute brand of hazing. "Are you serious? 'Cause if I go talk to Deborah and Rebecca yells at me, I'll tell her that you told me I could."

Hoyt shrugged. "Good. Because I did. If you get in trouble for doing what I told you to do, then that's on me." He looked her dead in the eyes, and she was starting to think he really wasn't pulling her leg. "Also, Deb's not a witness. Or a suspect. Or a possible suspect. You can talk to her alone."

Viviane followed along behind him as he continued his bluster about leaving her on her own. It was a fake-out, right? She could no longer tell. "But how do we know she's not a suspect? She could be the killer. Right?"

The older deputy stopped walking for the front door and turned on her. "Deborah Niece? Really? A murder suspect?"

"Well…" Yeah, it sounded completely farfetched in her mind. "Rebecca says to get rid of all our bias and look at every case with fresh eyes."

"True. But this is Deborah. You know her. Think it through, rookie."

Okay, she'd been right. This was a test. Forgetting her personal feelings, what facts did she know about Deborah that would preclude her from being Roger Biggio's killer? She said the first thing that came to her mind. "Deborah's a foot shorter than him and not nearly strong enough to carry his weight."

"Killers can be resourceful, and this one's allegedly short, so her size doesn't eliminate her from the suspect pool. What does clear her, though, is that she was on a women's retreat with Angie's church group, and they didn't get back 'til eight that morning."

"Wait. Really? She has an alibi?" Viviane clenched her jaw.

As Hoyt reached the end of the wall, he patted Elliot on the back with a grin as he stepped around the dispatch desk.

"No, not really." He turned back to Viviane. "Why would a church group for married women get back after dawn on a Monday? You have to get better at figuring out when people are lying to you, Darby. More importantly, the lesson here is that normal people can commit terrible crimes under the right circumstances. In my experience, money and power can tempt even the most straitlaced person. All joking aside, you need to always remember that. No one is above suspicion." He paused to make sure his message resonated before slipping out the door.

Mulling over her training officer's words, Viviane returned to her desk. She was disappointed in herself for not recognizing Hoyt's deception. Throwing herself into her seat, she glared at the papers.

Until now, she'd managed not to fall for any of Hoyt's ploys, but she'd stepped right into this one. She'd gotten excited and stopped thinking things through. If she had, she'd have known there was no church retreat. Her mom hadn't gone anywhere, and she was in the same group as Angie.

Contemplating it further, she was even more frustrated with herself because Deborah wasn't even in the church group. Her instincts told her she should go chat with the real estate agent. Even if Hoyt was messing with her, he'd told her she could go.

If I go, and I'm not supposed to go, that means he's the one who gets chewed out by Rebecca, not me.

Vindicated and vindictive, Viviane jumped out of her seat, snatched up her hat and gun, and rushed to the door.

"I'm heading out, Elliot. Hold down the fort 'til I get back."

"You got it, Vi...I mean Deputy."

Either Viviane would figure out why Deborah was on the list and get praised, or Hoyt would get into trouble for leading her astray. Both of those possibilities were fine with her.

17

Abe Barclay, the cemetery groundskeeper, parked his work truck on the street in front of the sheriff's station. But then he sat for a few minutes, chewing on his lip, debating whether to actually go in. He was in no mood to deal with that wannabe sheriff. She'd sashayed into her position without earning it or knowing her place. He didn't like being forced to work with know-it-all women. She was no Alden Wallace, that was for sure.

And it would be humiliating to have to get fingerprinted by a dumb blond.

If she was even there. He'd heard rumors a while back that she was always showing up to work late. And of course, she kept getting hurt on the job and had to recover while getting paid on the taxpayer's dime. Probably broke a nail and had to get an emergency manicure. He snorted a laugh at the idea.

Climbing out, he slammed his truck door shut and tromped up to the entrance. There were only a few people out and about, since it was basically the last few weeks of the summer season. With kids already back in school in most places, the sidewalks were empty. And there were only a couple of cars on the street.

He headed through the door and up to the new kid behind the desk. That was good to see. A man right up front to greet everyone.

The new fella was stuck on the phone, though. All he could do was lift a finger to signal to give him a minute. With nothing else going on, Abe wandered around, half listening to the conversation.

"Mr. Washington, Mr. Washington, sir, no I can't send anyone out to look for your wife. Sir…yes…sir. Yes, sir. Sir, is your son there?"

For a moment, Abe felt a twinge of something. He'd heard about Buzz Washington. The poor guy had lost his wife and his mind. It was a sad thing when a good man was deprived of a woman like Amy. Even sadder still when that same man lost his marbles too.

Turning away from the call, he inspected the lobby instead. He hated waiting. For anything. That was why he was here now, so he could talk to someone face-to-face and get things dealt with straight away.

Stepping to the right, Abe tried to get a view into the back. If he could flag down one of the men, he might be able to get this settled.

"Can I help you, sir?"

Abe stopped leaning over the half door and looked at the dispatch kid. He was sitting there with his hand over the mouthpiece of the headset. "I need to speak with Deputy Frost. He asked me to come in. Can you let me in to have a word with him?"

"I'm sorry, sir. Deputy Frost left a bit ago. I'm the only one here right now, but I can call Deputy Darby back to the station if you'd like to speak with her."

It took a moment for Abe to remember who Darby was.

Then he realized the boy had said "her" and scowled. "Not *her*. Is Deputy Abner here, then?"

"No, sir. Abner doesn't work until this evening." He jerked the phone back up to his mouth. "Mr. Washington? Were you able to find your son?"

Abe lifted his hands, twiddling his thumbs as he stared at the kid.

"Sir, that's your nurse. No, sir. I don't need to speak to her. Sir?"

Giving up on waiting, Abe started patting his pockets. He always had paper on him in some form or other. Feeling the crinkle in his back pocket, he pulled out a folded sheet. Miming to the kid, he made it clear he needed a pen. Once he got it, he scribbled out a note. Refolding it, he jotted Frost's name on the flat side and passed it over.

"Make sure he gets that. All right?" He popped the pen into his pocket, staring the kid in the eyes to make sure he understood.

Looking down, the kid nodded.

The last thing Abe needed was for the deputies to think he wasn't complying. Then they'd come poking their noses around again, and he didn't need that kind of hassle.

That taken care of, he turned to leave. It was past lunch, and he still needed to get home and make something to eat. There was only so much time he was willing to waste on the cops.

18

I knew something had to be up. There was no way Abe would willingly talk to a woman like that, not unless he was trying to screw her too. And she was way out of his league.

After she'd left Abe last night, she'd driven straight home and hadn't gone anywhere else. But considering what she'd said to him, I thought it would be wise to check up on Abe and make sure she hadn't talked him into doing anything stupid.

"Why are you going to the sheriff so soon after talking to her? *Hmm?*"

Abe parked his work truck on the street, and I drove past it. Maintaining the speed limit, I blended in with the rest of the thin traffic. Once past his vehicle, I parallel parked a few spaces ahead of him.

Using the rearview mirror, I watched Abe go inside. My heart sank a little. He was going to the damn cops. I'd have to get rid of him now. It was foolish to have hoped he'd ignore the rants of that bitch as she put stupid ideas in his head. He'd been useful to me once.

Hanging Roger in Abe's work shed should've sent a clear message to Abe not to mess with me. Put an end to the demand for more pay. As he had with all my other victims, Abe should've hidden Roger Biggio's body and kept his mouth shut.

But the cops found Roger before Abe had even seen him. My warning wasn't as effective without the bloat and rigor of decay.

And now Abe was walking into the sheriff's station.

A man who knew too much about me and my activities just strolled into a nest of cops like it was no big thing.

After only a few minutes, he came back out. He looked up and down the street. Not once did his gaze settle on me. He had no idea I was here. Even in the middle of the day, with only one car between us, this guy was so thick he still didn't notice me. Had he been this careless in our other transactions? Maybe there was a trail that led from Abe back to me.

"How can you be this blind? You should notice your surroundings and who's watching you."

I didn't bother to lean down as the oblivious caretaker drove right past me. He never even looked around, just kept his attention straight ahead. Even as I pulled into traffic directly behind him, Abe didn't seem to notice.

"Can I trust someone like you? If you're this thick, how much did you spill to the cops? If they called you in for anything, you'd still be in there. That means you went in on your own. What did you tell them, Abe?"

I kept talking to myself as I drove behind him through town, then out into the residential areas. As I considered the events of the previous evening and what that meeting meant for me, I wasn't sure if I was trying to talk myself into or out of killing Abe.

Really, it didn't matter. Taking his life wouldn't bother me one way or the other. It was only another thing to do.

As I expected, we drove straight to the caretaker's house. It was a run-down little duplex with a scraggly yard barely big enough to encompass the building. There wasn't even enough room for a driveway. Abe parked on the street, never looking up as he swung his door open.

I did the same maneuver as before, driving past him to the next intersection, and turned right. Once I could see the back of his house, I pulled over on the shoulder. With a resigned sigh for having to work in the middle of the day, I reached into the back seat. There was no one home to see me. Kids were in school. People were at work. The sun was bright and almost every window had the shades pulled to keep out the heat of the day.

Clipping my tool pouch to the back of my belt, I climbed out of my car. Time to take care of this shit.

19

A little bell chimed as Viviane pushed open the door to Shadow Homes Real Estate Agency. It was the middle of the day, so she suspected Deborah would be in the office. That suspicion was confirmed when a cheerful voice called out from the back.

"Welcome! Please come in. I'll be right there."

"It's Deputy Darby, Deborah." Viviane smiled at how silly that sentence sounded.

"Viviane! Girl, come on back here. I'm in the middle of a pile of brochures. You can join me."

"A paper-cut prison? That sounds like a fun time." Viviane laughed and wandered back, following the real estate agent's voice. The entire office smelled like the candle version of a home-baked apple pie. Despite the artificial nature of it, the smell instantly relaxed her, reminding her of life's simple pleasures. And it made her hungry. Maybe she should've told Hoyt to pick her up something after all.

Viviane turned the last corner and found the real estate agent sitting at a tiny, two-seater kitchenette table. The table, floor, and other chair were piled high with boxes filled with folded and flat brochures, business cards, and calendars, all featuring Deborah's face. She said the first thing that popped into her head.

"That's a lot of brochures."

Deborah laughed and started to wave her over. "I was going to tell you to take a seat, but it looks like the boxes got there first."

"Oh, that's fine. I spend so much time sitting in my new job, standing is kind of a relief." Viviane couldn't help but gaze into the boxes.

"I promise I'm not a narcissist." Deborah blushed as she watched Viviane stare at all her tiny smiling faces. "This is for my job. People need to know what I look like before I show up at a viewing or inspection. Sometimes I think this is the hardest part of the job. Or maybe it's getting my picture taken and deciding which one to use."

"You need all of these?"

She bobbed her head, glancing around. "Yeah, it looks like a lot, because it is, but I couldn't stand looking at the old ones. You know, the ones with Nat on them. Seeing her looking out at me from the shelves and racks. After…you know."

Viviane gulped, grateful she hadn't eaten before having that mental image in her mind. Natalie had been Deborah's best friend and business partner…until she became the third victim of a madman who killed her in an insane bid to keep his sanctuary and altar safe. Natalie's decapitated head propped up and staring at her own corpse next to the Old Witch's Cottage hadn't even been the most gruesome part of it.

Her body was also flayed and mutilated. Rebecca and the others found strips of her flesh the madman was using to create a book cover. And the prior crime scenes had been decorated with drawings in literal shit. Human feces. Viviane was thankful she hadn't been promoted before then, as she probably would've fainted.

Frost had puked a few times. So had Locke, from what she'd heard. Even Rebecca and Darian, the two strongest stomachs she knew, had been shaken by what they'd found. The whole thing had been incredibly creepy and disgusting.

Seeing Natalie's face staring at her from every piece of marketing material would've had Deborah weeping her eyes out on a daily basis.

Now Deborah took a sip of her drink and somehow managed to smile, despite it all.

Viviane coughed, trying to settle her stomach and keep from crying at the same time.

"Are you here looking for a home, hun? Or is this official business? Has anything changed with Nat's case?"

"No, ma'am." Viviane straightened, swallowing hard. "Kevin Garland is still dead. Thank god. And the case was cleared, with all the t's crossed. I'm sorry, but I'm actually here about a different case. Do you know a man named Roger Biggio?" This was more difficult than she thought it would be. Talking to the police again had to be triggering for Deborah.

"I don't think so. Why? Wait." Deborah pouted prettily, and Viviane gave her a moment to finish whatever thought had popped up in her mind. "What line of work is he in?"

"Cybersecurity."

"And investigations. Yes, I kind of know him. I never met him in person, but I did hire him years ago. That was back in 2012 or thereabouts, I think. He told me he was taking on side gigs in addition to his day job."

"What did you hire him for?"

"He worked for the company I contracted to figure out what was going wrong with my ledgers. And that's a scary thing when you run your own business. It was just me and my husband at the time, and neither one of us knew what was going on. That was back when we were Niece Real Estate."

"Oh, I had forgotten about that. What did you need him for?"

"My books weren't balancing, no matter what I did. The bookkeeper I used to double-check my work suggested there was something going on with my computers, since he was seeing different things from what I saw." Deborah picked up one of the brochures and sighed. "Turns out my husband was embezzling funds from the business to pay for his girlfriends."

That was a new layer to the rumors. Viviane kept her face neutral, even though she sympathized with the woman. More importantly, this was just the point Hoyt had made back in the office. Cheating and embezzling were the kinds of things a normal person just might kill over. Maybe Melvin had sought revenge against Roger Biggio.

"It ended up destroying my first business, but Natalie got her license and joined me. We opened Shadow Homes Real Estate Agency and built it up to what it is today. Maybe I should give up, though. Two partners down already. I think I'm cursed."

"You're not cursed. Not any more than the rest of us. Hey, you must have new contracts now that Coastal Properties is tied up with all those investigations and lawsuits and is virtually bankrupt."

"True. And that *has* been good for business."

"See? Not cursed. Just bad things happening to good people."

"I suppose you're right. So long as this new case of yours doesn't take down my new company." Deborah waved her hands over the stacks of smiling faces. "I've spent a lot of time and money on this crap."

Viviane smiled. "I hope not."

"And I suppose, if I'm not looking back through the gray-colored glasses of a broken heart, I can say that Roger Biggio saved me." Her shoulders twitched in what might've been the world's saddest shrug ever. "Because of what he found, I was able to separate myself from Melvin and his schemes. And I got my money and my dignity back when I kicked him to the curb."

"But I bet Melvin wasn't very happy with him." Viviane didn't want to point out the bad side of the situation, but she also needed to know more. "Did your ex hold a grudge against Roger?"

"Oh, Melvin never even knew about Roger or the big company he worked for back then. I took everything he dug up and gave it to my lawyers. We used what he'd found in the divorce trial, and I sent it to the IRS, but nothing had Roger's name on it."

"Do you think that was because Roger was worried about his safety?"

Deborah shook her head, her tight French twist hardly moving. "I don't think so. Or at least, he never sounded worried to me. He seemed more concerned about my well-being. According to him, a lot of people will lash out when they're caught or about to be caught. His company even gave me an action plan of how to move forward safely with what I was given. Which, in my case, was to take it directly to my lawyers and the Real Estate Board of Virginia."

This was where things got tricky for Viviane. She didn't want to sound accusatory. But she also wanted to make sure she covered all her bases. "Okay, last question, and then I'll get out of your hair. I have to ask this for the record. Where were you last Sunday night to early Monday morning?"

Deborah tittered a delicate laugh and waved her hands, palms up, over the stacks of boxes that surrounded her. "I was at the annual real estate conference in Richmond. That's where I met the vendor who printed all these out for me. Go ahead and grab one of the receipts if you want. There's one for each item."

Looking down, Viviane spotted a slip of paper that had slid between the printouts and the side of the box. She scanned it quickly. Order placed in person, photoshoot fees, dates, and location were all listed along with time of delivery and two signatures. It was as solid an alibi as she could've hoped for.

20

A be's window slipped out of its frame easier than the windows at Roger's home and office had. Four simple slices, and I was through the sealant. There was no second pane of glass either.

It always shocked and amused me how many people thought their houses were secured when it was literally silicone that was only meant to keep water out. Most of the time, that was all that stood between me and what I wanted.

I was breaking into his bedroom on the side of the house. This time of day, it was the best choice. People, adults at least, were rarely in their rooms sleeping during the day. Once I set the liberated glass pane on the ground, I reached up with my gloved hands and hopped up and through the frame still locked into the casing.

On the second step into the room, the floorboard creaked. I froze.

I could hear Abe. It sounded like he was in the kitchen. Water was running and what sounded like dishes were clinking, but nothing loud enough to cover the loud groan of hardwood floors.

Five seconds went by. Nothing happened. I nearly laughed out loud, which still might not have given me away. Of course. I should've known. Abe's head was so far up his own ass, he was clueless about anything around him. Which sealed his fate.

Abe had to go.

Slowly, I pushed open the bedroom door, already slightly ajar. Holding it firmly in my hand, I pressed my other hand against the hinge side, supporting it so it wouldn't squeak as I peered through the tiny gap. The bedroom connected to a front room. The couch was visible, as was the flat screen mounted on the wall, but I couldn't see the kitchen where the sounds were coming from.

Moving cautiously, I stepped out of the bedroom, leaving the door open in case I had to make a fast escape.

Abe never even raised his focus from the dishes as I stalked up behind him.

I was almost within striking distance when he finally glanced over his shoulder.

His eyes went wide when he saw me, and a thin, high-pitched squeal came out of his throat. He started flailing, as if he wasn't sure which way to run. Finally, he settled for stumbling back, dropping a dish towel as he tried to move toward a corner of the room.

Worried he was going for a weapon of some kind, I darted forward. I smashed the heel of my hand into his forearm, slamming his wrist into the tall cabinet next to him. He squealed again as I caught that wrist up and yanked it away. Twisting his arm, I sent him stumbling to the side. When he moved, it was clear what he'd been after.

A shotgun rested in the corner against his pantry.

Abe's remaining good hand jumped up in surrender. What a pansy. I shook my head in mock sympathy.

"Hi, Abe. Did you get my message yesterday?"

His wide eyes bulged even more, and I hoped he didn't end up pissing on my shoes. I hated it when people did that. I liked my shoes, and urine was a scent that stuck around. Not to mention I didn't want any of Abe's DNA on me.

"Message? Did you leave a note in our usual place? I don't know anything about a message."

"You don't? I'm talking about the message hanging in your shed. That was to remind you what I'm capable of and that you should be happy with the agreement we had. Greed is a dangerous business. Asking for more cash was your first mistake. Your second was not getting rid of the body before the cops stumbled upon it."

Sweat dripped down Abe's temple. "I—"

"Actually, you have too many screwups to list them all. I wouldn't be here right now if you'd handled things on your end. But now you have foolish ideas in your head and that's why you went for the gun, isn't it?"

"I was startled, that's all." Abe tried to back away from me. There was no place for him to go. The tiny kitchen barely had enough room for the stove, fridge, and us.

"You were startled? Was that before or after you went to the sheriff?"

His eyes shifted around, and I knew he was trying to think up another lie. "Um. After."

"Then why did you go to the cops, Abe? After leaving Biggio's body hanging like a tree ornament in your shed, I'd think you'd know better than to do something so stupid."

"Yeah, I never even saw his damn body, but thanks to that, I had to give the cops my prints! Said I had to come in. They'd be suspicious if I didn't go. I don't want them looking too deeply at me. And neither do you. Right? I went in there to look agreeable, throw 'em off."

Was he being serious? It didn't matter.

"Are you trying to insult my intelligence?"

"No. Of course not." He blinked as another bead of sweat dropped into his eye. "Why would I insult you? We're a team."

"A team?" I felt ill just saying it. I wasn't on a team with him. He provided a service that made my life easier, but there were other ways for me to discard my victims without Abe's assistance. The ocean was filled with creatures eager to feast on whatever I tossed their way. "Is that why you went for your gun as soon as you saw me? Because we're a *team*?"

"I'm sorry, man. I'm sorry. Really. I am. I panicked. That's all."

"Panicking isn't good. You can't do that every time things get a little dicey. It's bad for business." I shook my head sadly, distracting him as I reached into my pouch. The syringe was tucked neatly inside and ready to go. All I had to do was drag it out, sliding the loosened cap off the needle as I did. I'd practiced the move so many times, it was smooth and natural. Abe never even noticed it.

Gently, I placed my left hand on his shoulder, looking him in the eyes as he stared in horror at where I was touching him. "Do you know what'll keep you from panicking like that in the future?"

He was so focused on my fake niceness, he never even looked the other way. "No. What?"

"Plenty of sleep, Abe. You've got to get plenty of sleep if you're going to stay healthy."

The anxious bastard nodded stupidly. "Sleep, yeah. I sleep like a baby every night. No worries there."

"Maybe you should take a nap now, Abe." I swung my right hand out. My finger was already on the plunger. As soon as the needle sank into the flesh of his arm, I depressed it. A full dose shot into his system. "Can you count backward from one hundred?"

I grinned as the reality of what had happened washed

over Abe's face. He tried to jerk away, might've even tried to scream, but neither worked. His body flailed. I stepped back, letting the drug work. It was more of a spasm, really. His legs kicked and his arms finally came up, trying to defend himself.

But it was too late. Entirely too late for Abe.

Moving over to the corner again, I cradled the shotgun as I crouched next to him. His eyes were already glassing over, but I was sure he could hear me.

"Suicide is a weird thing. Sometimes it runs through a community like a virus. Taking out the weak, the old, and especially, the stupid. Who do you think will mourn at your graveside, Abe?"

21

Rebecca parked outside the residence of Niro Donato. She'd spent so much time in Coastal Ridge lately, she felt like an honorary citizen. Though their joint jurisdiction on a case had advantages, she found the extra layers of bureaucracy a pain in her butt. And the primary benefit of extra manpower was no longer so attractive now that the department was fully staffed.

She had her phone synced up to Bluetooth so she could use both hands while in her cruiser. "So Deborah was a client of Biggio's, but that was back before he'd opened his own business?" Rebecca leaned over to use the onboard laptop to check the files. Her ribs were healed enough that they didn't protest the movement.

"Yep." Viviane's voice was so cheerful, Rebecca could easily imagine her smiling as she spoke. "She hired the firm before her divorce, which was finalized in 2014 and took more than a year to settle."

"Was that the only name you managed to track down from the list I gave you?" With the case file open, Rebecca scrolled through the list she'd uploaded and saw there were no additional notes on it.

"So far, yes. I've left messages at a few businesses, and I know Frost has too."

"Well, good job interviewing Deborah. That tells us what those papers were about. It's probably a list of people who Biggio worked for in the past. Either he hoped to use the old clients as references or to build his new client base." Rebecca checked her mirrors again, hoping to see the cruiser she'd asked for.

"Why do I hear barking in the background? Does Patsy Biggio have a dog? If she does, that might help her stay safe in case the same guy tries to break into her house."

Rebecca glanced out the window where a man struggled to get his terriers under control as a squirrel taunted them from a tree. "Patsy doesn't have a dog, and I'm not there anymore. I left Jake there on protection detail after we called forensics to comb through the house. What you're hearing is some guy on the sidewalk. I'm actually parked outside of Niro Donato's house."

"Who?" The sound of high-speed typing came over the phone.

"He's an older subject of one of Biggio's investigations. I got his name from the widow. She remembered him because Donato threatened to get revenge on Biggio. I haven't updated my notes on the case yet, so he's not in there."

"Well, you need to add it. You're out there alone." The rookie had the audacity to *tsk* at her.

"Viviane, I'm not out here alone. Or at least, I won't be shortly. I've got a local officer coming out to join me as my backup with our shared jurisdiction. That's why I'm still in my cruiser, waiting and catching up with you." She checked her mirrors one more time. "Quick rundown on the guy, though. Three years ago, Biggio investigated Niro Donato.

Biggio ended up testifying at the trial against him for insider trading and bribery."

"Revenge is a good motive for murder."

"And considering where this guy lives now compared to where he used to live, I'm willing to bet he spends a lot of time thinking about what he lost." Rebecca glanced around at the run-down neighborhood.

The sidewalk was mostly weeds with a few tree roots trying to break through. Each house was pressed up against the next, with barely enough room to walk between them. There were no front yards to speak of, merely patches of mud with a few tufts of grass. From the marks left in them from the last rain, she bet they also doubled as parking spots for the few residents who could actually afford a vehicle.

"Anything I can do to help?"

"Actually, yes. I have a second name that Patsy gave me. Brian Dunmore. Could you look him up and get me his current information? I know he used to play football for Virginia Tech, but I want to know where he is now and what he's doing. His teen daughter was another target of Biggio's investigations. After she was found guilty of cyberbullying and lost her scholarship, he assaulted Biggio. Find out what came of that assault case and get back to me."

"On it, Boss."

A Coastal Ridge cruiser turned onto the street and slowed.

"My backup's here. I'll check in with you when I'm done interviewing Donato."

"Good luck." Viviane ended the call.

Rebecca swung open her door and walked over. Officer Walton stepped out of his cruiser and secured his hat onto his shaved head. His smile reached his brown eyes, and he offered his hand in greeting.

"Sorry to keep you waiting. Would you believe me if I told you I had to help a little old lady across the street?"

"I didn't expect an Eagle Scout. How did I get so lucky?"

Tipping his hat, his smile widened. "Happy to oblige. What's the situation here?"

She brought the officer up to speed before they approached the house. The windows were covered to keep the light out, and as they got closer, she could make out the floral print and realized they were actually bedsheets and not curtains. Niro had fallen very far indeed from his five-million-dollar home on half an acre of prime beach real estate.

There was no sound when Rebecca pressed the doorbell, so she knocked on the doorframe instead. Officer Walton shifted uneasily next to her as they waited. Right before she was about to knock again, the sound of approaching footsteps reached them.

The door swung open with a stuttering creak, revealing a young man. He was pale and gaunt, frowning at them through the ripped screen door. This guy was way too young to be Niro, and too old to be his biological child. Had she gotten the wrong address?

"Can I help you?" His gaze shifted between Rebecca and Walton, who'd tucked his thumbs into his belt.

"Does Niro Donato live here?"

The man shifted uncomfortably and turned away to point at the stairs behind him. "He rents one of the rooms upstairs. But I think he's sleeping."

A roommate situation certainly explained a lot. "Can you get him for us, please?" Rebecca smiled sweetly.

"Uh, yeah, sure. I don't want any trouble."

"Neither do we. We only need to ask him a few questions."

The man—he couldn't have been twenty-five yet—turned

to race up the steps, leaving the front door open. There was a muffled conversation at the top of the stairs, but she couldn't make it out.

A few minutes later, an older man wearing nothing but a pair of shorts stumbled down the stairs. His belly jiggled with each heavy step, but the rest of his body was toned. It was the body of a guy who ate poorly but worked a labor-intensive job. He didn't stop walking until he reached the door, then pushed the screen open, forcing Rebecca and Walton to step back.

The door slammed shut behind the man, whose face matched Donato's driver's license. Crossing his arms, he leaned back against the screen door. If he was embarrassed by his state of dress, it didn't show in his face or body language.

"I'm Donato. You'll have to excuse my appearance. I just woke up since I work night shifts now. What do you want?" His voice was gruff and his hair, which was in desperate need of a trim, was giving *finger in a light socket* vibes.

"You wanna get right to it, then?" Walton looked him up and down.

There was no place for Donato to hide a weapon. He didn't even have socks on.

"Yeah, I do. Like I said, I just woke up. Haven't had my cup of coffee yet. And I don't want my roomies thinking I'm in trouble with the cops. So get on with it."

Rebecca shrugged. "We're investigating the death of Roger Biggio."

Before she could say anything more, Donato's dull-brown eyes lit up. He uncrossed his arms and gave a single clap, smiling. "That bastard is dead. Oh, that is a good way to start my day. Thank you, Officers."

"That's not a good way to start off a line of questioning." Watching the life trickle back into his body, Rebecca didn't think he was behind Biggio's death. He was too shocked and happy to hear about it.

"Whatever. That man destroyed my life. He took my license, my job, my money, my entire career. My house. Everything I worked for. Finding out he's dead makes me feel a little bit better." Donato shrugged, crossing his arms again. After that tiny bit of exuberance, he returned to his previous stoicism. "Besides, if you're here asking me about him, you probably think I had something to do with his death."

Rebecca raised an eyebrow, but it was for show. "Did you?"

"Nope. Wish I did. Would've been nice to be the one to send him to burn in Hell where he belongs. But I guess someone hated him more than I did. Besides, I have an alibi."

"How can you have an alibi when we haven't told you when he died?" She was getting curious now.

"Because I work two jobs, have to use the bus to get anywhere, and have no time to do anything else. Low-wage slobs like me, we don't have a lot of free time. I swipe my card to use the bus, I clock in, I clock out, I swipe to use the bus home again, and then I sleep. Every day, no days off. Work is all I have time for now. It seems like hell, but in this case, it gives me an alibi for any day of the last year and a half. Since I got out on probation."

Rebecca glanced around them. "That doesn't sound all that different from prison."

"It's not. My wages are garnished to pay back my lawsuits, and I still need to live." Donato shrugged, his eyes as dull and lifeless as they had been when he first walked out.

Just as she was about to ask him another question, Rebecca's radio crackled, and Elliot's voice came through. "All units, 10-57 on Granger Drive. All units, 10-57."

"Thank you for your cooperation, Mr. Donato." Rebecca

nodded to Officer Walton before racing back to her cruiser, grabbing her radio to respond. "Dispatch, I'm on my way." She hit the lights and siren even as she turned the ignition.

Elliot had used the code for *shots fired*, and she was all the way across the bridge.

22

Dust flew from her tires as Rebecca slid to a halt in front of Abe Barclay's residence. Her anxiety tasted as bitter as old coffee...or dried blood. It had taken her just over half an hour to get there from Coastal Ridge. Thirty minutes when her people were on the scene with a possible shooter. And she hadn't been able to be there to make sure they were safe.

As she wove through traffic at a pace she knew was reckless, Rebecca was transported back to the tiny spit of land and its blood-soaked shoreline. She wasn't on Little Quell Island battling an ambush from more than a dozen men. Her deputies weren't in a fight for their lives while the deafening roar of automatic weapons reverberated in her ears.

Even when the all-clear call had broadcast over the radio saying they'd found a body, the pounding of her heart had only slowed slightly. It was an over-the-top reaction. She knew it. Her therapist had confirmed it during their recent consultations. He also said an exaggerated reaction was normal for what she was dealing with and that it would fade in the coming months with some effort on her part.

Until time and cognitive processing therapy could work its magic, she distracted herself from the anxiety by looking for objects that were all some random color her subconscious chose. She was cursing her inner prankster for choosing orange, because absolutely nothing inside or outside her cruiser was orange.

Perfect.

"Hey, Boss." Viviane gave a faltering wave as she looked up from the crime scene tape she was securing around the house. "Are you okay? You look nervous or something."

Rebecca's head rocked back in what could be considered a nod but felt too jerky. She couldn't tell her friend, now employee, about the many different ways she'd pictured her untimely death in the last thirty minutes. Viviane hadn't been on Little Quell during the attack, but every time she put on her badge and gun now, she risked the same fate as Darian.

Dammit.

"Just frustrated with the traffic." The best lies were always partly true, and Viviane seemed to buy that one completely. Since Rebecca's face often betrayed her emotions, she knew a half-truth was a necessary component to convince Viviane. The second tactic was to change the subject. "What do we have here?"

Viviane waved a hand at the front door hanging wide open. "It's pretty gruesome. Would you believe me if I said it's a suicide since he's holding a gun?"

Rebecca wouldn't believe anything until she saw it for herself. "Can you show me what we have?"

"We got the shots-fired call, but when we got here, there was no answer at the door. Then Hoyt saw the victim through the window, so we had to break the door down." They walked toward the front of the house, which seemed to be a duplex. The door was smashed in, a ram bar lying on the porch.

The tension finally left Rebecca's shoulders, and she smiled at the sight before her. She knew Viviane would've pleaded with Hoyt to let her break down the door. "You the one who used that?" She pointed, and Viviane squared her shoulders proudly.

"It's a lot easier in the field than it was in the practice halls. It was even more fun than I thought it would be. At least, until we breached the door and saw what was inside." Viviane waved at the house.

"That you, Boss?" Hoyt walked outside to join them.

"It's me. Who do we have?" From where Rebecca stood in the front yard, she saw bits of shattered door strewn through the front room.

Hoyt gestured for her to follow him. "You should come see this first."

"Outside?" That couldn't be good. "Is there another body around back or something?"

"Nope. Just the one body inside, or what's left of it. We saw it when we first got here, which is why I got the ram. As soon as we made it in, I knew there was no saving him. His face and a good portion of his head were gone. But I checked anyway." Hoyt turned the corner of the house, stepping wide, and she followed in his footsteps. "But I thought you should see this first, before going in."

He pointed at a window in the run-down, aging house. The screen was warped, like it had been jimmied. The panel of glass was still in the frame, but the caulking on the lower pane looked whiter than the yellowed, slightly cracked caulk on the upper pane.

"Didn't you report that the burglar at Biggio's office broke in by cutting out a windowpane?"

"I did." Rebecca knelt, inspecting it. "This was recently done. The sealant hasn't been damaged by wind or rain."

"I already got photographs of all this. The whole outside."

Rebecca turned her head up. "Which means you left the inside for me to take care of."

"I didn't do that on purpose or anything. Although, I'm sure the faceless man will get added to my perpetual loop of nightmares, that's not the only thing you need to see." Hoyt turned and pointed.

She looked where he indicated, but she saw nothing and cocked an eyebrow, questioning him.

"There are tracks. Not around the window. Only in the sandy spots farther away. They go from the road to the house. I can't find any tracks leading away, so I'm guessing someone entered through the window and left out the front door and used the walkway. Otherwise, we'd see another set heading in the opposite direction of these."

Standing, she could see what he was talking about. Or at least, where he'd put the evidence markers. "Any good prints?"

"Not really. Not to the naked eye anyway. All I can really see is heel prints, so I can't even guess at the size of the shoes. We'll need the techs to make casts, and then we can check." He shrugged. "But, hey, at least we know he was wearing shoes with a heel. Not flip flops or bare feet."

Rebecca rolled her eyes and harrumphed. "I can tell that from here too. There are at least five patches of stinging nettles between here and the road. Nettles are nasty. If they weren't wearing thick-soled shoes, they'd be in a world of hurt."

"You keep this up, and no one will even remember you weren't born on the island." He clapped her on the back.

"Yeah, right. Okay, stay out here and make sure no one messes up the tracks. The sand is dry, and I don't want to lose them because someone got too close or a bird landed on them." Rebecca turned for the front of the house. "I'll go take care of the inside. And we'll pretend you didn't orchestrate it this way on purpose."

As she made it to the front yard again, Rebecca noticed the same old white truck she'd seen at the cemetery, parked right out front. "Darby, did you confirm that Abe Barclay lives here? Did you check on the neighbor who called it in?"

Viviane spun around to face her from where she'd been standing guard in the front yard. "I tried. No one was home. The neighbor who called said there was one shot, but no bullet hole penetrated the shared wall. I've got Elliot looking up who lives next door. And he ran the property records and, yes, Abe Barclay is renting this house."

Rebecca pointed at the parked truck. "Go run those plates and tell me if they come back to Barclay."

"On it, Boss." Viviane took off, leaving Rebecca to observe the scene without distractions.

Hoyt and Viviane had already gone through the residence. They'd cleared the house, and Hoyt had also checked the body.

Now it was Rebecca's turn to take in the scene and get her own set of pictures. As she leaned inside the shattered doorframe, she craned her neck to get her first look. She could see why they hadn't wanted to come back in.

She didn't want to step into the home until she observed the scene from her current vantage point by the front door. To the left in the living room was where the corpse sat on the couch. The shot had clearly gone through the top of the head, painting the wall and even some of the ceiling. And the couch and low coffee table had been sprayed too. A thick layer of blood coated what was left of the skull.

His eyes, nose, right cheek, and jaw were pulverized. Bone had turned into shrapnel, and his features were erased. The chest and arms were covered in blood, as was the shotgun, still partially in his grasp. Blood spray had reached the door. So had one tooth, the four roots pointing straight up in the air.

"And I thought stepping on Legos was bad."

She shook away her irreverent observation as she continued to scan the room.

Viviane and Hoyt had left trace footprints through the house as they cleared it. When lives were on the line, crime scenes could get wrecked pretty quickly. To her right was a kitchen farther inside the house, where there appeared to be dishes resting in a drying rack. Nothing looked out of place.

Rebecca shook her head and turned to get booties and other protective gear. She'd only made it a few steps before Viviane met her, holding the box of booties.

"Thought you might need these. I heard back from Elliot, and I ran the plates."

Rebecca put her booties and gloves on. "What did you learn?"

Viviane passed her the camera. "The truck isn't registered to Abe Barclay. It's registered under the cemetery's name. Also, Elliot confirmed with the homeowner that this unit is being rented to Abe Barclay."

"I think he's done something different with his hair." Rebecca shuffled her shoes in her booties to get them settled.

Viviane laughed, but it sounded a little clunky as she swallowed hard.

"You okay, Darby?"

"No, but I can handle it." Her smile faded. "Why does it look like his face exploded?"

Rebecca stepped carefully to avoid the bits of Barclay. "Because it did. The sinus cavities over pressurize and explode outward due to the kinetic energy. Combine that with the slug following right behind, taking the jawbone along for the ride, and you get face-fetti."

She nearly regretted that last word as soon as she said it

as Viviane choked and coughed behind her. Face-fetti. That was what she'd done to three of the men on Little Quell Island when they had ambushed her and her men. And as she had learned long ago, what didn't kill her made her sense of humor that much darker.

At least I can laugh at it.

For her, reviewing the scene first from a distance and then a second time up close helped her to catch details others might miss. At least, that was what she told herself. If she was honest, she actually viewed each scene three times, with the final view being through the lens of the camera as she captured each aspect of the crime.

Careful not to disturb the body before Bailey Flynn and the forensics team arrived, Rebecca inspected what remained of the jaw.

All the blood had been blown upward. After the heart stopped pumping, there was very little blood left to trickle down and soak the spot where the chin had been. The throat was relatively dry with only a few tiny splatters from the entrance wound. Dark specks mixed in with the dots.

"He's got gun powder residue here."

She took several pictures of the entrance wound before examining the shotgun. The hand holding it had relaxed in death. *Or had it been relaxed even before then?* Instances of suicide on the island were rare.

Using the lens of the camera to zoom in, she focused her attention on the hand holding the gun. There were places that should have had gunshot residue that instead appeared clean. The crime team would need to bag the hands and check them in the lab to be sure, but she suspected Abe hadn't been the one to pull the trigger.

Bailey had just determined the Biggio death was a homicide. Hoyt found evidence suggesting the windowpane on the side of Barclay's home had been tampered with much like the one at CyberGuard Forensics. Despite the mounting evidence indicating a murder, Rebecca refused to get tunnel vision.

"He's holding a shotgun. Looks like a," she squinted to read the lettering engraved on the side, "Benelli M4. Check to see if Barclay had one registered in his name."

"On it." Viviane wrote the note down.

Rebecca took several more photos. "We'll need to get prints after Bailey's done, so we can positively ID him."

This whole setup looked staged. As such, she wanted to make damn certain that nothing could go wrong with gathering the evidence. "No one touches the body or anything else until Bailey's here."

"Right. No touching."

Remembering the mark the medical examiner had just shown her at the morgue, Rebecca carefully moved around the body looking for anything similar.

There.

"Viviane, when the M.E. gets here, please have her look at this." Rebecca pointed at a small dot on the side of Abe's arm. "I think our victim was drugged, like Roger Biggio."

"Will do. You sure it isn't blood spatter?"

"We'll let Bailey confirm it, but it's too perfect of a circle and the wrong coloring to be from the head wound."

"Head wound? Is that what we're calling this?" Viviane gestured at the nearly headless corpse.

Rebecca shrugged before entering the kitchen and noting the damp dishes and sink. She snapped several photos of the area, including a dish towel on the floor. Someone had interrupted Abe Barclay while he'd been washing dishes.

Straightening, she turned to the door. A patch of bright white on the coffee table caught her eye. Shifting around the body, Rebecca took several pictures of the piece of paper there. It had scrawled handwriting across it, and she leaned over to read.

"Found a note. It says, and I quote, 'Everything is too much. Life wasn't supposed to be like this with my shitty job and no woman to call my own. I can't take it anymore. I pray my next life will be better.'"

Viviane shook her head. "I'm not buying it."

"Neither am I."

23

"Honey, I'm home!" Rebecca closed the door behind her and looked around with a smile. It felt so good to say that again, and not just be talking to the walls. Seeing the pile of folded linens on the table added a cluttered and enticingly homey feel to the cottage that she hadn't felt before.

Ryker came in from the back porch, and his welcoming smile brought heat to her cheeks. They'd slept in the same bed last night. It had been tense at first. With neither one being well enough to start anything physical, she'd been forced to clutch her hands together to keep them to herself. That aspect of their relationship had been brand-new before they'd been separated for a month, and they'd need time to figure it out.

Especially since she'd thought he hated her guts until yesterday.

"Honey, you're home." Ryker closed the gap between them and gave her a kiss. "Are you done for the day?"

"I'm not really off yet. I wanted to come back and check on you." She walked into the kitchen and took a look at his pill scheduler. The midday pills had been taken, which was a relief. She opened the freezer and pulled out one of the casseroles. There was a plate in the sink, but she felt the need to ask anyway. "Did you remember to eat lunch?"

"I did. And I had a good visit with Meg. And another one with Larry. He heard I was out of the hospital and wanted to come say hi."

She set the casserole dish in the refrigerator to thaw. It should be ready to cook by the time she got back home. "Did he? Or did he want to know when you'd be going back to work? Frost mentioned that Larry's been struggling to keep up with all the work you two used to split. I know it's been a few months since the hurricane, but there's still a lot of reconstruction that needs to be done."

"Oh, don't I know it." His chuckle was rueful. "You have no idea how much I want to be back on the job. But I still can't load a dishwasher because I'm not allowed to bend over." He gestured to the dirty dishes in the sink. "Do you know how weird it is to leave dirty dishes sitting there when I'm home all day? I feel like such an inconvenience."

"Here's a trick to the dishwasher thing. When you can't bend over, squat down to load items. I learned that the first time I broke my ribs. It makes so many things more manageable."

Ryker's eyebrows quirked and he picked up the plate and tried it out himself. "Huh! That'll work. Thanks." He frowned. "I should have thought of that myself."

Rebecca squeezed his shoulder. "I know all kinds of work-arounds for different injuries."

He wrapped his arms around her waist, careful not to hold her too tight. "While I'm glad you do, because it's useful, I wish you hadn't needed to learn any of it."

Leaning her head back, she kissed him on the cheek. "I

appreciate that. And I wish I didn't have to share that wisdom with you."

"One more question, though, and I swear I'm not judging you. Do you usually meal prep so far in advance? I've never seen a freezer so full of ready-to-eat, homemade meals."

She laughed. "I didn't make a single one of them. The one we'll have for dinner is compliments of Nancy Neumeyer, the judge's wife. A lot of people sent me food while I was recovering. I think most of them forgot it's just me here, or they weren't sure how to make a meal for one person. That's why I have a ton of leftovers I never got around to. But, hey, they're all freezable, right?"

He nodded, rubbing his cheek against hers. It felt so nice to be able to stand there together. When she'd thought he was avoiding her, she mourned the loss of their relationship. This was like a miracle, having him here with her.

Though she did still need to ask him about his parents and their response to her. But not today, and maybe not anytime soon. That conversation could wait awhile longer.

"I'm sorry you have to do this for me. I didn't think about how much I was asking when I asked to stay with you. The fact that you're recovering hadn't even occurred to me. But it's clear a lot of people reached out to help you. That usually only happens with a major injury or death in the family. I know when you came to get me from the hospital, you probably didn't list all your injuries. But this seems worse. How hurt were you?"

Rebecca felt the blood drain from her face. That was something she'd never given any thought to. He didn't know about her injuries, not specifically. Even worse, did he know about Darian?

"Um…" He hadn't seen her new scars. She'd showered and changed into her pajamas—a long sleeve shirt and loose shorts—in the bathroom before they'd gone to bed. To herself, in the light of day, she could admit she'd done that on purpose to hide it from him. Partially out of self-consciousness, but also so she wouldn't rub it in his face how dangerous her job was.

Or the danger her job had put him in.

Ryker laid his hands on her shoulders and gently turned her to face him, having to move out of the way as her holster snagged on his shirt. "Rebecca Rose West." Oh, she knew she was in trouble now...he was using her full name. "How hurt did you get after I passed out on the boat?"

"You didn't pass out on the boat. You were shot and knocked unconscious." She didn't want him to downplay his injury.

His eyes narrowed and hardened. "Whatever. Stop stalling and tell me the truth."

"It was pretty bad." Feeling like a swarm of butterflies had suddenly taken flight in her stomach, along with a few crows, she gestured toward the front room. "Can we sit down for this?"

His face etched with dread and his eyes filled with worry, he agreed and followed her to the couch, letting her sit first. "I already know something happened to your eye and your ribs were broken. We never got a chance to talk about it last night. Tell me the rest."

Rebecca scrubbed her palms on her pants, trying to keep herself grounded in the here and now while revisiting that horrible night. "First, what do you know about what happened?"

He scowled at her deflection, then saw how serious she was and relented. "I know Darian had blood on his chest. Locke was bleeding from his leg. I pulled up and you all started climbing in. I got shot but then don't remember anything else. Frost said you stayed back to hold off the bad guys while he piloted us to safety. I was the last person to check out of the hospital, so I assumed I was injured the worst."

Ryker started to grin but froze as Rebecca took both of his hands. It was so much worse than she'd expected. Had no one told him what happened? Or been allowed close enough to do so? Had he forgotten due to his brain injury? Did they simply give up on reminding him of what they'd all lost that night? The thought made her shiver, and she blew out a slow breath.

"You weren't the worst off, actually. Ryker, Darian didn't survive his gunshot wound."

His mouth fell open. Furrowing his eyebrows, he shook his head. "No...he was wearing a bulletproof vest. I saw it. And I remember him getting in the boat and he was still talking and..." His grip tightened around her fingers. "How? When?"

"That night...oh, Ryker, I'm so sorry." He shook his head again, and she felt a tiny thread of fear. What if he forgot again? She pressed on, scooting closer to him. "He *was* wearing a vest. The bullet came from the side and got under it, hitting his lung. He didn't get medical attention in time."

"What about Lilian and Mallory?"

"Lilian got to see him before he passed. Got to say goodbye."

Tears trailed down Ryker's cheeks, and he let them run. "And what about you? What happened to you after you sent us off?"

"I..." Rebecca sighed heavily. Hiding how dangerous it'd been wasn't just useless, it could come back to bite her in the ass later. If she and Ryker were going to work out, and she hoped they did, then she couldn't keep things from him.

"I got the shit beat out of me. It was bad. I've seen kids' drawings that looked better than my face. On top of that, I was shot and had my side sliced with a knife, and I was straight-up pummeled. Because of all that, I lost a lot of blood." She swallowed hard, willing some moisture into her mouth. "I nearly died."

Face pale as death itself, Ryker squeezed her hand. "I...I'm so glad you didn't."

"Rhonda Lettinger, the GIS agent, and Bailey Flynn, the Coastal Ridge medical examiner, found me and helicoptered me to the hospital. By that time, I'd nearly bled out. I was in the hospital for several days myself. Then another week of sleeping on the couch for the most part. It was the twenty-first before I got released to go back to work, and I kind of fudged the truth with my doctor to get her to do that."

He stared at Rebecca, eyes glazed with horror. "You're kidding."

Her brain caught up with her, and she added the last two things she had been diagnosed with. "Oh, and dehydration and a fractured foot." It sounded so odd, tacked on at the end like that, she couldn't help but feel awkward as soon as the words left her mouth.

Ryker's lips twitched, and he shook his head. "Fractured feet suck so much." He was holding his eyes perfectly still.

Then Rebecca giggled and quickly smothered it. Clearing her throat, she bobbed her head, exaggerating a sad smile. "Dehydration does too."

"Takes like a whole bottle of Gatorade to get rid of it."

She shook her head. "No. Mine was really, really bad. It took at least two Gatorades."

Ryker snickered before putting on a neutral expression again. He didn't hold it for long and ended up laughing uproariously. Rebecca also lost it and joined him. There was probably a decent amount of hysteria mixed in, but they fell against the back of their couch, racked with mirth.

Wiping tears from his eyes, Ryker struggled to sit up. "Oh, man, neither one of us should be laughing this hard while we're still healing." He reached over and helped her sit up, pulling her against his shoulder and kissing the top of her head. "Okay, seriously, though, why did you look so nervous before you told me that?"

Struggling to catch her breath, Rebecca gasped. "Oh, I suppose I was worried you'd freak out about my job being too dangerous or want me to step down or something. As much as it sucks sometimes, I still love it."

Ryker leaned away and stared down at her. "Not saying your job is safe…everyone knows a cop's job is risky…but have you ever really thought about how dangerous it is to work in maintenance? On an island with boats on top of that?"

Rebecca looked into his eyes and searched for any hint of disapproval, anger, or contempt. There was none. Just amusement and love. She shook her head slowly as she debated that. "No. I really haven't." She narrowed her eyes. "How dangerous is it?"

"Less dangerous than meeting up with your girlfriend to take her out for a midnight cruise after she's been hanging out with her work friends." His lips quirked before stalling and drooping. "Not by much, though. There was that time I was cutting up a tree after a storm, and it bounced unexpectedly. Hit me right in the head. If I hadn't been wearing a hard hat, I would've lost more than just a month's worth of memories."

They sat there for a moment in silence. Rebecca thought about all the different ways Ryker could get hurt on the job. Electrical work was inherently dangerous. So were framing and drywall because of the heavy materials. Going into random people's homes must be fraught with pitfalls. Her eyebrows shot up as she realized that actual pitfalls were also a problem he might have to deal with. It almost made her career seem safe by comparison.

"So…you're saying I should wear a hard hat at work?"

The corners of his eyes crinkled up. "No. I'm saying we should both wear hard hats on our next date." He kissed her, and she held onto him, snuggling into his shoulder. "I'd never presume to interfere with your job, Rebecca. But I do have a confession, since we're spilling our guts here. Metaphorically, this time. I kind of, slightly, interfered in your personal life."

Rebecca snorted. "You *are* my personal life. Of course you interfered in it. Except for my coworkers, you're basically the only person I hang out with."

"Yeah, more than that. I was going to tell you about it when you first walked in, but…"

"You forgot?"

"I got distracted. And I wasn't sure how to tell you. Mrs. Shuping heard I was staying here and stopped by."

It took Rebecca a moment to remember that name. "My landlady?" He dipped his head in agreement. "Does she want you to do some work or something? I thought everything was fixed."

"It is. But that wasn't why she called. She wanted me to help her out with some paperwork and…" Ryker shifted uneasily. "To cut to the point, since I'm sure you need to get back to work, she came by to tell you that she might not be able to honor your rental agreement for the rest of the month, let alone extend it another month like you'd asked."

Rebecca went still as her heart chilled. That was a tricky problem she'd never considered. Where else could she live on the island? This place was starting to feel like home. Before she could think of anything to say, he continued.

"Then I found out why. She got a bill for back taxes. The county reevaluated the value of the house and decided she hadn't been paying the proper amount. They want her to pay it all now or they're going to place a lien on the house."

"Can they do that?" Rebecca jerked up, pulling away from him.

He let her go, shaking his head. "No. They can't, not on a whim like this. County mandate is every two years, which isn't until next year. I know because I made improvements before the last one. Also, the value they placed on the house doesn't make any sense. I helped her contact the local board of assessment to file an official appeal with the Board of Equalization and Assessment Review. They had no idea what we were talking about and said the property assessment hadn't been changed."

Rebecca squinted, trying to figure out what it all meant.

"They looked into it while we were on the phone. Longfellow was the one who filled out the change, wrote the bill, and pushed it all through. None of it was legal or binding. We got the bill cancelled."

"Longfellow? He's—"

"It gets worse."

She gaped at him. That wasn't the end of it?

"It was such a shock for her that she's thinking about selling the house now. Before the new assessment happens."

"I'll buy it." Rebecca spoke before she could think. Just saying the words made her happier, though.

"Wait. What?"

"I'll buy it." It sounded even better the second time. "I'll call Mrs. Shuping and ask her how much she wants. I've given enough blood for this island that it feels like home. I can't leave. Not anymore. This is my home."

Ryker's lips slowly pulled back. "Are you sure?"

"I'm as sure as I can be without knowing how much Mrs. Shuping would want for it." The idea of owning this warm, cozy place filled her with tingles.

His smile kept stretching, but it was interrupted as Rebecca's phone rang.

"I'm sure that's work calling you back in. You get that, and I'll call Mrs. Shuping and let her know." Ryker darted forward and kissed her. "I'll leave you to it." He got up, heading for the phone in the kitchen.

Rebecca stood and answered her own phone, not surprised at the caller ID. "Yeah, Frost, what do you need?"

Her senior deputy cut right to the chase. "Sorry, Boss, but I need you to come back to the office. Abe Barclay made one final stop before going home and losing his life."

"Oh, yeah? Where?" Rebecca made her way to the door. A door she might soon own if things worked out right.

"Here. At the office. And he left me a note." She heard paper crinkle. "It's handwritten, and it doesn't match the writing of the supposed suicide note we found at his home."

24

When Rebecca walked through the door to the station, both Hoyt and Viviane were standing on the lobby side of the dispatch desk. Elliot appeared to be sweating buckets as he shuffled back and forth. He looked like a kid who'd been caught with his hand in the cookie jar and wasn't sure if he should beg for forgiveness or make a run for it.

"Sheriff, I swear I didn't know the man who came in was the same one Viviane was asking me about. I never got his name."

Rebecca walked up to the desk to join the rest of them. "It's fine. I'd be pretty weirded out if you did, Elliot. No one expects you to know the name of every person who walks through the front door. Now sit down and tell me exactly what happened."

"It was twelve minutes after one this afternoon. I marked it on my log, like I'm supposed to. I was on a call. It was Buzz Washington again, trying to find his wife. And I was reminding him that Mrs. Washington was deceased when this guy walked in. Viviane had just left. Hoyt was at lunch. I told the man I could get Viviane to come back. He insisted on talking to Hoyt."

"Barclay's a misogynist." Hoyt stepped back enough to let Rebecca move up in between him and Viviane. "He kept trying to talk to me when Viviane was interviewing him too. I can totally see him doing the same thing here."

Elliot jerked his head up and down, then pointed at a sheet of paper in an evidence bag. The paper looked like it had been folded in thirds before being straightened. "Yeah, he insisted it had to be Deputy Frost. When I couldn't help him, he wandered off. I didn't see what he was doing, but then he handed me that paper and told me to pass it along when he returned. To Deputy Frost, that is. So that's what I did. I handed it to him as soon as he got back."

"We didn't even have a chance to walk through," Viviane confirmed, shooting sympathetic looks at Elliot. "I would've done the same thing."

"Yeah, that's what you're supposed to do. Good job, Elliot. Get yourself some water now." Rebecca gave him a reassuring smile.

He still looked like he might wet himself at any moment. "No, I'm—"

"Elliot," Viviane leaned over the desk, getting close enough that there was nowhere to look but right at her, "walk it off. It helps." She unplugged his headset, then made shooing gestures at him until he finally relented and moved off.

"What's the note say?" Rebecca reached over to Hoyt, and he let her spin the note around to read it.

Deputy Frost, I stopped in like you asked me to so I could be fingerprinted. I do not trust that new woman Sheriff. She's just window dressing to appease the libturds. I no your the man whose really doing all the work within the police depart. You understand, the way Wallace did, how to get things dun round here the right way.

Rebecca raised her gaze to Hoyt. His cheeks were red, not with embarrassment or guilt, but with anger.

"That's the same kind of nonsense he was spouting before, all that sexist crap. Also, he can't spell." His right hand clenched into a fist, and she raised an eyebrow. For Hoyt to be so riled up, Barclay must have been saying far worse than some immature comments about Rebecca's abilities as sheriff.

"Well, considering our windows are reflective and you can't see in them, being called window dressing isn't much of a compliment either way. And doesn't say much for Barclay's powers of observation."

"Agreed."

"But I don't care what Barclay thought about me personally, or my gender collectively. All I care about is, do you have any idea what he was talking about?"

Hoyt lifted his hat and ran his hand through his hair. "I told him he needed to come in so we could fingerprint him for elimination, since it was his work shed. He didn't really need to, I just had to say something so I wouldn't punch him in the nose after the sexist shit he was saying."

"He deserved a good face-punching." Viviane cleared her throat. "No disrespect for the dead intended."

"Well, it appears someone thought he deserved more than that. So let's try to avoid our own biases and steer it back to what Barclay might have known." Rebecca looked at her two deputies. "Go sit down and try to recall everything he said to you while you were interviewing him. Subconsciously, he may have stressed certain words. Recreate the conversation as best as you can. Write down everything that was said and go over it 'til you have it right."

Elliot came back, holding a cup of water.

"When you get a moment, make a copy of the log and give it to Frost to enter into evidence as well."

"On it, Boss."

Rebecca jerked her head to stare at him. "I've left you too long with Frost and Darby. You've been corrupted."

His mouth split into a stunning grin, and his voice was no longer rushed or shaky. "The term suits you. I'm keeping it."

Knowing there was no use telling them not to call her *Boss*, Rebecca shook her head. Using her fob, she let them into the bullpen. "While you're making the copy, I'll be in my office. If we have a killer using staged suicides to cover up their murders, they might be a professional. We need to find the connection between our victims and stop the killer before they strike again."

25

Once in her office, Rebecca closed the door before sitting down at her desk. Signing in under her login, she pulled up the security camera footage for the station. It was a fairly new addition and one she hadn't pointed out to anyone else on the island. Well, no one except for Hoyt. She trusted the man enough to give him the login information.

After the ambush on Little Quell Island, it had become clear to her and to Special Agent Lettinger that someone in town had known of their plans and been able to communicate them with enough time to be ready for their arrival. Shadow Island was closer to Little Quell Island than any other land mass. Even if both boats had left at the same time, Rebecca and her crew would've gotten there first or at least seen the others pulling up.

That hadn't happened. Which meant someone knew they were leaving the island and where they were going before she'd been able to reach the dock.

Once Rebecca and Rhonda had both agreed on that, they'd devised a plan to have one of Rhonda's trusted techs come down to install the cameras in a secured, closed circuit.

Only two accounts were allowed access to that footage. One was Rebecca's. The second one she had insisted be Rhonda's.

In case Rebecca didn't survive the next attempt on her life, she wanted to make sure someone out there knew what had happened.

Hoyt she trusted with her life. Rhonda she trusted with her death. It was good to have friends like that.

She scrolled the video back to one that afternoon and started watching. At 1:09, Elliot picked up the phone. He started talking, and it quickly became apparent he was speaking with Buzz Washington. A few minutes later, Barclay could be seen walking up the sidewalk then opening the door to come in.

It went exactly as Elliot had described. He tried to take a message and offered to have Viviane return to the station. Barclay refused, borrowed a pen, pulled a piece of paper from his pocket, wrote out the note, folded it, and wrote Frost's name on the front. He stole the pen after ordering Elliot to make sure the note was passed on.

Because of course he did. It would be too petty to charge him with theft after his death, but Rebecca let herself be amused at the idea.

She switched to one of the outside cameras and set it for the same time frame. With this perspective, she watched Barclay drive down the road, park, and walk inside. He wasn't the only vehicle on the street, though. A gray sedan came into view, and the front end was distinctive enough she knew it was likely either a Buick Regal or a Ford Crown Victoria. Then again, it could've been a Lincoln Town car too. The car of choice for so many people who didn't want to be identified.

Did that driver stare at Barclay as he drove past?

Rebecca backed it up and watched it again. The gray sedan came into view, and she paused the video. She thought she could almost make out the driver of the second car, the one that came down the road immediately after Barclay. It seemed like he turned his head and watched as Barclay parked his truck before driving past, but she couldn't be certain. The glare on the windshield was too strong.

There was more than one way to identify a driver, though.

She switched to the other camera out front, this one pointed the other way. Barclay's truck came into view, and moments later, the car followed behind it. The Buick emblem on its trunk was clearly visible, but the license plate was a blur.

"Dammit."

The driver must have used a reflective coating of some kind. While the plate would be totally readable from directly behind, it would be obscured when viewed from other angles. Rebecca silently cursed the existence of reflective tape to avoid red light camera tickets.

This footage wasn't a complete waste, though. She saw the car park, wait while Barclay was inside the station, then pull out to follow Barclay again when he left.

"Was that what got you killed, Barclay? Did he follow you home after catching you coming here? Did you know something he didn't want shared?"

Rebecca captured stills of the car to print out and add to the murder board for everyone to see. She also sent out an APB on the Buick Regal. If he wasn't on the island anymore, then he would likely be driving through Coastal Ridge.

Thinking of Coastal Ridge and Barclay's death reminded her of something else. Picking up the phone, she dialed Deputy Coffey's cell.

"Coffey here."

"Are you in Patsy Biggio's house?"

"Yes, ma'am." His voice was cheery, which seemed strange.

"Is she right there?"

"Yes, ma'am." He chuckled. "That is why you called, right?"

He was good. Instead of asking questions that might give away who he was talking to, he made it sound like a personal conversation. "Instead of using the radio? Yes. I didn't want her to overhear me."

"Well, is it important? Should I come over now?" She could hear the soft thud of his boots as he started walking.

She understood what he was asking. "No, you're not in any danger that I know of. But I do want you to go outside."

"Sure, you want anything in particular? I can pick it up on my way home tonight. Yeah, let me get somewhere private."

"Look for any other signs of a break-in. We did a cursory check, but not room by room when we thought it was a suicide. M.E. has ruled it a homicide, as you know, so we need to look at the scene with fresh eyes. Check to see if any of the windowpanes have recently been cut out of their frames. That's the method that was used at Biggio's office in town and on our recent victim here who was murdered right around two this afternoon."

"I can do that, yeah." When she heard a door close, he dropped the fake cheerfulness now that he couldn't be overheard. "Look, I can tell you no windows were cut out, but there's a screen missing from a living room window. The window itself probably wasn't latched, so our guy could've made it in without cutting glass. I'll make sure everything gets closed and locked down tonight." Coffey paused. "Do you think he's about to come here, or do you think he already has?"

"I think he already has, but there's nothing to say he won't come back. He's already killed two men. This time, in the middle of the day. Keep your head on a swivel."

"Yes, ma'am."

"And keep an eye out for a gray Buick Regal. It was spotted trailing Abe Barclay before he was killed today."

"Mrs. Biggio is planning to go stay at her sister's as soon as she's done packing. That'll get her out of the danger zone, at least."

"Let's work to make that happen. Can you call the Coastal Ridge PD and request to have an officer stay with the women?"

"Yes, ma'am."

Rebecca ended the call, then dialed another number.

"Rebecca, did something else happen?" Bailey Flynn sounded distracted.

"Were you able to confirm the mark I found on Barclay's arm was from a needle?"

"Yep, just like you thought. And before you ask, I've already drawn blood and sent it off with one of my guys to get the test rushed."

"You're the pinnacle of professionalism and excellence. Any chance you've gotten the test results back from the first one yet?"

"Not as far as I know. I'm in the field at the moment, and with my hands full, it's hard to check email."

Rebecca silently scoffed at herself and opened her own inbox. Of course Bailey couldn't know. And she would get those results at the same time anyway. "I've got nothing from forensics, so that's a no."

Injection sites on both bodies couldn't be a coincidence. And with the same break-in method at Barclay's home and Biggio's office, those two scenes were linked as well. Rebecca started typing an email to send to Chief Morrow of Coastal

Ridge. She added a request to check Biggio's office parking lot cameras for a Buick Regal with a reflective license cover.

"Thanks, Bailey. I won't keep you on the phone."

"I appreciate it." The line went dead.

Rebecca walked to her printer and picked up the picture of the car. With all three scenes now connected, it would be much easier to pinpoint other similarities. Once they identified commonalities, they could start closing in on the killer.

26

Rebecca stepped back from the murder board and turned to face her deputies. They had gathered in the bullpen to try to sort through the details of the two crimes. "Darby, did you ever manage to track down the man who punched Biggio in court after his daughter was found guilty of cyberbullying?"

"Brian Dunmore, yes." Viviane tapped on her keyboard. "He has a solid alibi for both crimes, and I corroborated it with not only four other witnesses but also with receipts. He was on a fishing trip with friends. He didn't even check out of his hotel in Colorado until this morning. And he sent me this time-stamped picture of him posing with the trout he caught in the upper Colorado River."

"And I was talking face-to-face with Niro Donato when Barclay was killed, so we know it wasn't him." Rebecca put a line through both names on the board. "Okay, what else do we know about our victims?"

Greg Abner had come in to start his evening shift, and they'd been tossing around theories for nearly an hour. "They didn't attend the same schools or work in the same field. The only connection I can see between them is where Baggio's first wife was buried."

"Except Barclay wasn't working the day she was interred, and he doesn't have the information on who is getting buried, only when a burial will be happening." Viviane leaned forward on her desk, inspecting the board as she rested her chin in her hand. "So it's the location of the burial that links them, not the service or attendants."

"Barclay lived here all his life, and Biggio's only connection to the island is, again, his wife's grave. And her history, which he wasn't a part of." Frost was sitting in the middle of the aisle, rolling his chair back and forth as he spoke. "Perhaps Biggio was hired to look into Barclay for some reason. Heck, Barclay probably wouldn't have known if he was being investigated or even who Biggio was."

"That's true." Rebecca underlined the words *Biggio's clients/targets* on the board. "And we won't have that full list until computer forensics manages to crack his passwords."

"The only past client connected to Shadow Island, as far as we can tell, was Deborah." Viviane rocked her head, stretching her neck. "Could it be another land grab thing?" She scowled. "No, that doesn't make sense either. Barclay didn't own his home. And Biggio owned land but not in an area where Deborah typically works."

Rebecca glanced at the clock. Viviane and Hoyt's normal shift was over hours ago. She remembered how tiring it was to be a rookie—learning to think in new ways, having to implement procedures she'd only memorized but never practiced. Still, they needed to keep sorting through the similarities and discrepancies so they could find the overlap. "Let's expand the social circles on both our victims."

Viviane leaned back in her chair. "We should track Barclay's path, accounting for every hour of the day, from the time Biggio died to when Abe was killed. Maybe he crossed paths with the killer."

"That's possible. Viviane, get a warrant for Barclay's financials and start tracking his movements. Once you know where he was, look for cameras or witnesses. Ask around and find out if anyone saw him being followed or if they saw this car." Rebecca taped the picture of the gray Buick Regal on the board.

"You got it."

Rebecca wrote *information/computers* under *injection sites* next to each victim, then stepped back to look at the board. "When I told him what to look for, Jake said he'd found a similar method of entry at the Biggio house. That means the same unsub was in Biggio's home, CyberGuard Forensics, and Barclay's home."

With the end of a marker, Rebecca tapped the name *Biggio*. "At the Biggio home, the computer hard drive had been erased. We haven't been able to tell if any paper files went missing. But considering the same person then broke into CyberGuard, I'm guessing he didn't find what he was looking for at the house."

"So is that the only connection between these men and the killer? They both knew him, but they didn't know each other?" Viviane sat up.

"It could be. And he wanted their deaths to look like suicides." Greg crossed his arms and glared at the board. "He's not doing this for kicks. He has a reason to kill these men, and he's fairly good at it, like a professional."

Rebecca agreed. "Have we followed up with the person who reported the gunshot?"

"Elliot's notes say it was Jacob Jones." Melody leaned back in her chair so she could be seen. "He lives three houses up from Barclay's rental and was walking to a friend's. When he heard the shot, he screamed, then hid and called us."

"Jacob Jones?" That name sounded familiar to Rebecca, and she remembered a pair of red swim trunks. "You mean Jake? He's a seventeen-year-old boy?"

"Yes, ma'am. You know him?"

"He was a friend of Dan Miller's. The first person I ever interviewed here. I liked him. He was very forthcoming and wanted to do the right thing even though he was scared. Seems like he hasn't changed much."

He'd also been the first person to openly talk to her about the Yacht Club. In that moment, they'd morphed from myths and legends into criminals, assassins, and sex offenders. What a crazy summer.

Rebecca's phone buzzed, and she looked down at it. "Hold up. Forensics emailed me." The bullpen went silent as her team waited for her to read the message. "It's confirmed. Barclay was drugged. Midazolam, a benzodiazepine."

Frost pushed himself to his desk, but Viviane's internet search was faster. "According to Wikipedia, Midazolam is used for anesthesia and procedure sedation. Also, to treat severe agitation. Let's see, it works by inducing sleepiness, decreasing anxiety, and causing a loss of ability to create new memories." Viviane kept summarizing. "It suppresses the nervous system."

Greg's face contorted. "So they were anesthetized before the killer positioned them to fake their suicides?"

Viviane made a small retching noise. "Looks like. I hope they weren't aware of what was happening." Her eyes raced back and forth across the screen. "Oh, thank god. It puts you to sleep. They didn't know what was happening to them."

"A tiny silver lining there." Greg grunted.

Frost spun on Viviane. "How can someone get their hands on that drug?"

"Only under direct supervision of your doctor."

"This links both victims to the killer." Having added the

drug to the board, Rebecca circled the name. "He had to acquire the drug before going after Barclay and Biggio. Start looking into the medication and see who has it locally. Find out if they're missing any. Dig up everything you can about it."

"It's stored at room temp, anything below seventy-seven degrees Fahrenheit." Hoyt looked up, a proud grin on his face for finding the information faster than Viviane.

"Actually, it should be stored between sixty-eight and seventy-seven degrees Fahrenheit." Viviane's tone was perfectly neutral.

Frost seemed not to hear her. "That means he wasn't keeping it in his car in this heat unless he had a cooler. Also, it doesn't last more than twenty-four hours after it's prepared."

"Or an insulated travel mug." Greg shook his thermos for effect.

"Well, you know what you're looking for, so get to it. I'm going to check ViCAP and reach out to the staties to see if there are any other," Rebecca curled her fingers to make quotes, "'suicides' in the last five years that match ours."

27

R egardless of how smooth and practiced the killer's methodology was, Rebecca could not find any cases that directly matched in ViCAP, the Violent Crime Apprehension Program used by American law enforcement agencies to track criminals, crimes, and methods.

These two murders had been nearly identical. That was unlikely to happen without a lot of practice.

"Special Agent Lettinger, how may I help you?"

"Hey, Rhonda, it's Rebecca." She relaxed into her chair's lumbar support as Rhonda's voice went from flat and professional to warm and welcoming.

"Hey, girl. It's after hours. Is this a social or business call?"

Their relationship had recently grown from pleasant coworkers to something more like true friends. In fact, all the restaurant meals that had been delivered to her house had come from Rhonda and her love of all things takeout. "Sadly, this is work."

"Ugh, fine. Let me put my thinking cap back on, then."

Rebecca's lips twitched at Rhonda's faux petulant tone.

No matter her protests, Rhonda didn't hate working. She just preferred it to be during business hours.

"Okay, hit me. What do you need?"

"I've got two murders down here that have been made to look like suicides. The killer injected them with a benzodiazepine called Midazolam. It causes weakness, knocks them out, and interferes with memories. It's the type of drug they give you before a surgery."

"Interesting way to go about things, but smart. I don't like it when the killers get smart. Did you find something linking it to another case outside your jurisdiction? Or was there one here in Norfolk?"

Rebecca rested her cheek in her hand, staring at the few suicide cases she'd found that stood out. "That's where I'm not sure. The other tricky thing about Midazolam is that it's undetectable in the body after forty-eight hours and sometimes as little as twelve hours. I may have found related cases. I can't be sure because I can't prove that Midazolam or another benzodiazepine was used."

"Ahhh, but I can. Okay, I'll check into those. Give me the case numbers and the jurisdictions." There was a brief pause on the line. "Are you going to be working late tonight, like normal?"

"Hopefully not too late. But I also know these drugs could be used for other crimes. Basically, any crime where you want your victim compliant and their memory fuzzy."

"Which is what all criminals want, but especially killers and rapists."

"It did occur to me it might be getting used as a new date-rape drug now that we're cracking down on roofies so hard."

"Exactly. Give me a minute. I want to jot down a few notes."

Rebecca rubbed a hand over her forehead while she waited. She really wanted to get home to Ryker so they could continue their talk from earlier. With everything else being so shaky in her life, she didn't want to worry about housing too.

Though she might be able to move in with Ryker at his house until he was better or she managed to get a place of her own.

No matter how enticing it was to stay with Ryker, she didn't want to leave Sand Dollar Shores. It might've been her independent streak, but she felt more secure staying someplace where her name was on the lease or title. A hard lesson she'd learned with her ex.

"I have a...colleague in the Virginia Drug Enforcement Section. I'd be happy to cross-check with him to see if he's run across this medication being moved, used, or supplied anywhere. I'm sure he could be helpful."

There was something a little bit off about Rhonda's tone. Rebecca couldn't quite put her finger on it, but it had her senses tingling. It wasn't her cop gut but her woman instincts telling her something was up.

"I'd be interested in talking with him as well. Are you going to pump him for information?"

Rhonda chuckled, and it was low and thick in a way Rebecca had never heard from her friend. The undertones of lust were unmistakable. "Oh, I do that all the time. I'll call later if I can get my hands on him."

28

Rebecca's cell phone rang. The caller ID sent a thrill along her nerves.

"Hey, Ryker, how you doing?"

"Hey, babe. I'm doing good."

His voice made her toes nearly curl.

"Wondering if you wanted me to put that casserole you were thawing in the oven or not."

A twinge of guilt wormed through Rebecca. "Oh, I'm sorry. You didn't have to wait for me. I thawed it so you'd have something to eat."

"Oh, that was never going to be an issue. Meg showed up a couple hours ago with a warm lasagna. It even had squash from her garden in it. That thing was so good."

Her stomach rumbled. "That does sound good. I love squash with basically any kind of tomato sauce."

"Hmm." He sounded guilty. "Does that mean I should've saved you some?"

"No, that's fine." Rebecca tightened her stomach, trying to quell its angry outburst. "I still have the casserole."

"You still have the lasagna too." Ryker laughed. "Or at

least, you will if you can manage to get home before I eat it all. I've only had three servings so far, but I think I hear it calling my name again."

Three servings? How many servings had Meg brought over? Rebecca glanced at the clock, surprised it was already nine fifteen. "I'll be home as soon as I can. I'm waiting for one more phone call and—"

The phone on her desk rang, showing the number for the state police out of Norfolk.

She spoke in a rush. "That's her now. I should be able to take this call and then come straight home."

"Sounds good." With that, Ryker hung up.

Switching phones, she tried to ignore her hunger. "Rhonda, I hope this is you with good and fast news. My boyfriend is blackmailing me with lasagna."

"Boyfriend?"

Rebecca dropped her head into her hand and briefly explained the unexpected turn of events that led to Ryker living with her.

"Wow. So is the lasagna blackmail, like, for sexual favors or just as a way to get you to come home?"

Rebecca had to think about that. "The second one. Sadly, the first one isn't an option until he's fully healed."

Rhonda snickered. "Oh, damn, that sucks. But as strange as the circumstances are, I like this boyfriend of yours already. We should meet. For now, let's get you some answers. I haven't been able to positively identify any cases linked to your guy's M.O. However, I spoke with Jason Peele in drug enforcement. He checked, and there's no surge of anesthetic-linked murders made to look like suicides happening in the state of Virginia. He also checked with his counterparts in North Carolina, and there's nothing going on there either."

"What about any other sedative usage in recent murders?

He may not have always used Midazolam. It's pretty hard to get and administer."

"We've always had a few such cases, but nothing new and not enough unsolved to make it so you should worry about them being linked. That's classified as a poisoning."

Rebecca butted in. "Would a physically smaller man feel the need to make his victims more compliant before attacking them?"

"That is a possibility. I saw your report on the break-in and thought to check up on that too. We don't have any known felons of that height who've been involved in any unsolved murder cases using sedation or staged suicides."

"Well, that's not a good thing." Rebecca sighed.

"You expect these aren't his first murders?"

"Right. They're too well-executed. This guy knows what he's doing. Hell, he cut a windowpane out and replaced it, caulking and all, after he staged our first second to look like a suicide. Do you know of any rookie killer who would seal up his entry point before planting a red herring like that?"

"Not offhand, but I bet I could find some. That's a stupid way to try and kill someone if you don't know what you're doing."

"Exactly. So what's giving this guy his bravado? Killing someone in the middle of the day after following one of his victims home from the sheriff's station?"

"He's got a Napolean complex?"

That simple answer had Rebecca snapping her mouth closed over her response. That actually made a lot more sense than anything else she could think of. "You're right. I should look into that." She cleared her throat. "Thanks for checking with Peele."

"No problem. Any excuse to get him to join me on a case is worth pursuing."

Rebecca shook her head. "I take it there was more than one reason you reached out to him."

"Lord, yes. Girl...have you ever heard the saying I hate when he goes but still enjoy the view every time?"

"Oh, yes, I have. I've got one of those waiting at home for me now."

"And he's got lasagna!" Rhonda gave an indignant screech. "Rebecca, get off the phone and go to that man now. We won't have any more leads to follow until tomorrow anyway. Even if he's off-limits for the time being, you can still enjoy that view."

Rebecca smiled through the phone at her friend and counterpart. "Have a good night, Rhonda. Thanks for your help."

29

Hospitals were terrible places, and Hoyt had come to loathe the Coastal Ridge one in particular. It was nothing against the staff. The layout wasn't even that confusing once you got to know the place. His main problem was he'd simply spent entirely too much time there recently —at a place where you only went if something was terribly wrong.

But like all things, even that had a silver lining. Now he could easily find his way through the corridors and back hallways to where the hospital pharmacy was located.

It wasn't a place that most visitors had cause to look for. This wasn't where you'd get a prescription filled when you were being discharged. Here was where the heavy-duty drugs were stored and dispensed to staff for procedures within the hospital.

And it had the security to match. There was a tiny placard sticking out from the wall with the word *Pharmacy* on it and a matching one on the thick plexiglass barrier over the desk. There was no obvious door showing how to get in. That was probably hidden somewhere down a staff-only hallway.

No one was visible when he approached the window, nor were any drugs or bins. All he could see were rows of bookcases stacked with binders. Still, when he rang the little bell sitting on the counter, he was greeted quickly.

"Morning, Deputy. Can I do something for you?" A tall woman about his age walked up, a polite, professional smile on her face.

"I sure do hope so, ma'am." He paused and made a show of thinking. "Or maybe I don't. See, I'm here because we ran into the illegal use of Midazolam in a felony, and I need to track down where it came from."

The woman straightened at the mention of the drug and her eyes narrowed sharply. "That's a Schedule Four controlled substance. Not something that's used for recreational purposes or abuse."

Hoyt leaned his elbow on the tiny counter separating them. "I did mention it was used in a felony, right? That's not recreational use. You can trust me on that."

She opened her mouth, then closed it in a scowl as the implications of such use hit her. Once she understood, she leaned forward and lowered her voice. "How can I help you?" She held up one regal finger. "Without breaking HIPAA laws. I will not divulge any patient information."

"That's perfectly fine, ma'am." He smiled his best smile, the one that always put people at ease. "First, you could tell me your name." Some people called it flirting…he called it good old-fashioned manners. And he suspected this lady would appreciate some of that.

The pharmacist blushed, dropping her eyes. "My name's Hazel Stevenson. Please, call me Hazel."

Straightening, Hoyt gave her a nod. "I'm Deputy Frost, as you can see." He tapped his name tag. "But you can call me Hoyt."

"What is it you'd like to know, Hoyt?"

"Well, ma'am, Hazel, I was hoping you could explain to me, in layperson's terms so I understand, how you secure your supply of Midazolam."

"Oh, that's easy. It's kept in a controlled system. Not just under lock and key, but electronic locks. Midazolam isn't prepped until it's ready to use. That's another reason it's so rarely abused."

"When would you all prepare it, then?"

"Only when we get a prescription from a doctor with a patient's code so we can check their charts for contraindications." She blushed again. "That means we make sure they're not on any other medication or have a medical condition that might create a negative reaction to the prescribed drug. We often have to double-check the doctor's orders to make sure they don't end up killing their patients." Hazel glanced over her shoulder.

"The lifeblood of the hospital. I knew it. Nurses are the soldiers, but nobody can do their jobs properly without people like you making sure the medications are correctly dispensed."

Hazel ducked her eyes bashfully, hiding her proud smile for a moment. "I'm not certain how anyone could get their hands on Midazolam." She shook her head. "Not just ours, but anyone's. I've worked in the pharmacy business for most of my life. Hoyt, you would not imagine how secure we keep these drugs to preserve their viability. The one you're asking about is sensitive to light. Did you know that?"

"Light?" He shook his head. "I did not know that. Which is why I needed to come speak to a professional like you. There's no better way to learn than directly from the experts. What kind of safeguards do you need to go through to gain access to a Schedule Four controlled substance?"

"Here, we have an automated system that dispenses it. Someone would need their personal passcode and their ID badge…and only a pharmacist's badge will work for that. They'd also need a patient ID number and the doctor's prescription. With all those measures in place, I simply can't see how anyone could get their hands on the drug without triggering an alert. And our inventory is tightly controlled and monitored. We'd know if any was missing."

"But what if it wasn't missing, according to the system?"

"How do you mean?"

"I mean, what if it went missing after it left the pharmacy?"

She blinked rapidly. "You mean like when a nurse is carrying it up to a room or about to administer it?"

He shrugged. "The best time to steal something valuable is when it's in transit."

"But then the patient wouldn't get the proper medication. I'm sure you've never witnessed it yourself, Hoyt, but it's very obvious when a surgery patient hasn't been properly sedated." Her expression was as stoic and calm as possible, and her eyes spoke of things she'd never wanted to see.

The blood drained from his brain at the possibility, and Hazel sagely bobbed her head.

"Trust me, the whole hospital would know if that had happened even once."

"That sounds…gruesome. I need to remember this when I start to think my own job is hard." Hoyt hadn't thought about that, but she had to be right. If the only time these drugs were administered were for procedures, doing one without the proper sedative would be obvious. "Can you think of a situation where the drug might go unaccounted for?"

"I suppose a bottle or syringe could become compromised. Then we'd have to order a replacement." Hazel stilled. "Things like that do happen. I wouldn't say they're commonplace, but they aren't rare either. It happens most often with patients who are afraid of needles. The poor souls…we end up having to get them a second needle after they damage the first one by jerking away."

Hoyt's eyebrows shot up, and he wondered if he was finally on track. "Has that happened for any orders of Midazolam in the last month?" He pulled out his notepad and started making notes.

"I can't remember any, but I could check for you. It might take me a bit, though. There are some new procedures. Paperwork, you know?"

"I know paperwork. Why do you have new procedures?"

Hazel shrugged. "They're always changing things around. Making it more 'efficient.' But the rumor is they hired some hotshot cybersecurity firm, so my guess is the higher-ups are trying to cover their butts."

The hair on the back of Hoyt's neck stirred.

"A new hotshot, huh?"

"Yep. You still want me to check on the Midazolam?"

"Would you? That would be immensely helpful." He gave her his winning smile again. Though, truth be told, he'd been smiling this entire time. The woman was a delight. And more helpful than she even knew.

Roger Biggio was a hotshot cybersecurity expert.

She stepped to the side to pull out a keyboard on a tray that had been hidden by the wall. As she typed, he jotted down everything he'd learned.

"There's nothing like that happening with the medication in question. Not in the last thirty days." Hazel leaned closer to the plexiglass barrier between them, peering down. "What are you writing?"

Hoyt happily flipped the notepad around so Hazel could read what he'd written. "I'm taking notes on all the things you've taught me. This way, when I have to interview someone less helpful, I won't sound quite so ignorant."

She blushed. "Oh, you. You're doing fine."

"Well now, I can't figure out any way that a dose or two of this drug could've gone missing. Can you?"

Hazel shook her head, folding her hands on the counter. "I'm sorry, but no. All our inventory is accounted for."

"One last thing then. Would it be possible for me to get a list of every time you've administered Midazolam in the last thirty days?" She opened her mouth, eyes starting to narrow, but he held up his hands in surrender. "Not with the patient's name or anything that would violate HIPAA. Just how often and when a prescription was filled."

She mulled that over. "I might be able to do that. But," she held up her finger again, "I would have to clear it with the privacy office first."

"I'm already on overtime, Hazel. Standing here and waiting for a response isn't going to ruin my day any. Especially when my morning's already been so lovely."

"Let me go check with them then." She turned and left, her cheeks pink.

Hoyt kept smiling as he watched the woman walk away. Despite his charming attitude, he knew this might be the person who'd taken the drugs and killed Roger Biggio and Abe Barclay. He leaned an elbow on the desk, and casually rested his hand on his gun.

30

F rost jumped as another woman in a white lab coat approached. "Is there something wrong, Officer?"

"Deputy, actually." He composed himself. "Deputy Frost. And, no, I'm just getting schooled by your coworker Hazel. She's helping me figure out the technical aspects of my case. And being quite helpful about it too." His winning smile had less influence on the new woman, but it still softened her around the edges. "What's your name?"

The woman gave him a sideways appraisal. Her brown skin looked rich against the sterile white lab coat, and the brightly colored scarf wrapped around her head gave her a more elegantly casual look than anyone should've been able to pull off in a hospital. "Loshetta Diamond. You can call me Loshetta. What kind of case are you working on?"

"Loshetta, well, it's a felony case where the victim was injected with a benzo."

"That's locked up pretty tightly around here. And I can't imagine…" She paused, chewing on one dusky-pink lip. "No, I *can* imagine a few ways that could be used to victimize people."

"Then you understand why I need to get answers and stop whoever's doing this."

Loshetta crossed her arms. "And you think we had something to do with this? What drug is it?"

"I'm not sure who had anything to do with it. My sheriff is worried this might be a statewide problem. And you're the closest hospital to the station, so I came over to learn all I could and to double-check things as well. As for the drug, it's, um, *mid-zalam*." He purposefully mispronounced the name.

"Do you mean Midazolam, Deputy?"

"Yeah, that's it. And please, call me Hoyt."

Loshetta smiled. "That's in a secured system requiring a passcode, a badge, a prescription number, and a patient ID number."

Hoyt nodded along. "That's what Hazel was telling me. She was also helping me figure out how someone could get their hands on a dose of it." He checked his notes, even though he didn't need to. "She told me this drug, when it's injectable, is mixed up here?"

"That's right. Midazolam doesn't have a long shelf life, and we need it at full potency in order to work properly." Loshetta glanced over her shoulder, leaning back slightly.

"Am I keeping you from your work? I don't want to interfere. I've already taken up so much of Hazel's time."

"No." She waved him off. "You're fine. We're not doing anything wrong, but that doesn't mean our boss won't try to get us in trouble for something. If it's not you, it'll be something or someone else."

"A real ballbuster, huh?" Hoyt grinned ruefully.

"Not just that, she seems to thrive on making things harder on us."

He leaned forward, opening his eyes wide as if he was intrigued. "Really? How so?"

"Like this shift. She knows I'm looking to get promoted and advance my career. I don't even necessarily want her job, just a better one than I have now. What does she do? Puts me on seconds for a couple weeks. The shift with the least work but the one most guaranteed to interfere with any kind of homelife." She looked around, then leaned both hands on the counter. "Thank goodness I'm back on days. That's when I get the best gossip too."

"Oh, do tell." He glanced around in the same way she had. "Truth be told, the reason I took this job as a deputy was because it had the best gossip. Cops in small towns always know what everyone else is getting up to. You were supposed to be home by five for your wedding anniversary? Well, I pulled you over leaving your high school girlfriend's neighborhood at six."

She grinned, shifting closer. "See, I always thought that would be the coolest job. Like, I'm not interested in all the shooting and having to stand out in the weather, but you guys know what's going on better than some people's besties. You see it all. I would love to have something dirty on my boss."

"What's her name?" Hoyt pulled up his notepad and pen. "Maybe I already do. You never know."

Loshetta laughed, then clamped a hand over her mouth to stifle it. "Oh, you're bad. That doesn't sound like a terrible plan, though. Sophia Maryland. But if you want to find the dirt, look into her new boyfriend."

"He's trouble? The dangerous kind?"

She shook her head. "I don't know if he's the dangerous kind. He comes by late at night. She hops in his car. Sometimes they just sit there and talk. Other times, they drive down to the back parking lot, and let's just say they stay back there for a few minutes. If you know what I mean." Loshetta winked.

Hoyt winked back. "Oh, I know what you mean. Maybe I should take a quick drive through the parking lots here. Just to make sure nothing untoward is happening. It's out of my jurisdiction, though, so I'd have to hold whoever I caught, in the light, while waiting for the local PD to come pick them up."

Loshetta giggled, swiping a hand back and forth between them. "I like the way you think, Hoyt."

"Do you happen to know what kind of car that boyfriend of hers drives?"

"I'm afraid I don't know anything about cars. And it's too dark to even know what color it is. About all I can tell you is it isn't a dark color."

Hoyt tried to get a description of the man instead. "Maybe she has other reasons she keeps him hidden away. You think he's short? Unsightly? You would not believe the number of people I have to ticket with public indecency because they don't want their friends to see who they picked up at a bar."

If he was short, that'd be an interesting coincidence. The guy Rebecca had a recent scuffle with was short for a man.

"Could be." Loshetta checked to make sure no one was close enough to overhear. "He's never gotten out of the car. What kind of woman stays with a man for three months but is too ashamed to be seen standing next to him? Knowing her, the guy is cheating on his wife. The hospital security even caught on, and they're always keeping an eye on them."

"Oh, this might be back in my territory now. Any idea what they're looking for?"

"No, no clue. But I'd love to see Sophia knocked off her pedestal for once." She turned her head and waved. "Like if she was involved in those drugs you're looking for. That would be the best."

"Oh, you're griping about Sophia?" Hazel asked as she walked back to join them.

"We are." Loshetta shrugged.

"Can't say I blame you, Lo. Here you go, Hoyt. I managed to get a list. It's only of the dates and times when a dose of Midazolam was fulfilled. That's all I can do without a warrant."

Hoyt thanked her, then squinted. Stretching up to his full height, he looked over their heads, scanning the area around them.

Both women turned, trying to see what he was looking at.

"You see something? What's up?" Loshetta frowned at him.

He shook his head and waited until they had both turned back, then *tsk*ed at them.

"Tell the truth now, ladies. Are you hiding the Fountain of Youth back there? That's the only way I can figure out two beauties like you having so much wisdom, grace, and knowledge."

They both burst out laughing, and he joined them.

"Okay, and to make sure this still counts as a work trip and not the pleasure jaunt it's been, can you ladies tell me where you were on the thirtieth?"

Hazel blushed and crossed her wrists in front of her waist. "Sunday. I was here working of course. That's our normal overnight shift. Clock in on Saturday evening and clock out Sunday morning. Worked Sunday to Monday as well."

"I was working too."

The older woman faced her colleague. "Oh, that's right. Saturday evening was when you were supposed to be off because your sister was in town or something. Right?"

Loshetta nodded. "It was my cousin from Virginia Beach.

We'd made plans to go out that night. Then Sophia called me in to cover."

"Except I was already here." Hazel shook her head. "It didn't make any sense, forcing you to come in. I had everything under control, and she knew that."

"And then she ended up sending me home early, too, because my badge went missing." Loshetta sighed and rolled her eyes. "It was such a messed up night."

Hazel bobbed her head in irritated solidarity. "That goes to show you how poor of a manager Sophia Maryland really is. She didn't even have your new one ready to go the next day when you came in for your scheduled shift."

"And that's her job." Loshetta shook her head. "I *should* make a play for her position."

"You should."

Hoyt looked up from the pages in his hand. "Well, thank you for imparting your wisdom on me, ladies. Now I can take this back and appease my own ball-busting boss."

31

So many people feared death. Those people were cowards and losers. There was no way to live life without also embracing the death that came with it. Walking through the disheveled rows of headstones, the old and new testaments to lives ended, wasn't all that different from walking through a field of flowers.

Sure, these flowers were granite, marble, and concrete, cast or chiseled into whatever trite saying or figure made people feel better. A landmark pretending to celebrate life when we all knew that living meant dying. Even prettied up, people still avoided the cemetery.

At least, the cowards did. Not me. I'd spent many happy moments here. Revisiting my kills buried under other identities. Folks who'd died without my involvement but whose graves offered a final resting place for my victims. With them hidden, I could continue doing what I did best and even look forward to my next visit. That would have to change now.

Abe wouldn't be here to make sure things moved smoothly. It was so sad he'd chosen to end his life. And in such a gruesome manner. There were less painful paths in life than to cross me. Too bad he didn't find one.

Which was why I was out here, looking for those final loose ends I needed to tie up. I'd searched through Abe's computer and come up dry. It seemed like the only thing that poor bastard used it for was porn and bookkeeping. I was shocked about the latter. Not an extra dime charged for his work, not a rounded-up receipt, not a single extra expense added to his report.

The man had been meticulous and trustworthy with his employers. If he'd continued to show me that same loyalty, I could've let him live and would've continued to pay him for his body disposal services. But after he accepted whatever Sophia gave him and then went to the police the very next morning, I couldn't trust him.

That Jezebel had gotten to him. Turned my loyal man against me. Not that I blamed her. She knew the kind of man I was. Her mistake had been thinking she could get the upper hand on me. No one could.

Losing Abe's unique skill set wouldn't stop me. I wouldn't quit until I wanted to. My job was too thrilling.

I doubted news of Abe's despondent need to take his own life would've reached that Jezebel all the way on the mainland. Although, she had a habit of always watching and listening. She was like a bat, and bats carried diseases. And diseases needed to be eradicated.

The chitter of bats overhead as they flew above the tombstones made me chuckle. Perfect. I walked through the empty cemetery's cold and hot spots as the stored heat from the grave markers mingled with the cool ocean breeze.

I headed for the mausoleum that was entirely too well taken care of for its age. It was the same one my two coconspirators had entered last night. The one where Abe hid the things that were important to him.

With my casual stride, a bystander wouldn't view me as imposing or suspicious.

Sure, I worked out and was stronger than most men. But women, all people really, looked down on me.

Until they were at my mercy.

I smiled. They all looked up to me then, when I was looming over them with my tools. My hands caressed my tool pouch around my waist. What had started out as a job had become my passion. My reason to live. Killing people the Yacht Club found inconvenient garnered me the respect I deserved.

No one was around to watch as I made it to the mausoleum and pulled the key Abe had given me long ago from my pocket with a gloved hand. I had a moment to wonder if the key would fit or if Abe had changed the lock. With an easy twist, the padlock popped open.

Good old reliable Abe. I'd miss him. Stupid fool should've at least changed the locks before trying to backstab me.

Tucking the lock into a pocket, I opened the iron-wrapped door. The well-greased hinges didn't make a sound, just as they hadn't on my numerous drops when I'd left Abe's payment for his services. Early in our partnership, I'd instructed Abe to maintain the hinges so my late-night visits wouldn't draw unnecessary attention.

The mausoleum was spartan, a waist-high platform in the middle with a cobweb-covered casket resting on top. Each wall had a shelf built into it with stone vases where flowers could be left, but they'd been empty since I started coming here.

When I'd searched his house and found nothing, I knew the evidence she'd given him was here. Whatever it was had to be important if it had convinced him to go to the police. Abe had nearly as much to lose as I did if the cops got involved. Once Abe had begun burying my victims, I made sure to remind him that he was on the hook for multiple felonies.

What could be so compelling that he was willing to risk jail time, or worse, my vengeance? Did he think the new sheriff could keep him safe? I pulled the door closed behind me and flicked on the light, illuminating the small stone building where one of the founding members of Shadow Island rested.

No, Abe wouldn't trust the sheriff. She was a woman, and Abe looked down on them. Then what could convince him to turn against me? It still didn't make sense why he'd chosen betrayal after so long. He'd been asking for more money recently, citing the stronger police presence in the cemetery after the old sheriff was buried here.

That was why I'd hung Biggio in a place personal to Abe and a location that should have been safe from prying eyes. To remind him of how quickly I could make someone disappear and never get caught. And he'd still gone to the sheriff's office.

Why?

Abe screwed up when he took off work instead of following his usual routine. He should've been at his shed first thing in the morning. The message would've been received, and he could've disposed of the body. But he screwed up royally, and the sheriff herself found Biggio swinging from the rafter of Abe's shed.

Looking at the thick layers of dust inside the tomb and the tracks through it, my mouth dropped. That was when it hit me. The only thing Abe feared more than me or jail time was the Yacht Club.

My blood ran cold. That had to be it. It was the only reason he'd risk turning against me.

Abe wasn't going to turn me in to the cops for justice. He was going to turn me in to one of the corrupted deputies so they could hand me over to the Yacht Club. If they learned the body in Abe's shed had been my doing, there would be hell to pay.

Biggio hadn't been a Yacht Club hit. I'd done that one to get What's Her Face out of some trouble. That was why I'd staged it as a suicide. Any hit I performed outside of the Yacht Club's direction was made to look like the poor sap took their own life.

The powerful men who called the shots from the Seaview Marina didn't approve of freelance work. They said it brought unnecessary attention to the activities on the island, and they were right.

I wasn't a fool. I knew I was only one of many who they sent out to get rid of a nuisance. But I was the one they sent when they wanted to keep it quiet. They had other people they could call in when death needed to be loud and messy, to make a statement. There were men they'd bought and paid for who would take great joy in slowly beating me to death.

Following the tracks left on the dusty floor, I began to inspect the vases. They were above my eyeline, so I had to reach up and feel around inside them. The first two were empty.

I reached into the third and jerked my hand back. Not sure what I'd been expecting. At least it wasn't something alive. I reached over my head again, tapping along this time instead of sliding. With the restriction of my gloves, when I pinched my fingertips together, I barely grasped whatever Abe had stashed in there.

It was a thumb drive. Making out the writing on the dirty label, a shiver ran down my spine. There for anyone's curious eyes were my initials. And below it was written *Sleep Talking*. That bitch Sophia had recorded me.

If she thought the information was juicy enough to serve as an insurance policy of sorts against me, then I had a pretty good idea what I'd discussed while deep in REM sleep. Names of my many victims. Locations of their bodies. I maybe even gave up the identities of my contacts within the Yacht Club. She'd be playing with fire if she tried to reach out to any of them.

But the thumb drive in my hand was useless in its current state. It was busted.

I suddenly realized why she'd been so pissed at Abe that night after they'd left the mausoleum. He'd taken what she'd offered, whatever dirt she'd collected to use against me, and he destroyed it. Regret—something I hadn't felt in so long I almost didn't recognize it—curdled my stomach.

Pulling my burner phone from my pocket, I texted her. *Need another syringe today for a new target.*

After a brief pause, she replied as I knew she would. *Need more notice next time. I'll see what I can do.*

My response was direct and left no room for excuses. *Just get it.*

Pocketing my phone, I stared at the broken plastic gadget that proved Abe had been loyal to me 'til the very end. Sophia had done this. She was the cause. I'd gone after the wrong person, punished the one loyal man I knew.

I clenched the gadget in my fist. "I will avenge you, Abe. And I'll make her death so much worse because of what she did to you."

32

"Morning, Boss. You know this is supposed to be your day off."

Rebecca gave Hoyt a disgruntled wave as she entered the bullpen. Working extra hours was a normal part of her life. "Gotta make up for all that time I was on medical leave eating bonbons and watching my soaps."

"Aw, she's just crabby that she's here instead of being home with her little cutie." Viviane's eyes twinkled as she walked past Rebecca and sat down at her desk with a box of neon markers.

There was no reason to deny that, so Rebecca didn't. "Since we're all here, how about we go ahead and get each other caught up on what we've learned? That way, we can all get out of here on time tonight." It was a crazy pipe dream, she knew, but it was something to work toward at least.

"Your timing couldn't be better." Viviane waved a stack of papers at her.

Hoyt tipped his head at his trainee deputy and held up his notepad along with some papers of his own. "I hit up the hospital pharmacy in Coastal Ridge, where I had a lovely talk with both women on shift. Turns out our killer's drug is heavily controlled."

"I had a conversation with Rhonda, who talked to a guy named Peele from the Drug Enforcement Section, and she said the same thing. It's not even on the DES radar because it only has one real use and is rarely, if ever, abused." Rebecca ambled to the back of the room to top off her coffee. There hadn't been time for it to get cold, but knowing what she was going to spend her morning working on, she wanted a full cup to get her through.

"Yeah, getting knocked out and waking up feeling sick without being able to remember what happened isn't the best high." Viviane shrugged. "I did research too. There's no one on the island who even knows what Midazolam is except for the doctors and nurses over at the community health center. Since they don't perform surgeries there and the only other medical use for it is to treat people with severe epilepsy, they don't even keep it in stock."

"The ladies I spoke to over at the Coastal Ridge Hospital pharmacy were willing to give me the dates, times, and reasons why the drug was dispensed." Hoyt once again motioned at the papers he and Viviane were going through. "There's no patient information attached, but we don't need that anyway. I can't see a patient pocketing their own medication then leaving the hospital instead of getting surgery."

Rebecca swirled the coffee in her cup while she thought. "Yeah, getting yourself scheduled for a surgery just to steal your own drugs doesn't seem like a good plan. Doing it twice would certainly raise eyebrows."

"And the pharmacist assured me everyone in the hospital would know if someone went through with their surgery without getting the proper dosing." Hoyt's grim expression made Rebecca flinch.

"Oh, I haven't had enough coffee to think about that." She took a swig from her cup. "You two are going through the known hospital orders for the Midazolam?"

"Yep. But we've just started." He held up a sheet so she could read it. "It lists who ordered the drug, who filled the order, who delivered it, and who signed for it."

"Which is why he made two copies, so we can both check the lists. There's a lot of names to double-check. And why I got myself a set of highlighters." Viviane shook the box at Hoyt. "Want a set of your own?"

"Why did I never think of doing that?" He picked out a full set for himself, and Rebecca snorted.

"Because you've been doing this since before highlighters were invented." Viviane smiled.

Rebecca hid her face behind her coffee cup as Hoyt scowled at the younger woman.

"I'm not that old. I remember using them in school. Well, high school."

Viviane's smile got tighter as she struggled to hold back laughter. "Back when they only had yellow."

"Okay, focusing on the data from Coastal Ridge makes sense to begin with. But if you don't find anything suspicious, we'll need to widen our search to see if any hospitals in the region have had the drug go missing. While you two go through the list Frost got, I'm going to check in with the labs to see if we have any updates on the forensics. When Jake shows up, he can help you two streamline the process."

As Rebecca walked between them to get to her office, neither of them looked up or noticed her amused expression as Hoyt muttered on about disrespectful kids these days and Viviane kept tittering with laughter. It was never boring with those two working together.

There was an email waiting for Rebecca when she sat down at her desk and fired up her computer. It had been sent by Justin Drake an hour ago. Opening it, she was relieved to see that he'd gotten access to some of the files on Biggio's computer. Different parts of the drive had been encrypted with their own layers of security, so he'd only managed to gain access to one portion so far.

"Better than nothing." Rebecca signed in to the secure server to get access to the files. There was a stack of them, all titled, but named with some sort of randomized system or one she simply didn't understand yet. Wanting to test a theory, she opened a search bar and started typing in the names of the people from the paper files they'd already gone through.

Rebecca opened the folder for Deborah Niece and started reading through it. It was marked as *Inactive/Closed* and confirmed everything Deborah had said about her dealings with the man and his company.

Opening another one, she saw that everyone on the list was marked *Inactive/Closed*. Catching on, Rebecca opened file after file, and each was labeled the same way. None were active cases at the time of Biggio's death. Most were years old. Rebecca backed out to the main folder and tried different search terms. *Shadow Island*, *Abe Barclay*, and *Midazolam* returned no results.

After more than an hour of hopping from folder to folder, she was debating refilling her coffee when there was a knock on her doorframe. Looking up, she saw both Hoyt and Viviane standing there.

"We've got something." Viviane was clutching a sheet of paper, smiling.

"I assumed from the smiles. What is it?" Rebecca reached for the paper Viviane held out to her.

"It's not a gun, but the next best thing. We found the smoking syringe."

33

"This might take a bit of explaining." Hoyt walked into the office and sat in his usual chair. "Remember I told you I visited the pharmacy at the hospital and talked with the ladies over there?" He waited as Viviane handed Rebecca the paper she'd marked up before she dropped down into the other chair.

When she was settled, Hoyt continued. "One of the ladies I spoke to was named Loshetta Diamond. She's a real sweet woman, very helpful, and likes to talk. When I asked her where she was the day of Biggio's death, she remembered it all too well. She was supposed to have the day off but got called in by her supervisor. Then she lost her badge somewhere in the pharmacy and was sent home early. That was corroborated by her coworker, Hazel Stevenson, who was also working that overnight shift."

"And…?"

He pointed at the page in Rebecca's hand and waited 'til she went back to reading it. "Loshetta Diamond, without the ID required to access the drug supplies, left the hospital at three that morning."

"But this says the pharmacy received a prescription for Midazolam that was filled by Loshetta Diamond ten minutes after she left." Rebecca raised her eyebrow at him, and he nodded.

Viviane was nearly bouncing in her seat at that point. "And look who delivered it to the patient's room."

Rebecca's eyes tracked down the page while Viviane waited like an impatient puppy. "Sophia Maryland? I take it that means something to you two?"

Hoyt grinned at his trainee's actions and slouched lower in his chair so he could prop his feet on a nearby box of copier paper. "Sophia Maryland is the supervisor who called Loshetta Diamond in to work on her night off, despite Hazel already being there. The regular overnight shift, as their human resources person explained to me, only requires two people. There was no reason to call in a third person. That's something Hazel corroborated as well. Loshetta and Hazel also complained that the night was slow."

"So why did Maryland call in a third person if she wasn't needed?" Rebecca rested her chin on the back of her hand, a slight smile on her face.

"Because, as the supervisor of the pharmacy, Maryland knows what procedures are scheduled ahead of time. Maryland knew that surgery was going to happen days in advance and what medication would be required for it." Hoyt paused only a moment to take a breath.

Viviane, unable to hold back, cut in. "Medications like Midazolam. Look at the drug fulfillment record. I marked it in pink."

"Maryland filled an order for Midazolam and delivered it to a nurse named Schumer." Rebecca looked at the paper again. "These prescriptions were filled within moments of each other on two separate machines."

Viviane practically quivered with excitement. "Right.

Now, if you want to fill a prescription, you have to have a badge and all the drug details. Fine. But if you wanted to fill the same prescription again from the same machine, using the same badge, the machine won't let you. It's a safety feature to keep employees from stealing."

"How do you know that?"

"I called the machine manufacturer."

"Good work."

"Thanks." Viviane beamed. "Anyway, if you enter the same prescription on a separate machine, with a separate badge, before the prescription is recorded as closed, you can get a duplicate."

Hoyt noted Rebecca was as amused as he was at Viviane's excitement. Rebecca examined the highlighted section again. "How could they fill the prescriptions back-to-back so fast? The machines would update pretty quickly, I imagine."

"The machines are right next to each other." Hoyt tilted his head at Viviane. "When Viviane found the duplicate prescription fulfillments, I called down to the pharmacy and asked Hazel how the machines were situated in the back. She told me they were side by side, which she hated because they were close enough to bump elbows if two people were trying to place orders."

"Close enough one person could use both of them at the same time?" Rebecca leaned back in her chair.

"Precisely—"

Hoyt was once again cut off as Viviane leaned forward to point at the paper. "Now look at the day Abe Barclay was killed. There's another duplicate fulfillment, recorded as placed by Sophia Maryland and Loshetta. But Loshetta had been sent home early that day. Yet her 'lost' card was used to fill an order, which was later delivered by Maryland."

Rebecca's heart picked up speed. "This is good."

Viviane took a quick breath before enthusiastically

plowing ahead. "When we followed up on it, HR told Frost that Maryland had called in the night before to get a replacement for Loshetta's lost card. Then Maryland returned it hours later, claiming Loshetta had gone behind her back to get her own replacement made. The second card was destroyed by HR right after that, and Loshetta was never even informed."

"So one lost card, and Maryland was able to get extra prescriptions of Midazolam." Rebecca sipped her coffee, then frowned and set it down.

Hoyt sighed and set his feet on the ground, getting ready for what he assumed was coming next. "And the patient was charged twice for one medication, which isn't unusual enough for any insurance company to catch. By the way, Maryland just got off from working the night shift again. Hazel said Maryland was planning to go straight home."

Rebecca set the paper down, turned to her computer, and began typing. "I also have an update. Forensics cracked Biggio's computer files. I was looking through them before you came in."

"Find anything interesting?" Viviane leaned forward, barely able to rest her elbows on the edge of the desk.

"Not anything we didn't already guess. I found the digital files for the people on the list we've tracked down. Those contracts were all closed…" Rebecca's voice trailed off as something caught her attention.

Hoyt got out of his chair and stepped around the desk to look over her shoulder at the screen. Rebecca had searched for Coastal Ridge Hospital and Sophia Maryland. Several pages came back with results. This was a possible motive if Maryland was the killer.

Could Rebecca have been mistaken and the short male burglar was actually a woman? That seemed unlikely to him from what Rebecca had written in her report. She'd been certain it was a man.

"The smoking syringe indeed. Biggio was investigating the Coastal Ridge Hospital, at their request, due to a DEA audit. Someone noticed several complaints of overbilling, and they wanted to see if the machine they used was malfunctioning. Biggio tracked all the extra orders to one name, Sophia Maryland." Rebecca reached into her desk drawer and pulled out her cruiser keys, which she handed to Viviane.

"His case was almost completed, and preliminary findings were turned in to the hospital last week. If they spilled the beans, or gossip moves as fast there as it does in our small town, then Maryland might've known she'd been found out."

Viviane cleared her throat as she took the keys. "Um, Boss, one more problem. There was another duplicate order late last night. Well, technically this morning, since it was just after midnight."

Hoyt straightened as Rebecca stood. "This time she used Hazel's badge. We're not sure how she got her hands on it yet."

Rebecca leaned over the desk and took her keys back.

"Then we need to find Sophia Maryland. And we need to hurry, before we find another involuntary suicide."

34

Sophia Maryland closed the door behind her, leaning against it with a sigh. It had been another long night at work. Loshetta had called in sick and nearly ruined her plans for getting the next dose of Midazolam. She'd had to improvise by "accidentally" knocking Hazel's lunch onto the woman's lap. When the woman had gone to change into a clean uniform, Sophia had snagged the ID badge she'd left behind and completed her orders.

Midazolam was one of the drugs they always used in a hospital setting, so it was fairly easy to acquire. The hospital's blind spot was thinking the security in the pharmacy was foolproof, so they didn't pay much attention, which suited her needs nicely. As long as she had a coworker's badge, she had fairly open access to any type of drug she wanted.

It was only fair. The hospital admins and their constant demands on Sophia were what led to her being stressed and needing other drugs to help her cope. They should've been the ones covering her medical needs.

A little codeine never hurt anyone, despite what the law

said. And selling an occasional pharmaceutical here and there made up for the raises Sophia never received.

She kicked her thick-soled shoes off, then straightened and headed for the kitchen. Although she longed for a glass of wine, it was midmorning. She'd have to settle for a relaxing hot bath before going to bed.

As soon as she stepped out of her foyer, she noticed she wasn't alone. For a moment, adrenaline attempted to race through her tired veins, but then she recognized the man sitting in her recliner, one leg crossed over the other.

"You really couldn't wait 'til I got some sleep?" Setting her Louis Vuitton bag down on the couch, she pulled out the syringe. "It would have been fine sitting in my fridge until tonight, babe."

He bristled when she called him that, and she smirked. His Napoleon complex always flared up when she called him by a nickname. Riling him up was so much fun. They'd been together off and on for years, though nothing serious had ever grown between them. Theirs was more of a transactional relationship.

A few months ago, he'd discovered that Midazolam made his job easier and, in his words, more enjoyable. It was his use of that drug that had eventually brought the heat onto her at the hospital. Which was why she'd gone to him, insisting he clean up the mess he'd created.

"I've asked you not to call me by your little pet names. And no, I couldn't wait for you to get your sleep. Some of us work in the middle of the day." He held his hand out, and she slapped the syringe into his palm as she walked past him into the kitchen.

There was no love lost between the two of them. If she got caught by the police for stealing drugs, she'd name him as her accomplice. He'd known that. Which was why he hadn't argued when she told him about the rumors of an investigation into her and insisted that he get rid of the man conducting it.

Since everyone who worked in the hospital, even contractors, had to wear badges with their names on them, learning that Roger Biggio was the one doing the digging had been child's play. She'd passed the name on to Dwight soon after.

That had been what one of the syringes had been used for. Sophia didn't ask, and didn't want to know, his purpose for the other one. What she'd seen of him in bed a few times made her realize she didn't want to know about his darker side. She'd never told him that he talked in his sleep.

If he'd known, he might've wondered what he'd said.

Based on his nighttime ramblings, he kept dangerous company. From the bit he'd said about the Yacht Club, she recognized they were a group she'd never want to cross. They had a nasty habit of sending men like the one seated in her recliner after people who asked the wrong kinds of questions.

No, he could never know how much she'd learned about his dark dealings from his bouts of somniloquy.

His ramblings had led her to Abe. Sophia had recorded Dwight after dozens of their trysts when, unsurprisingly, he'd immediately dozed off after he'd finished. She'd gone to Abe attempting to broker a trade for the dirt Abe had on Dwight and their dealings.

It could have served as their dual insurance policy. Instead, the foolish bastard had destroyed her offering, then ignored her when she'd tried contacting him again earlier today.

That was fine. She wasn't any worse off now than she'd been before. All she had to do was find a way to separate herself from this situation and hope the cops never found the connection between her and the missing drugs. Although

Biggo had been eliminated, the efficiency with which Dwight had dispatched the man made the room swim around her.

Opening the fridge, Sophia pulled out some fruit juice and poured herself a glass. After this whole thing was taken care of, and she knew her career was safe, she planned to move to a different hospital and town, not leaving a forwarding address.

Initially, their relationship had been mutually beneficial. She'd even been fascinated the first few times he'd spilled his guts while sound asleep. Once she realized what he was confessing to, she decided it was best to get a little extra *insurance*.

Not knowing whether she'd ever use the information, she hatched the plan to record his confessions. But once her workplace thefts raised suspicions, she calculated he could put his contract-killing skill set to work and eliminate the investigator the hospital had hired.

Win-win.

Still. Working with a hired killer was playing with fire, that was becoming clearer to her every time she slept with him. That was one reason she'd ended that part of her relationship. It had been too unsettling, hearing the details of his work.

She turned and found he was sitting at the island counter. "Now that you have what you came for, you can go. You know the way out. I need some juice and a bath. Then I'm going to bed. I have to work nights for the rest of this week, and I need some sleep."

He stood as she turned toward the bathroom, already debating which scented bath bomb to use.

"Where are the files you shared with Abe?"

Sophia's hand shook, sloshing her cranberry juice, and she lowered it so he couldn't see. "Files? Abe? I'm sorry, but I don't know what you're talking about."

She saw the darkness in his eyes, the same feral hunger that had scared the hell out of her a few weeks ago and convinced her to shift their relationship to strictly professional with no more sexual benefits.

"The files you put on the flash drive you gave to Abe. I know you wouldn't have handed over your only copy. And I know he destroyed that copy. It's too bad I killed him."

"Killed?" She stopped before she gave herself away. "I don't know any Abe."

His chuckle was eerie, and she couldn't help backing away from him. Her juice-dampened socks stuck on the linoleum of the kitchen floor.

"Don't lie to me. I followed you to the cemetery. Why would you meet with Abe? How did you even know him? I needed answers, so I broke into Abe's house. And then I made sure he couldn't reveal any dirt on me. The poor guy didn't even have a mouth left to tell anyone anything about me when I left him with his brains splattered across his living room wall. But you were the one spreading secrets. A good man died because of you."

He pointed the syringe in his hand directly at her.

She would've been less afraid if he'd been holding a gun. At least with a gun, the pain would be over quickly. Who knew what he would do to her once that drug got in her system?

She'd delivered her own demise.

Feigning innocence, she prayed he believed her as the lies tumbled past her lips easily. "I didn't give him anything he could use against you. I, uh, just wanted to know what kind of work he did for you because I thought I could use him myself. You know, take care of my own dirty work so you wouldn't have to do it for me. I felt so bad asking you to kill Biggio."

She felt a sudden weight on her bladder as he smiled. "I already found the flash drive. And since you labeled it…"

Sophia clenched her pelvic floor muscles. If she wet herself now, he'd know she was lying. She had to play this cool and distract him. She laughed.

"If Abe had something incriminating, I didn't give it to him. What you do with the drugs I give you is no concern of mine. In fact, I'd rather not know. I'm not interested in your work, just your body." She smiled seductively and dipped her head toward the bathroom. "Why don't you join me in the bath, and we can both relax. How does that sound?"

There were no weapons in her bathroom, but there was a bottle of drain cleaner. If she threw that in his eyes, she could get away. Then she could call the cops and claim he was an intruder who'd tried to rape her. She could still get out of this clean if she could convince him to join her in the bathroom.

"That's how our little arrangement works, right? I scrub your back, you scrub mine." She batted her eyelashes.

"I don't know why you thought you could lie to me and get away with it. You recorded me in my sleep. After drugging Abe, I blew his brains out. That should've been you."

Shivers ran down Sophia's legs, and she opened her mouth, trying to come up with something to say. Anything that could stall him or get her out of this mess.

Dropping her glass, Sophia ran. She'd only made it a few steps before he slammed into her from the side. His short stature didn't take away from his strength, and he easily pinned her against the wall.

Facing him, she raised her hands to gouge out his eyes. If she could hurt him enough, maybe she could still get away.

His hand wrapped around one wrist as he expertly knocked her other arm out of the way. Her heart clenched. He knew exactly what he was doing. Before she could even blink, he spun her around, pressing her face into the wall and twist her arm behind her back.

Sophia tried to back-kick him, but his legs weren't where she thought they would be, and she missed.

"Don't worry, *babe*, I'll make sure whatever you think you have on me will never see the light of day. One way or another."

Following the sound of his voice, she punched backward, trying to catch him in the nose or mouth. Her hand hit his shoulder. Once again, he'd anticipated her attack and dodged it. Terror filled her chest, surging to greater heights as she felt the needle enter her arm.

"You were fun and useful for a while. I might've even kept you around if you hadn't made me kill Abe because of your schemes." His body pressed against hers, pinning her so tight she couldn't move as the drug raced through her body, making her muscles go slack.

Sophia tried to remember precisely how much was in the syringe. The prescription she'd swiped only this morning had been for a larger man. Her smaller body would metabolize the drug much faster. Even if he didn't kill her after this, the drugs still might. Her lungs would...her thoughts swam away on a tidal wave of warmth.

She should be doing something. What was it?

"Goodbye, dear Sophia. It was fun while it lasted." His lips pressed against her neck. "And don't worry. I remember you said you always wanted to be cremated."

The world shifted, and Sophia was suddenly looking up at her ceiling. Sunlight streamed in through the windows. She hadn't covered them yet. It didn't matter. She was so tired she could go to sleep right here. The sounds of her cupboard doors opening and closing echoed off the endless surfaces of her mind.

Something was wrong. Why could she smell cooking oil if she was in her bed?

Everything was so soft and fluffy around her. She no longer cared about curtains or cooking oil as she gently closed her eyes.

35

Rebecca kept her eyes on the traffic around them, swerving as she needed. Viviane started to hand Rebecca's phone to her but set it on the closed laptop of the onboard computer instead. "Coastal Ridge police are sending two squad cars."

"And you told them to put a rush on it?" With the cruiser's lights flashing, she passed a speeding car on the left as it wiggled back and forth, not sure if she was trying to pull them over. Morning traffic across the bridge was thick enough that she hadn't had a spare thought to give toward listening to Viviane's conversation with the city dispatch.

"I did. I told them she most likely had a syringe on her too. Dispatch has warned the responding officers." Viviane had to brace her hands on the door as Rebecca cut through an intersection without slowing. "I still don't get why she killed Barclay. Let alone who might be her next target."

Rebecca had to change lanes to avoid rear-ending a slower vehicle. "There's something else going on. A piece we don't see yet. It wasn't a woman who attacked me in Biggio's office." She sighed, frustrated. "Barclay was the only one we talked to at the scene. Maybe she was there and saw him? We won't know what her reasoning was until we talk to her."

She swerved across two lanes, sliding through the next turn while keeping the SUV under firm control. They were only two more turns away from Maryland's address. Hopefully, the local officers were close. So far, she still couldn't hear any sirens.

"Um, Boss. I think we've got a problem."

Rebecca shot a glance over at the passenger seat. "What is it?" When Viviane pointed, she shifted her gaze to follow her finger.

Thin wisps of smoke were rising up into the air ahead of them.

"Shit. That's by Maryland's. Might even be hers."

Viviane knocked the phone down as she flipped open the laptop and pulled up a map, having to hold on as Rebecca flipped on the siren and took the next turn. They were getting closer to the smoke.

"Yes, that looks like it could be her house." Viviane's voice was strained as she tried to keep her seat.

"Keep an eye on it. We're almost there." Rebecca turned onto Maryland's street. Heavy smoke roiled from a bungalow. "Is that it?"

"That's it! That's her house on fire!"

"Call it in!" Rebecca slid the cruiser to a halt, the tires bumping into the curb enough to jerk them to a stop. "Her car is in the driveway. Get fire out here, now!" Without looking back, Rebecca flung the door open.

As she ran for the burning building, she scanned the area for anything that stood out. Nothing. A few curtains from neighboring homes twitched as people on the block peeked out at the ruckus, but no one had moved outside to gawk yet. On the porch, she carefully touched the doorknob. It wasn't hot, but it was locked.

"Sophia Maryland! Are you in there?" Rebecca pressed her ear to the door but heard nothing.

Pulling away, she raised her foot and smashed it against the door, aiming for the spot just above the knob. The door held. Rebecca had to kick it once more, hoping the fire hadn't gotten any closer in the meantime, before the door finally gave and sprang open.

Acrid smoke so thick she couldn't see through it rolled out the open door, rushing toward the sky. Rebecca ducked under it. Every fire lesson she'd ever had in school, Girl Scouts, Quantico, and public service announcements ran through her mind.

It wasn't the fire that killed most of the time. It was the smoke, then the heat, and finally the fire. The fat column of smoke over her head was the real threat, so she had to stay under it.

Before moving inside, she grabbed her shirt and pulled it up to cover her mouth and nose. The other hand pulled her flashlight, and she shined the light inside. Her light hit the smoke, which might as well have been a brick wall.

Dammit! How was she supposed to figure out if anyone was inside when she couldn't see?

Another lesson, one she wished she'd remembered sooner, came to her. Opening the door fed fresh air to the fire. As soon as she'd kicked it in, the timer on how long the occupants had to live shortened.

Smoke filled most of the interior, but there was still nearly three feet of clear air along the floor. Rebecca crouched lower.

Viviane was yelling on her radio as she hurried across the front lawn.

When Rebecca stuck her head through the open doorway to try to hear or see any signs of life, the heat rushed her and dried her eyes in an instant. She had to blink repeatedly to see.

Rebecca crawled forward.

Inches from her face, she saw a pair of nurse's shoes discarded haphazardly in the entryway. In front of her, a purse sat on the couch, another sign that Maryland was likely inside. Unless she was willing to risk her life going deeper inside a burning house, Rebecca wouldn't be able to see much else. She couldn't even see the rest of the furniture, just darker shapes in the smoke.

Shit. I've got to find her.

Fear raced through her. Every primal instinct in her DNA told her to run back out. Run until she couldn't smell the smoke anymore.

Rebecca crawled out the door and fell against the side of the house.

Viviane was still on the radio, not even looking her way. No sirens pierced the air. The seconds dragged on with no help in sight.

"If I got that far in a few seconds, and if I can hold my breath for two and a half minutes, and if I can get in far enough in to find Maryland, I can do this. If I hold my breath." Rebecca tried to psych herself up. Fears be damned. She couldn't sit there with a woman inside about to burn to death.

Even if that woman is most likely a murderer.

Sometimes, having such strong morals really sucked. This was one of those times.

Taking slow, full breaths of the clean air, Rebecca did the breathing exercises her doctor had given her for physical therapy, which had helped strengthen her lungs. He'd called it a "singer's breath," and it was all about using her diaphragm to fill her lungs to capacity.

Once they were full, she held it all in. Knowing she didn't have long, Rebecca scrambled inside on her hands and feet.

For the briefest nanosecond, her thoughts jumped back to the treacherous night on Little Quell Island. Every step had been filled with pain and a growing certainty that she would die before she reached the med kit Darian had given Locke to tend to the gunshot wound in his leg.

She never believed she'd experience something worse than that night, but her current discomfort was another level of hell. Her lungs screamed to expel the oxygen they held and breathe in some fresh air.

As she made it through the entryway past the couch, she saw a pair of legs and moved toward them. Sophia Maryland was on the floor, face up. From the linoleum under her, Rebecca guessed she was in the kitchen. It was too hard to tell through the blackened smoke.

But she spotted the flames dancing just beyond her. The stove looked like the ignition point, with bowls melting from a collapsed cupboard in front of it and a bottle of cooking oil tipped out.

The heat from the fire made sweat bead all over Rebecca's skin. Next to Sophia's body, the kitchen cupboards burned.

How far has the oil spread?

If the flames touched the puddle Sophia was lying in, Rebecca wouldn't be able to save her without catching on fire herself. That was a lesson her mother had taught her as a child. Oil fires spread fast and would cling to whatever had oil on it.

Shit. Shit. Shit!

There was no time to waste, and she couldn't spare the breath of air to shout for Viviane to come help her.

The smoke was a sickly yellow-gray where her light touched it. The area of clean air along the floor was shrinking by the moment. Tears blinded her further, her eyes stinging from the fire's assault. It only got worse as Rebecca scrambled toward the flames and the oil-soaked body lying so close to them. All she wanted to do was let out the stale breath in her lungs, and she nearly did as the wall of heat hit her.

So many thoughts careened around in Rebecca's head. She ignored them all, focusing on what was in front of her instead. Give her a firefight with bullets any day of the week. That was a walk in the park compared to what she was dealing with now.

The back of the couch suddenly burst into flame, adding another source of thick black smoke, likely toxic. Visibility vanished completely. There was no more clean air, only the dark haze and fluttering ash.

Rebecca dropped her useless flashlight, using her hand to feel in front of her instead. Her fingers landed on fabric. Creeping forward, thighs screaming with fatigue as lactic acid built up in them, she managed to get a grip on the woman's top.

Using the fabric as a handle, Rebecca rolled Maryland onto her stomach. It wasn't much, but if she could keep her face down while she dragged her out, maybe she wouldn't choke on the smoke and soot.

Rebecca gripped her waistband next for more leverage. Ready to finally give in to her instincts to run, she turned and was met by the same sight she'd just been seeing.

Shit, am I facing the right way?

Everything looked the same no matter which way she turned her head. It was worse than getting caught in a blizzard. She had to take a moment to think.

Fire erupted over her head, and she flinched. No time to think. They had to move!

Air currents brushed along her cheeks.

Rebecca processed where she'd seen furniture. The wind

was coming from the open door, and she just had to navigate toward it.

Where the hell is the fire department?

She crept forward, dragging Maryland behind her. Keeping low only made things harder on her body, and she tried to straighten. Her hand slipped, almost losing her grip on the waistband. Sweat and oil soaked the woman's clothes, making it hard to hold onto her.

Releasing her own shirt, which she'd been holding against her mouth, she reached back and doubled her grip on the unresponsive woman's shirt and waistband, twisting her fingers tightly into the fabric.

"Boss! Where are you!"

Rebecca pulled Maryland in a low stoop toward the voice screaming her name. She wanted to scream back, to call for help, but the roaring fire behind her was so loud and the air so thick, she feared she wouldn't be heard. And then she'd have given her breath up for nothing. And that breath she held was the only thing keeping them both alive.

Her head swam as her legs churned.

The black smoke turned gray, then yellow. It parted as a hand burst through.

"I got you, Boss!"

A dark hand wrapped around Rebecca's uniform, pulling her forward and dragging Maryland with her.

Clean air hit her face like a slap. Air burst from Rebecca's lungs, and then she greedily sucked more in. It was bitter and hot and tasted so good. Her legs melted underneath her, and she pitched forward.

"Not yet! We're not clear!" Viviane's voice screamed into her ear, chasing back the rushing roar of the fire.

Rebecca had no strength left to respond, but she kept her hands tight on the woman she'd risked everything to save.

Just being able to breathe again renewed some of her strength, and she stumbled along.

Together with Viviane, they each looped one of Sophia's arms over their shoulders and hauled her to safety. Rebecca's eyes stung, and it was hard to make out shapes. Her next step landed on something soft.

Grass had never felt so good under her feet. She blinked repeatedly against the grit in her eyes, her chest still heaving. Another set of hands fell on hers, and she lifted her head.

Two men in Coastal Ridge uniforms were standing beside her, trying to take Maryland. Rebecca released her hold and fell against Viviane. As Rebecca watched, the officers pulled Sophia Maryland away.

She didn't move, not even to blink. Sophia Maryland's eyes stared blankly up at the sky.

Shit. I was too late after all.

36

"**K**eep the mask on." The paramedic warned Rebecca, and she held it firmly against her face as they lifted her into the back of the ambulance.

Firefighters had arrived right on the heels of the local PD, and they'd quickly given up on the idea of saving the house. Instead, they focused on keeping the blaze from spreading as more police showed up along with three ambulances.

Rebecca was still struggling to catch her breath even though the paramedics had placed an oxygen mask on her. Viviane was still surrounded by uniforms, explaining what happened as the paramedic pulled the door closed behind her.

"Can you get your top off?" He moved around her, pulling various things from compartments.

The oxygen was already helping, but Rebecca's throat was dry, so she simply nodded and started unbuttoning her top. As she pulled her shirt over her head, she saw the scorch marks on the back of it.

"We're going to check your airways then get you cleaned up. Sound good?"

The medic kept talking, explaining everything he was doing as he went. His partner, a woman with fire-red hair secured in a tight bun, climbed in from the front and helped them.

Rebecca nodded at the EMT she recognized as Anna Partridge, the same paramedic who'd transported Chester Able to the mainland.

In short order, Rebecca was declared healthy with only slightly singed skin on her left hand and along her back. That was treated, and Anna gave her a blanket to cover herself with. The EMT driver was distracted, listening to something on his radio that Rebecca couldn't hear over the sound of the oxygen mask and beeping machines.

"They're having trouble with the other woman." The first paramedic was talking to his partner, but Rebecca butted in.

"My deputy or the woman I pulled out? I thought she was dead when we got out of the house."

He frowned, as if debating whether to tell her. "The woman you pulled out. The one in scrubs. She's alive, but unresponsive. Her breathing is incredibly shallow, and she's not reacting to stimuli. Do you know anything about that? They're about to take off for the hospital."

The memory of the missing prescription that had led to them racing to Maryland's house suddenly popped into Rebecca's mind. Maryland had seemed possibly good for the crimes.

But Maryland hadn't attacked Rebecca in Biggio's office. It certainly didn't seem like she was their killer now. In fact, it looked like she was the killer's most recent victim.

"Tell them she might have been dosed with Midazolam, an anesthetic that acts like a paralytic. Have them check her for a fresh needle mark." Rebecca tucked the blanket she'd been given under her arms.

The two paramedics shared a confused look.

"That's why we're here. She was connected to a—"

"That's good enough for us." He waved her off and spoke into his radio, passing on what she'd told him, then looked at his partner. "I'm going to run over to assist. You'll be okay here?"

Partridge looked at the screen over Rebecca's head. "We'll be fine. If her ox sats keep coming up like this, she'll walk out on her own."

Once he was given the go-ahead, the man climbed out through the front, leaving the back doors closed.

Rebecca appreciated the gesture, as she was basically half naked. She closed her eyes, finally able to start relaxing. They'd rinsed her eyes with saline, and they no longer burned, but she had to keep dabbing at her face with the cloth they'd given her as tears continued to flow.

Sitting forward with her legs out in front of her wasn't comfortable, and she kept shifting around as she waited in silence to be declared fit to be released. Her mind wandered back to the case at hand. If Maryland wasn't the killer—the person who'd attacked her in Biggio's office had been shorter and stockier than the woman she'd just pulled from the burning house—then what did she have in common with the other victims?

Perhaps she was working with the killer. Anything was possible at this point. If she was, who was it? Idly, she wondered if forensics had finished at the Biggio house.

Coastal Ridge PD was handling that scene, and she hadn't had a moment to check in with them. Of course, they were right outside the ambulance.

She opened her eyes and stared at the closed doors. If she could get dressed and out of here, she could ask one of the officers standing outside. Considering all the twists and turns this case was taking, she wouldn't be surprised to see Chief Morrow out there.

A knock on the door made Rebecca and the paramedic jump.

"What the hell?" Anna maneuvered around Rebecca and carefully opened the door a crack to see who it was.

Rebecca leaned away from the open door, wishing she had another blanket to use as cover. The medic turned to her, pulling the door closed as she did so.

"Your partner is here with an update. Do you want to let her in? She says she also has your spare shirt."

Trust Viviane to know her well enough to look for a spare uniform in her cruiser. The door barely opened, and Viviane squeezed her way inside, holding not just the shirt but a bottle of water as well.

Rebecca saw the smile on Viviane's face, and it brought her more relief than the water or the shirt ever could.

"You really pulled my ass out of the fire this time, Vi."

Giggling at the terrible attempt at humor, Viviane let the paramedic close the door. Her deputy sat on the gurney near her feet.

"I only pulled you out of the smoke. You pulled Sophia out of the fire and saved her life. I didn't even think to tell the paramedics about the drugs she stole. But they did find a mark on her arm, thanks to you. She's being rushed to the hospital now. Once they figured out that her symptoms were caused by Midazolam and not just the fire, they got optimistic about her surviving."

Rebecca reached out for the shirt Viviane was holding. "Can I put this on now?"

"Go ahead. Your back wasn't really burned, just a little singed. Remember to put lotion on later and you should be fine." Anna looked up at the monitor again. "And you can take your mask off too. If your sats stay stable while you get dressed, we'll release you."

Not needing to be told twice, Rebecca pulled the mask

from her face, dropped the blanket, and reached for the bottle of water in Viviane's hands. She chugged it, the tepid water feeling spring fresh as it slid down her throat. "Oh, Deputy Darby, what would I do without you?" Half the bottle drained, she sighed happily.

"Wear a dirty shirt and get your own bottle of water. You didn't even really need me today. You're the one who saved Maryland." Viviane slapped Rebecca's leg. "But seriously, as your friend, don't ever do that to me again. Running into a burning building? What were you thinking?"

Swinging the shirt over her head, Rebecca started buttoning it. "That I could see the victim on the floor and the fire creeping nearer to her. I couldn't stand there and watch her burn." She smiled at the paramedic despite her disapproving glare. "Besides, I knew you were right at my back. And I've been doing breathing exercises and was pretty sure I could make it through on one breath."

"Exercises you only know because you broke your ribs and were having problems breathing properly until, like, a week ago." Viviane slapped her legs again, and Rebecca was grateful she couldn't reach her back. It was already starting to itch as the burn gel dried. "I'll take you home so you can get cleaned up and take the rest of the day off."

"No. We need to get back to the station." Rebecca shifted her shoulders, wiggling her uniform back into place. "There's still a killer out there. It's not Maryland like we thought. We need to get back to the drawing board and figure out who it is. He was willing to burn her house down to kill her. Once he finds out he failed, there's no telling what extremes he might go to or who he might target next."

37

V iviane hadn't stopped pestering Rebecca until she agreed to at least take a quick shower in the locker room once they got back to the station. It had taken Viviane sweetening the pot by taking her through the Bean Tree's drive-through to get an extra-large cup of iced coffee.

The heat of the day had never stopped Rebecca from enjoying a cup of hot coffee, but the burns around her lips did.

Running into a fire had been a bad plan. She'd been lucky. All she'd lost was a few strands of hair that had been so tightly twisted in the rubber band of her ponytail that they were torn free when she let her hair down to wash it. The singed ends said more about how close she'd come to serious harm than anything else.

Cool, clean, and slathered in lotion, Rebecca was ready to get back to work. Unlocking the locker room door, she headed out to give Viviane back the bottle of lotion she'd borrowed.

Hoyt walked in from the front as she arrived in the bullpen. "Perfect timing, Boss." He held up a cardboard carrier with four large Styrofoam cups in it. "I figure after the heat from the fire, you and Darby could do with some cool refreshments. And we need to share the wonder of Betty with our new guy too."

Rebecca put some pep in her step. Betty's milkshakes were legendary. "Strawberry?"

"Of course. What else would I get for you?"

"What new wonder am I being introduced to?" Jake looked up from his computer as they walked in from opposite directions. Rebecca accepted a cup, then Hoyt handed Jake one.

"Betty's homemade milkshakes." Viviane stood up to reach for the cup being held out for her.

"Now that we're all protected from the heat, let's get back to our case." Rebecca's lips felt as chapped as they would after an entire day on the slopes. "Maryland was clearly not our murderer, or at least not our only murderer. If nothing else, she's at least an accessory. Do we have any updates on her? Is she conscious and able to tell us who did this? What about the house fire?"

"Maryland is still being evaluated, and they're giving her oxygen for the smoke inhalation. As for the house, they're still trying to put it out." Viviane shook her head. "The fire chief said it will be hours yet. And more after that before they can determine a cause. They're going to look for proof of arson, considering everything we already know."

Jake stirred his shake with the straw. "And forensics hasn't found any fingerprints at the Biggio residence. I called them about it while you were out with Darby. Once we knew what to look for, it was clear enough that someone broke in. And they found signs that Biggio was dragged from his office into his garage. We can assume he was loaded into his car there, then taken to the cemetery."

He took another sip of his shake and savored it before

continuing. "I guess that's when the skid steer came into play. He probably drove it right down one of the narrow paths and loaded Biggio's body into the bucket. Then it would've been easy enough to open the double doors of the work shed, raise the bucket, and tie the rope around his neck. They also found that his computer was wiped at eleven twenty-six."

"Which is probably shortly after the killer drugged him. Was anything salvaged from the computer?"

Jake shook his head. "Yes and no. They said everything was wiped. Best guess is some kind of EMP or magnetic field. The monitors also showed signs of magnetic interference. But they'd also taken in the home printer for processing. When they plugged it in, it pinged that it needed paper. Once it was operational, a letter Roger had composed to his wife spewed onto the output tray."

Viviane's mouth dropped open. "A love letter?"

"An apology, by the sounds of it."

"Closure." Hoyt directed his comment at Vi, but everyone nodded their agreement and took a moment to process the implications.

Moving her mouse around, Viviane started clicking. "If we add Maryland's name to the victim pool, what do we have that links her to Barclay and Biggio? As a victim, I mean."

Over her Styrofoam cup, Rebecca glanced at Viviane. "We know she was stealing drugs from work. Drugs the killer used to attack all three of his victims. We also know Biggio was working on something at Coastal Ridge Hospital. Patsy said so."

Hoyt chimed in. "And Hazel, the pharmacy tech at Coastal Ridge, said some hotshot cybersecurity firm was causing changes in procedures."

Rebecca eyed the whiteboard littered with information. "I imagine Biggio's project was the drug-dispensing discrepancies, and Maryland was apparently the cause of the drug discrepancies...so Maryland might've been a loose thread the killer tried to get rid of after he killed Barclay and Biggio."

"That would make sense if the killer was getting drugs from her. We're making an educated guess that the hospital was suspicious and hired Biggio to look into the drug transactions. The killer offed Biggio. Then he killed Maryland so she couldn't turn on him." Hoyt leaned back in his chair, his eyes losing focus, apparently mulling over his theory. "Doesn't explain Barclay."

Jake turned to face him. "And why go through the risk of transporting Biggio all the way over to the island in order to kill him? Why not hang him in his own house and be done with it? Taking him to the cemetery where his first wife was buried doesn't make sense."

"Maybe Biggio's suicide being staged at the cemetery had nothing to do with his first wife at all." Rebecca knew it was a shot in the dark, but they had to look at this from all angles. "Maybe it was a message for Barclay. Warning him he was next."

"Then why didn't Barclay tell us about it?" Viviane looked to the older, more experienced deputies for a clue.

"No idea." Rebecca shrugged. "It could've been anything. But I think it's telling that none of the locks in the cemetery were picked or showed signs of being forced open. If the killer's the same guy as the burglar from Biggio's office, then we know from the condition of the locks at the office that he prefers to pick a lock or use a bump key."

"Which we saw no traces of at the cemetery. But we also know from Barclay's statement that all the locks share one key. The killer could've had a copy."

Hoyt raised a good point—one Rebecca had no way of verifying without asking the killer himself.

"Jake, go through the forensics in both break-in cases. Coastal Ridge is sharing their files with us on those. See if there's anything we missed. Hoyt, go through everything we got from Barclay's house. Check for anything that might link him to Maryland or Coastal Ridge hospital. Viviane, follow up on that APB we put out on the Buick Regal. Hopefully, someone's seen it by now."

"Hey, Boss." Hoyt grew serious. "About that car. The sweet ladies at the pharmacy mentioned a 'boyfriend.' They said he'd drive his car back by the hospital, and Maryland would go out and sit in the car with him."

"And you're thinking that could be our killer?"

"It seems logical. Only problem is, when I asked about the car, the only thing they could tell me was that it wasn't a dark color."

Rebecca swiveled around to address Viviane. "Did you get all that?"

"Sure did."

"Good. If you come up empty on the APB, check cameras around Maryland's house for when the fire was set. Based on what Deputy Frost just shared, I'm going to call the Coastal Ridge hospital. If Maryland is awake, she can tell us her boyfriend's name. Even if she's not in a condition to speak yet, security might have him on tape."

One of these trails had to lead them somewhere. Without his supplier for Midazolam, the killer might switch to a different drug. And so far, that drug was the only thing that connected these three people. If they lost that, the killer might just get away with his crimes.

38

"I'm afraid I don't understand." The hospital lawyer repeated himself, looking at the signed warrant in his hand. He was walking beside Rebecca and a security guard, who was studiously ignoring everything as he escorted them through the hospital. "Why do you think that Ms. Maryland's home arson attack is related to our hospital?"

Once again, the man tried to slow her down by stopping, but Rebecca didn't care. She kept walking down the narrow concourse of the hospital toward the security room. Viviane and the two police officers who'd met them there stepped around the man standing in the middle of the hallway.

With a heavy, flat stare, Rebecca motioned for the security guard to keep going. If the lawyer wanted an explanation, he could catch up to them to get it.

As she assumed he would, the lanky man used his long stride to catch up after realizing they weren't going to stop. She had no idea why he was trying to stall her, but she wasn't going to put up with it. "And I'm afraid, Mr. Geller, that you don't need to understand. The judge understood my reasons the first time he read them. That's why I was able to get that warrant for your security footage so quickly. We have two dead bodies and a third victim who might not survive the attack. Time is of the essence."

"I know that. After all, Ms. Maryland is being treated here. And we're all very worried for her recovery and safety. I don't see what this has to do with *us*."

As they approached a door marked *Security*, the guard pulled his badge out, ready to unlock it. He, at least, was professional enough to deal with the matter in a timely manner.

"Coastal Ridge Hospital is her employer." Viviane held up a hand and started ticking off reasons without slowing down. "This is the last place she was seen alive. She stole drugs from your pharmacy. And her attacker used those drugs to incapacitate her so he could burn her alive. This is the third time we've explained this to you. Do you understand why now?"

Her voice had been getting progressively and incrementally louder with each sentence until people from up and down the hall were turning to look at them. It was an impressive tactic for cowing lawyers, and one Rebecca was going to have to remember as it sent the stalling man into a fit of silent shock.

The guard unlocked the door, and Rebecca pulled it open, leading the way. "The more you stall us, the farther away the killer is getting. If you continue to get in our way, I will have you charged with interfering with a police investigation." She pointed at the officers, one of whom pinned the lawyer with eager eyes. "I'm going to collect my evidence now. Officers, please use your discretion regarding his interference."

The guard sitting at the bank of monitors turned at the commotion flooding his domain.

Rebecca handed him a list of times and dates. "I need video footage of the pharmacy for these times and the footage from all exterior doors for an hour before and after. I'll also need it for the times after Sophia Maryland's work hours on each of these dates. Any additional footage with her on these days would also be appreciated. I called about an hour ago to let you know what I needed. Is there any chance you've already compiled this footage?"

The seated guard flicked his eyes up to the one who had escorted Rebecca in. At his nod, the man grunted. "I don't have it all yet. That's a lot of searching. But I do have the pieces for the times you asked for." He pointed at six monitors, all with frozen images of Sophia Maryland on them. "If you have the warrant."

Rebecca gestured at the lawyer, who was still hanging out in the doorway, keeping it open. "He's got your copy. Go ahead and start playing this one. Where is this?" She leaned over the desk, tapping the monitor that showed Maryland about to walk through an employee entrance with a Buick Regal parked at the curb.

"That's the delivery door for the pharmacy." The guard started the video. "And this was recorded on Saturday, the twenty-ninth of last month."

As the video played, they all watched Maryland walk out of the hospital and slip into the same car Rebecca had seen outside the sheriff's station before Abe Barclay had been killed.

There wasn't a hint of fear or reluctance as she sat next to the man who might have just tried to kill her. And it was, indeed, a man. The angle of the camera was much lower, just above head height, and she could see the driver.

"Viviane, brown hair, cut short. Dark eyes, probably brown. He might be the guy I ran into at the office as well. License plate ends in three-four-nine-nine. Call that in to update the APB."

Rebecca watched as the car pulled forward and parked

for a few minutes before pulling around again. This time, she caught a glimpse of him before the glare from the lights obscured his image through the windshield.

"Same thing happens on the other date." The security guard pointed at a different screen and started playing that video. "Same time too. This is her meal break. And she makes a phone call about thirty minutes before that car shows up both times. On the other days, when the car doesn't come, she doesn't make a phone call."

Rebecca looked at the other four screens. They all played out as the guard had said.

"He didn't need to pick up the drugs from her today. He met her at her house because she was the victim, and it was much easier to have her bring it to him where he was going to kill her." Viviane moved closer, staring at the images on the screen. "She was carrying a bag when she left, but I don't see it in the pharmacy. Does she have access to a locker or something?"

The security guard who'd escorted them spoke up. "All employees have access to lockers if they want one."

"And we would be more than happy to show you hers." A new woman, dressed in a stylish tailored business suit, stepped into the room.

Finally moved out of the way, the lawyer let the door close as he handed over the warrant.

The new woman glanced at it briefly before handing it back. "I'm Ms. Tyler, the Chief Administrative Officer. Sorry, I wasn't here to meet you when you arrived. I trust my associate has provided you with everything you need?"

This was why Geller had been stalling. He was waiting for backup from his superior. Now that she was here, he stood calmly behind her.

"After he tried to slow us down, we were able to view the evidence despite him." Rebecca motioned at the monitors.

She wasn't about to fall for the verbal trap the CAO had laid out by agreeing she had everything she needed. "We have not taken possession of any of it yet. We'll still need that."

"Of course. Gentlemen, if you would please go ahead and make copies of everything Sheriff West asked for. Sheriff, if you'll follow me, I'll take you to Ms. Maryland's locker. It's hospital property, and we'd be glad to hand over all the contents to you now that Ms. Maryland has been fired for theft. I've just gotten off the phone with the DEA. They said you called to give them a heads-up. I'm sure you'd like to discuss your findings with them as well."

Rebecca smiled broadly. "Oh, I'd love to have another chat with them. Now, which way to the lockers?"

REBECCA AND VIVIANE stood to the side as the security guard entered the combination to unlock Maryland's locker. She hadn't expected something so retro in a modern hospital. Even the one she'd had in high school hadn't been this old, with the locking mechanism built into the door. It was no wonder the lawyer hadn't been concerned about privacy issues.

Popping the handle open, the guard stepped aside and let Rebecca see what was there.

"A spare coat, change of scrubs, toiletries." Rebecca put the objects in a large evidence bag that Viviane held open for her. At the bottom of the locker were more items. "Bath towel, stack of takeout menus." That was when a handle came into view. Picking it up, she saw what it was. "And a metal lockbox, latch still intact, but..." She tugged at it, and the mechanism popped open. "Unlocked."

Rebecca opened the box. "A thumb drive and..." She reached inside for the lone piece of paper. The writing on it caught her attention. "Viviane, you might have found the smoking syringe earlier, but we've just found the jackpot."

Flipping the paper around, she showed everyone what was written there.

"I didn't commit suicide. If you find my body, it was Dwight Stokely who killed me."

39

It was time for me to go. With Sophia eliminated, my last loose end was gone. Moving around the spartan motel room, I tossed my clothes into bags. It was a dance I'd done so many times, I no longer had to think about it.

Despite searching her home thoroughly before torching it, I hadn't found any of her files. That could be a problem. I knew from firsthand experience that the Yacht Club didn't like exposure.

Over the summer, the members had grown more paranoid. Their fuses were shorter, and there was no way I'd survive if they believed I was a liability. Hopefully, it wouldn't come to that. I had wiped Sophia's computer and every device she had before starting the fire.

As long as I kept moving from town to town, the cops never noticed how many bodies I dropped. My work for the Yacht Club had lined my pockets nicely. More importantly, the kills stirred something deep within me, something that was now part of my DNA. I knew I'd never stop killing. But I was smart enough to know my days of working for the most powerful men along the East Coast were over.

We'd had a good run. Longer than most of the other employers I'd worked for. They'd provided an endless stream of targets for me. Most of the hits were on stuffy old men who were behind on hush money payments or who'd tried to skim funds from the club's coffers. When people thought they were smarter than members of the Yacht Club, they tended to die early.

The tides of this island were threatening to pull me out to sea and drown me. Time to head back to the solid ground of the mainland where I could lose myself in the larger crowds. Maybe I'd move across the country to escape the Yacht Club's reach.

People would be surprised how many individuals made their living the way I did, men and women. I'd find a new employer after lying low for a few months and letting the dust settle from Sophia's mess. Without Abe to stash my bodies under legitimate corpses, I'd need to get creative. Maybe the fish on the West Coast had a voracious appetite, and I could fill their bellies with fresh meat.

I glanced around the motel room one last time to make sure I'd left no trace of myself behind. Scooping up the motel key with its little plastic disk attached, I grabbed my bags and opened the door. The air was finally cooling. There was the faintest hint of fall crispness to it.

Yes, definitely time to move on. The California coast was calling my name. Although I wanted to leave before the Yacht Club decided I was a liability, I'd need to gas up the car and get some dinner. And if I was leaving this island for good, then my last supper had to be the infamous steak and baked potato from the shack on the beach.

I deserved a moment of relaxation. Pondering my next move while tearing into a dry-aged ribeye with a cold beer was just what I needed. With a clear head, I could turn my sights to choosing my next hunting ground.

40

"Everyone, follow me." Rebecca swept through the bullpen on the way to her office with Viviane right behind her. They'd just left the forensic lab in Coastal Ridge, and she was still trying to wrap her head around what they'd learned.

"What's going on?" Hoyt asked as soon as Rebecca closed the door to her office.

It was a tight fit getting all four of them in the room together, but this was something she didn't want to risk being overheard by anyone who might walk into the lobby.

"Give me a second, and I'll start showing you what we found. Quick update, though, the Buick Regal we saw trailing Barclay picked up Maryland the night before Abe's death and the night before Biggio's death as well. It probably belongs to the man Maryland accused of killing her by the name of Dwight Stokely."

Rebecca dropped into her chair and opened her email. They'd given the drive to the forensics unit, and they'd sent her back several audio files and a few Word documents.

Another email popped up, and she realized the techs were still transcribing.

"Maryland left a thumb drive along with her note. The Coastal Ridge forensic team accessed it, and it's a bunch of recordings of Stokely talking in his sleep. They're still processing, but they've listened to him talk about debt collection for the Yacht Club."

"Good thing Mr. Dwight Stokely works for the Yacht Club rather than the CIA. State secrets would be out the window." Hoyt clicked his tongue.

"Dwight Stokely." Rebecca felt that frustrating feeling of recognizing an actor's face but not remembering their name. "Why does that name sound familiar?"

"'Cause we've got a folder on him." Hoyt stood up and moved to the filing cabinet where they kept the Yacht Club files they were still reviewing.

In truth, the files were scattered in various places, including her rental home, the utility closet in the locker room, and any space she could spare in her office.

He started digging through them. "Here we go. This was a weird one that went nowhere. We got a call about a man lurking in the cemetery. I went out and found him with dirty hands. Before I had a chance to do more than just talk to the guy, Wallace showed up and said he'd take over."

Pulling the folder from the drawer, he turned and handed it to Rebecca. It was distressingly thin, and she opened it to find a single piece of paper. It was a quick read. "Possible trespassing case but the cemetery didn't want to press charges, so Wallace left it alone." She flipped the folder inside out so they could all see the giant question mark in red ink that had been drawn there. "Clearly, he didn't know what to do with this."

"That's what made me remember his name. Like I said, it was a weird case. We never figured out what he was doing or how he'd gotten so dirty. When I called to follow up with them, I was told that nothing was disturbed."

"And who told you that?" Rebecca closed the file and slid it over to him. There was another memory in the back of her head. She opened the other files connected to this case and did a quick search.

Hoyt's head jerked back. "Abe Barclay. Dammit. Barclay covered for Stokely back then. But that's the only time Stokely ever came on our radar here."

"There's the Barclay and Stokely connection." Jake pointed at the file on the desk.

"Now we've connected Maryland, Barclay, Biggio, and Stokely." Rebecca nodded to herself. A picture was taking shape.

"And the Yacht Club," Viviane pointed out. She looked quickly at their newest member. "Wait, should we be talking about this in front of Jake? No offense."

"None taken?" Jake shrugged and looked at the other three, his eyes troubled. "Is this some old guard secret or something?"

Rebecca had thought about this exact issue the entire way back. If she couldn't trust the people she worked with, especially one that was recommended by Special Agent Rhonda Lettinger, they'd never get anywhere. Breaking it to him bluntly was probably the best way to move forward.

"We've got a gang of rich assholes that keeps dropping problems on our shores. They're responsible for Sheriff Wallace's death. They're involved in human trafficking, or prostitution at the very least. Drugs. They pissed off a cartel and cost me one of my people." She paused long enough to let that sink in. "If you don't want to get involved in the deeper stuff, you can step out now."

"The Yacht Club? I'm familiar with them." Jake crossed his arms, his face grim as he lifted his chin and clenched his jaw.

Hoyt dropped his hand on his knee with a loud slap. "Why am I not surprised that the ex-statie knows about them too?"

Jake shook his head. "Just rumors, mostly. But too many to think they aren't at least based on the truth. What's the real name of their group? The American Pirates? Billionaires and Bloods?"

Rebecca chuckled as she pulled the copies from the machine. "They really are called the Yacht Club. It's a terrible name, I agree. But they seem proud of it."

"Wait, you've actually spoken to them?" Jake shook his head, uncrossing his arms long enough to rub a hand over his neck.

Viviane nodded. "Several of them. Go figure, they've all been pompous, blackhearted assholes. Every case that involves them also ends real bad."

"Like the guy who cared more about his reputation and retaining his power in the club than finding out who killed his son." Hoyt shook his head in disgust.

Rebecca had been reading through the transcription while they talked and clicked the print button. "Speaking of Albert Gilroy."

"You've got to be kidding me. Maryland was linked to that jackass? What is this?"

"Turns out, Stokely talks in his sleep. Maryland recorded it. Why, I'm not sure. But these recordings were stored in her locker along with her note about her death. I'm guessing she knew she was in deep shit and decided if she went down, she was going to take Stokely with her."

"A woman scorned." Hoyt mumbled as he read through the transcription. "Is this enough to nail the Yacht Club? What's this string of numbers here?"

Rebecca printed off the next transcription. "We don't know what the numbers are yet. This all might come in handy later, but right now, we need to focus on finding Maryland's attacker. Were you able to track down that car with the plate numbers I gave you, Frost?"

"I handed that off to the new guy." Hoyt waved his hand at Jake and kept reading.

Jake shifted forward. "I saw the stills you sent over too. And I noticed that the back and front glass had barcode stickers on them. That got me to thinking, what if the car was a rental? Combining the rental aspect with what you gave us, I was able to track down a car that matched. It was rented three weeks ago in Coastal Ridge. They got a copy of the guy's license. He's a frequent customer of theirs too. There's a copy in the folder."

"Frequent, huh?" Hoyt rubbed his chin. "So Stokely's a debt collector for the Yacht Club, and he was caught hanging out in the cemetery. And Barclay was the one to tell us that nothing was dug up, but I found Stokely himself with fresh dirt on his hands."

"Barclay was covering for Stokely's crimes? Stokely's an Aqua Mafia enforcer?" Jake frowned, but Rebecca and Viviane both snorted with laughter.

"Aqua Mafia, as bad as that is, actually sounds cooler than their real name." Viviane shook her head with amusement.

Rebecca opened a new window on her computer, searching the DMV for Stokely's license. "I'll put out a BOLO on him and update the APB information on his car. We need to find him before he leaves town. If he thinks Maryland is dead, then I don't see any reason why he'd hang around this area anymore."

41

Thankfully, Judge Neumeyer had been available so that Viviane acquired a warrant for Stokely's bank records with no issues. The credit card company didn't even give her a hard time when she asked for his statements. Everyone was shocked to learn he'd made a purchase a little more than an hour ago.

At the Tidepool Motel in Shadow Island, Virginia.

They all spilled out of the station at a run. Viviane and Hoyt headed for the motel while Rebecca and Jake headed for the bridge. Viviane hadn't even gotten the cruiser to a full stop before Hoyt jumped out the door and into the tiny lobby.

She lost sight of him for a moment as she got out of the SUV to follow. Before she could even make it around the front of the cruiser, he was turning and running back outside.

"He's already checked out!"

Viviane spun on the ball of her foot, her gaze raking over the parking lot, looking for the Buick Regal. There were very few cars, none of them the right vehicle.

Hoyt snatched his radio off his shoulder. "Boss, he's gone. But he didn't check out that long ago. Maybe fifteen minutes. He might still be on the island."

As Hoyt glanced at the time, Viviane dropped into the driver's seat again. "We need to make sure he doesn't leave town."

"Is that him?" Rebecca turned to look where Jake was pointing but only saw buildings. "He's on the next street over."

Keeping to the speed limit, Rebecca waited for the next intersection. A gray Buick Regal coasted through the green light a moment before she did.

"That's him." Rebecca pressed her foot down on the gas slowly. She didn't want to draw his attention. "That road leads to the bridge. But it's not the fastest route, since it swings around the park. This way is at least three minutes faster."

She continued to accelerate, crossing the next intersection without any sign of Stokely. It was the start of rush hour, but the traffic was all heading in the opposite direction. Once she had enough distance between them, she pressed the pedal all the way down.

One problem with a town this small—you couldn't use your sirens if you didn't want the perps to know you were coming.

Still, they got to the bridge ahead of the Buick Regal. If they stopped there, Stokely would see them.

"He's right there." Jake tapped the window again.

Rebecca cursed. "Remind me to add speeding to the charges we press against him."

A sound that might've been laughter escaped Jake's

throat.

Stokely followed them onto the bridge. There were no cars between them. He had to have seen them by now.

"We can't let him get to Coastal Ridge. Traffic is only going to get heavier there. We have to stop him here." Rebecca threw on her lights and siren, then slammed on the brakes and slung the steering wheel to the side. Two lanes of traffic were blocked off, but that left the other two open.

The driver's door was facing Stokely's car, and Rebecca kept her eye on it as she jumped out of the SUV. "Coffey, get the spike strips from the back!" She sighted down her gun, aiming for the shape that should be Dwight Stokely's head.

Was it him? The car matched the description. *But I can't see the plate.* There was a barcode sticker on the windshield, like Jake had said, which marked it as a rental. *Or that could be some poor schmo's easy pass for toll roads.*

Doubt and uncertainty warred inside Rebecca, fighting against her training. Sweat poured down her spine. Her soul and her body were not in agreement, and she couldn't make a decision.

I don't want to die. I don't want to have to kill again either.

Rebecca couldn't remember the names or faces of all the men she'd killed over the last few years. But she knew she didn't want to have another death on her conscience.

The front end of the Regal lifted as the driver stomped on the gas pedal. Dwight Stokely had killed two people and tried to kill a third. Did he deserve to die for it when she had killed so many more?

"There's no time! Take the shot!" Jake yelled loud enough to be heard clearly over the crash of the waves on the bridge's pillars and the chaotic hum of approaching traffic.

She shook her head, keeping her eyes open and focused on the driver. "I don't have visual confirmation!" The words were true as she started them, but by the time she'd finished, he was close enough. An outline of a head came into view even through the dark tinting on the glass.

It was too late now. He was too close.

Stokely swerved to the right, aiming for the lighter-weight back end of her cruiser. Right where she'd sent Jake.

Rebecca fired at the same moment that metal screeched against metal. She wasn't aiming for the driver, but for the tires. Her aim was true, and just as the car was about to push past, the driver lost control as both left-side tires suddenly went flat.

She had a sudden sense of *déjà vu* as she watched the car rock wildly, careening around the SUV. This was almost exactly what had happened with Rod Hammond. She'd hesitated then, too, and put Locke's life at risk. The same way she'd endangered Jake's today.

This time the car didn't roll. Instead, the Buick Regal slammed into the railing of the bridge.

"Get out of the car. Hands up!"

The dread that had been wrapping around her heart eased as she heard Jake yelling orders. Sprinting around the car, she joined him. They both had their guns drawn and pointed at the cab.

"The tint's too thick. I can't see inside."

Rebecca gritted her teeth. "I know, that's why I couldn't take the shot earlier!" She stepped to her right, getting a tighter angle on the driver's window. Once she had it, she squeezed the trigger.

Glass exploded as her bullet went through both the window and the windshield, allowing Jake to see inside the car.

"He's going out the passenger window!"

Rebecca ran around the back of the car to get to the other side while Jake ran around the front.

Stokely was crawling out the window, the door panel crumpled up against the thick railing.

"You've got nowhere to go, Stokely. This is the sheriff's department. Put your hands up and don't move."

The trapped man turned to face Rebecca. As soon as she saw his eyes, she was certain. This was the same man she'd fought with in Biggio's office. His gaze was devoid of fear. He had Shadow's darkness within him.

"Nowhere to go? Oh, I don't think so." On his knees, he waved his arm out in front of him, gesturing at the ocean that spread out all around them. "I have at least one place to go."

"And then what? Do you have a gold medal in swimming I'm not aware of? I can shoot you just as easily in the water as I can right here, Dwight. Don't be stupid." Rebecca started inching forward. His car was pressed too tightly against the side of the bridge. There was no way she could reach him from this side to prevent him from leaping over the railing.

Maybe if she kept him distracted long enough, Jake could reach him from the front.

"I don't plan on swimming. I expect to die. Sometimes death is the best answer. I can't be caught."

"Come on, Dwight, jail isn't all that bad. Free room and board, an exercise yard, cable. It's not much, but it's not as bad as Hell."

Stokely laughed as he twisted and pulled his lower body out of the window. He didn't even try to straighten up, instead responding to Rebecca nearly upside down.

"It's not jail that scares me, lady. It's the guys who'll find me in jail. They'll make me suffer before killing me. I've screwed over the Yacht Club. As soon as you start digging, you'll find out. I'd rather take my chances in Hell than let them get their hands on me." He stood upright and glanced over his shoulder at the water below.

"We can protect you!"

The car rocked as Jake jumped onto the hood and into her view.

"We'll put you in protective custody. All you have to do is tell us what you did for them." She was close to begging. If she could turn this man, she would be miles closer to shutting down that damn rich man's club.

"Protective custody!" Stokely shook his head, looking amused. "Nah. You two aren't bought, but you're the minority. Like I said, I'll take my chances in Hell."

With those final words, Stokely dove over the railing.

Rebecca and Jake rushed to the guardrail.

The bridge wasn't exceptionally high, so Stokely hit the water quickly. Rebecca saw the immediate splash. But he'd gone headfirst into the shallow, marshy stretch where the island coast faded into the ocean. Stokely's prone body floated up to the surface, face down, almost as fast as he'd fallen.

With his head tilted at an impossible angle, Rebecca knew he was dead.

42

"You okay, babe?"

Rebecca startled, turning away from the ocean view to look at Ryker. They were sitting on her back porch. The glass bottle of beer in her hand was still cool, so she knew she hadn't been zoned out for too long. "Sorry, I was lost in my thoughts."

"Still thinking about how Dwight Stokely killed himself over going to jail?"

"Yeah. It's just…the look on his face. I can't get it out of my head. He said he would rather take a chance on Hell than let the Yacht Club get their hands on him. When the divers recovered his body, he'd suffered a broken neck from slamming into the shallow marsh. Bailey ruled that he drowned after being paralyzed from the fall."

"Oh, that's disturbing." Ryker took a sip of his beer.

"Yeah, it was." She picked at the label on her bottle. "One good thing, we were able to deliver Roger Biggio's final note to his widow. Officer Hooper told me Patsy was deeply moved by it. She'd been racked with guilt over their fight, but his note indicated he knew how much she loved him and he that loved her just as much."

"Aww, I'm glad they recovered that for her." Ryker whistled for Humphrey. They'd moved the dog in the day before, and Rebecca had been obsessed with him ever since.

"But that's not the only thing on your mind, is it?"

"Hmm?" Rebecca had watched as the dog ran up, leaving his exploration of the sand for another time.

"I said, there's more on your mind than just Stokely. What is it? Don't make me pull out the big guns." He shook his finger at her, and she chuckled.

"Big guns?" She scoffed at him. "What big guns?"

Ryker looked her dead in the eye, his expression completely deadpan, as he pulled a potato chip out of their snack pile. "Humphrey, get it, boy." Then he threw the potato chip in Rebecca's lap.

The chocolate lab, always eager and single-minded when it came to any form of snacks, launched himself after the chip, landing in Rebecca's lap.

Her squeal of laughter did not deter the hungry pup, and he spun in circles looking for his treat.

"I warned you! Don't make me up the ante." Ryker held up a piece of beef jerky. "Are you going to tell me what's wrong, or are you going to suffer the 'give me food dance?'"

"No!" Rebecca wrapped her arms around Humphrey, covering his eyes before he could see what his master was holding. "I'll talk. I'll talk!"

A sense of relief washed through her, and she realized she really did want to talk. In fact, that was occupying most of her mind. How to tell Ryker. When to tell Ryker. What he would think of her once she had. And she was half worried that he would think she was overreacting. She took a deep breath and started.

"William Jake Christensen was dubbed the American Jack the Ripper. They suspect him of killing up to twenty people."

"Okay. We're starting with a history lesson?" Ryker wiggled the piece of jerky in a threatening manner. "Or are you trying to distract me? Because we both know you can't distract Humphrey."

"It's a bit of both. Just hear me out. The Seminole Heights serial killer, who we think is Howell Donaldson, only killed four people. He's still in jail while his case is being heard. Michael Gargiulo, the Hollywood Ripper, only killed three people and attacked a fourth who survived."

"These are strange but interesting facts I'm not surprised you know. What about them?"

This was the difficult part. Rebecca took a swallow of her beer before going on. "In order to be considered a serial killer, you only have to have killed three people in a similar fashion. That's really all there is to it."

Ryker waited for her to continue while she played with Humphrey's ears. "Okay."

"Do you know how many people Richard Ramirez the Night Stalker killed?" She bit her lip.

Ryker shook his head, his gaze firmly set on her face. Rebecca knew her expression was probably telling him more than her words were.

"Thirteen people in a year. It took Justin Black an entire summer to kill fourteen. I'm responsible for more deaths in *one day* than Richard Ramirez and Justin *freaking* Black managed in *months*." She stopped petting Humphrey and stared at the ocean. She couldn't stand to watch Ryker's face as she said the next part. "Even discounting the rest of the year, I've killed or at least caused the deaths of fifteen men in only a few hours. All on one tiny island. Most cops never fire a single bullet. I've killed so many."

"You're not a serial killer." Ryker's voice rang with sincerity and pain.

Rebecca gulped down the knot that formed in her throat. "I know that. And yet, it doesn't feel any better, knowing I've killed more people than the Night Stalker."

"How many people do you think soldiers kill on the front line? Coast Guard?" He stopped and shook his head. "It doesn't matter. The numbers don't matter, not really."

She stared at him as he leaned over and took her hand. Humphrey put his mouth on their joined hands and started chewing, making her laugh.

"I am sorry you had to do that. I wish every day that it hadn't turned out the way it did. But it did. And you had to do what you did to save lives. You saved my life. You saved Locke's life. You saved Frost's life. You gave Darian a chance to say goodbye to his family even after those men killed him."

A sob broke free from Rebecca, and she had to muffle it with her hand, the one not covered in puppy slobber.

"You fought," Ryker choked on tears that trailed down his cheeks, "and bled and got shot and were beaten. You were bleeding to death. And you still fought to stay alive. Sometimes staying alive means killing those who are trying to kill you and your loved ones."

Humphrey jerked his head up, huffing in confusion as they cried together. He whined and headbutted Rebecca's chin. She couldn't help it and started to laugh as he licked at her tear-stained cheeks.

Ryker got up and walked around the table to kneel carefully in front of her, having to catch Humphrey as he lunged forward. "Thank you, Sheriff, my beautiful, loving Rebecca West with a heart so big she feels remorse for even the criminals she arrests. Thank you for saving my life and living long enough to be reunited with me."

Rebecca could barely speak. "I thought I'd lost you."

He cleared his throat, wrapping his hands around Humphrey's muzzle to get him to at least slow down with his licking. "When I was stuck in the hospital, I told you I kept forgetting things and had to be reminded over and over again. They told me the first thing I asked was if you were okay. And it was the question I asked most frequently, more often than 'Where am I?'"

She pressed her lips together. "How can you even remember that?"

"I couldn't." Ryker shrugged. "That's why it was the top question and answer on my memory board at the hospital."

She laughed, and Humphrey's tongue landed a direct hit on her open mouth as the pup tried to comfort her. She wanted to ask why he wouldn't allow her to visit or accept any of her calls, but this conversation was already more than she could take.

"Thank you. I didn't mean to make this all so emotional. I wanted you to know the type of person you've been living with."

Ryker pulled his dog out of her lap. "I knew who I was living with already. You're an amazing woman who will go to extremes to keep her friends, neighbors, and most importantly, herself safe from anyone who tries to hurt them."

Rebecca thought back to the way she had frozen on the bridge. It had been a hard decision to make...to pull the trigger or not. And then she realized Jake could be in danger, and she fired the shot. She didn't tell him about that part.

"That's enough big thoughts and feelings for now. How about we sit here and enjoy our view of this beautiful ocean as the sun sets?" Ryker looked into her eyes, reading her every expression again.

She smiled, caught up in the love and acceptance she saw in his gaze. "That sounds like a great plan."

"Good." Ryker groaned and turned around, settling down

onto his rump and leaning back against her legs. "Because kneeling like that was killing my knees."

Rebecca laughed and leaned forward, wrapping her arms around his neck and snuggling into him. Humphrey climbed onto his lap, twisting himself into a knot to lick Rebecca again.

It was the perfect way to end the day. Together, all three of them stared out at the ocean, content to sit together in silence.

"Is that a storm cloud blowing in?" Ryker rolled his head to the side.

Rebecca followed his line of sight. "That looks too low to be a cloud. Do you guys get fog like that? I've never been here past the summer before."

"We get fog, but not in a vertical line like that."

A thread of worry worked its way down Rebecca's arms. "That looks more like smoke the bigger it gets. Leftover fireworks from the past Labor Day celebrations?"

As if on cue, her phone rang.

Rebecca answered, keeping her focus on what she realized was a growing plume of smoke. "West here."

"Boss, we got a problem." Viviane's voice was rushed. "There's a big boat on one of the docks that's on fire. Fire teams are en route. People are already forming bucket lines."

"I think I see the smoke from here. How bad is it?"

"Bad and getting worse. Boat fires are always dangerous. And this one is docked near fifteen others." There was a pause, and when Viviane spoke again, her voice was muffled as if she'd wrapped her hand around the receiver. "And the fire is heading toward the refueling station."

The End
To be continued...

Thank you for reading.
All of the *Shadow Island Series* books can be found on Amazon.

ACKNOWLEDGMENTS

How does one properly thank everyone involved in taking a dream and making it a reality? Here goes.

In addition to our families, whose unending support provided the foundation for us to find the time and energy to put these thoughts on paper, we want to thank the editors who polished our words and made them shine.

Many thanks to our publisher for risking taking on two newbies and giving us the confidence to become bona fide authors.

More than anyone, we want to thank you, our readers, for sharing your most important asset, your time, with this book. We hope with all our hearts we made it worthwhile.

Much love,
Mary & Lori

ABOUT THE AUTHOR

Mary Stone

Mary Stone lives among the majestic Blue Ridge Mountains of East Tennessee with her two dogs, four cats, a couple of energetic boys, and a very patient husband.

As a young girl, she would go to bed every night, wondering what type of creature might be lurking underneath. It wasn't until she was older that she learned that the creatures she needed to most fear were human.

Today, she creates vivid stories with courageous, strong heroines and dastardly villains. She invites you to enter her world of serial killers, FBI agents but never damsels in distress. Her female characters can handle themselves, going toe-to-toe with any male character, protagonist or antagonist.

Discover more about Mary Stone on her website.
www.authormarystone.com

Lori Rhodes

As a tiny girl, from the moment Lori Rhodes first dipped her toe into the surf on a barrier island of Virginia, she was in love. When she grew up and learned all the deep, dark secrets and horrible acts people could commit against each other, she couldn't stop the stories from coming out of the other end of her pen. Somehow, her magical island and the darkness got mixed together and ended up in her first novel.

Now, she spends her days making sure the guests at her beach rental cottages are happy, and her nights dreaming up the characters who love her island as much as she does.

Connect with Mary Online

facebook.com/authormarystone
x.com/MaryStoneAuthor
goodreads.com/AuthorMaryStone
bookbub.com/profile/3378576590
pinterest.com/MaryStoneAuthor
instagram.com/marystoneauthor
tiktok.com/@authormarystone

Made in United States
Troutdale, OR
02/16/2024